# SULLIVAN'S TRACE

## ALI SPOONER

# Also by Ali Spooner

**Single Books**

The Blank White Page
From the Cradle to the Stone
Holy Water and Whiskey Scars
The Ghost of East Texas
The Trophy Wives Club
The Bee Charmer
Forever Home
Ruined
Back in the Saddle
Open Your Heart
South of Heaven
Shotgun Rider
The Settlement
Love's Playlist
Cowgirl Up
Twisted Lives
The Epitaph
Terminal Event
Bailey's Run

**Erotica**

The Wolf and The Unicorn

**Series**

*The Island Series*

Neptune's Ring
Venus Rising

*The Hunter Series*

The Devil's Tree
Bound

*Sasha Thibodaux Series*

Sugarland

Bayou Justice

Line of Sight

*Strong Southern Women Series*

Diamond Dreams

Gator Girlz

True North

Footprints

*Cast Iron Farm Series*

The Mountain Whispers

The Star Child

Soul on Fire

The Sky People

Turn the Page

*Songwriters Series*

Six Strings and a Dream

Midnight in Nashville

Out and Loud

**Co-authored with Annette Mori**

Heart Strings Attached

Free to Love

Trouble in Paradise

**Co-Authored with K.L. Gallagher**

Hat Trick

# SULLIVAN'S TRACE

ALI SPOONER

Affinity
Rainbow Publications

2024

Affinity E-Book Press NZ LTD
Canterbury, New Zealand

1st Edition

ISBN: 978-1-99-104085-5 (paperback)



Editor: A Koenig
Proof Editor: Lisa M
Cover Design: Irish Dragon Design
Production Design: Affinity Publication Services

## ACKNOWLEDGMENTS

I thank my fans for following my stories and providing great feedback and encouragement. Writing wouldn't be so much fun without you. Thanks to Affinity, Irish Dragon, for the cover art and the team of editors, readers, and publishers who continue to help me grow as a writer.

## DEDICATION

To Mark R., I know you will love this story. Thanks for all of your support!

# TABLE OF CONTENTS

# Chapter One

---

Camille Graves sat on the front porch, staring across the railing at the approaching dust swirls. For the better part of the sixty years she had been alive, she had worked for Doc Barton and his family. She watched as a large red truck approached. The two-year drought showed no signs of letting up soon, and the image of the truck shimmered in the heat waves as she squinted against the sun's brightness.

"That would be Miss Bryn," Camille said to herself as the truck slowed and turned into the drive a few hundred yards away.

Miss Bryn would be Bryn Barton, Doc's granddaughter, who was expected to arrive today. Camille had not seen her for almost five years, and she was excited to see the young woman.

Doc Barton had been the area's veterinarian for over forty years and had built a reputation as the best large animal specialist in the south. He had brought some of the finest

American Quarter Horses and thoroughbreds into this world. He would soon be passing on his practice to his granddaughter, Bryn, to finally go into full retirement. Since his wife's passing five years ago, Doc Barton found that he had lost a step or two and was not able to put in the long hours and late nights like he used to. As he aged, it seemed like a prized foal or calf would often choose to be born between two and five in the morning, frequently after many hours of painful labor.

†

The flash of the hot sun reflected off the truck, catching the attention of Micah Sullivan, "Sully," to her friends, as she climbed up to sit on the top rail of the corral fence.

"Damn, Glen, go easy on his mouth, will ya?" she barked from her perch.

"Sorry, Sully," Glen said as he eased up on the reins.

"He's got the instinct, so just sit back, hold on, and let him do the work," Sully shouted.

It was never easy for her to train a new rider. The horses she bred were born with the instinct to herd cattle, but to compete and establish their reputation, they still needed a rider. Sully's back injury a few years earlier prevented her from competing as much as she liked, hence the need for a quality trained rider. Glen was talented, and Sully had been working with him for over a year, but she still had to remind him to give the horse free rein to make the instinctive sharp movements of a cutting horse. All the rider had to do was point out the animal they wanted to be cut and separated from the herd, and then sit back and let the animal do the work.

Sully watched as the truck stirred up a cloud of dust as the owner maneuvered the hulking machine down the drive. Doc Barton had stopped by the previous day and informed her that his granddaughter would be arriving today to begin orienting to his practice in anticipation of his retirement. Even though Sully had joked with Doc, she knew the portly old man was weary and ready to retire. Still, Doc Barton was the best vet for hundreds of miles, and she would miss the comfort of knowing he would be available at the drop of a hat. He did his best to assure her that Bryn was competent and had gained valuable experience working at some of the country's premier racetracks.

Sully watched the truck slow as it approached Doc's house. She had taken over the management of Sullivan's Trace three years earlier after the sudden death of her father. She was named after her grandfather, Micah Sullivan, an immigrant from Ireland who found work as a cowboy in Texas before relocating his small family to Florida.

The first Micah had an eye for quality horseflesh and began breeding some of the best American Quarter Horses in the states. His experience driving cattle in Texas also helped him train cutting horses, and his talents quickly became well-known across the southern states. His first grand champion, Sullivan's Sun Dancer, became the root of his stock and sired numerous champions. With the birth of artificial insemination, the bloodlines would last for many generations.

Doc Barton had been out to complete a prebirthing check on one of the mares carrying a foal of the famed Sun Dancer. Much to her delight, Doc had informed her that the foal would be a colt, a rather large one. The size did worry him about the birthing process.

"He's going to come out half grown at this rate," Doc had said as he finished his examination. "I will give her two to three weeks left at the most," he said as he removed the disposable gloves from his hands. "Bryn will be here just in time to help bring him into the world," he said proudly.

"Are you sure she is ready to take on your practice?" Sully asked curiously.

Doc chuckled, which made his eyes sparkle brighter. "She is young, but her education is the best money can buy. Besides that, she still practices some of the timeless methods I taught her when she first graduated," he added.

"I know you wouldn't turn the practice over to just anyone," she said.

"Just wait until you meet Bryn before you judge her based on youth. She is only two years younger than you," Doc said with a mischievous grin.

"Point taken," Sully said as she returned his smile. In a male-dominated world, she remembered the constant doubters who challenged her farm management when she first returned to take over.

Doc had been the farm's vet as long as Sully could remember, and it would take some getting used to, having anyone else provide medical care to her stock. With a thousand acres and several hundred horses in her breeding stock, Sullivan's Trace was a large account for Doc Barton, and he had proven to be an invaluable member of her team. Sully planned to send him into retirement with style as she prepared to expand her annual Fourth of July cookout with a surprise retirement celebration for Doc. Sully would serve up the best BBQ and steaks in the county and add a fireworks display. She had also ordered an exceptional gift for Doc, which would be delivered later this week. With Camille's help, it would be an extraordinary celebration.

†

Bryn slowed as she approached the house. Besides a fresh coat of paint, it didn't look any different from the last time she had been here. That was nearly five years ago when her grandmother had ended her year-long battle with cancer that had eroded her body from the inside out. She could still feel the pain in her grandfather's eyes as the casket was lowered into the ground, and he said his final goodbye to the love of his life. Bryn knew the pain would never leave him, but she hoped the spark of life had returned to her grandfather's eyes.

She smiled when she saw a slight figure rise from a rocking chair on the front porch and saunter toward the front steps. Camille had been a part of the family forever and had been a rock of support for Doc when his beloved had passed.

Bryn put the truck in park and switched the ignition off. She exited the truck and walked toward the house with a huge smile.

"It is so good to see you again, Camille," she said as she reached to take the small woman in her arms.

Camille welcomed the embrace, saying, "I thought this day would never come. Your grandfather has been eagerly awaiting your arrival but got called away on an emergency a few hours ago."

"How is he doing?"

"He has slowed down a bit but still tries to work from dawn until dusk," Camille said with a chuckle. "Deep down, though, he is drained and ready to meet the retirement challenge."

"I hope my presence here will allow him the confidence to do just that," Bryn said, her arm slipping around Camille's waist as they walked onto the porch.

"Can I pour you some iced tea?" Camille asked as Bryn sat in one of the rockers.

"That would be fantastic. I have found nothing better to beat this summer heat than a glass of your sweet tea."

Camille chuckled as she handed Bryn the cool glass. "Just as smooth a talker as your grandfather, I see."

"It must be a family trait," Bryn said as she smiled and took a long drink.

She lowered her glass and looked across the lawn at the heat waves radiating from the ground. "How long has it been since it rained?"

"Six weeks and counting," Camille said. "Every now and then, dark clouds form, giving us hope of at least a shower, but just as quickly as they form, they disappear without a drop of rain."

"That must be really tough on the farmers in the area."

"The corn's bone dry, and the beans are wilting in the heat. Lake levels have dropped dangerously low, so the farmers can't use the water to irrigate like they have in the past."

Bryn gazed at the dancing heat waves until the metal clanking sound of a gate rang in the silence, and she looked off to the right.

"Is that still Sullivan's Trace?" she asked.

"Yes, it is. Old man Sullivan died a few years back, and Micah returned home to take over the running of the farm, and the breeding and training program," Camille said as she watched Bryn closely.

"I still remember the summer I spent here as a kid when Micah and I became friends, only to dissolve once the summer ended and I went home," Bryn said.

"That was the year your father had surgery, wasn't it?" Camille asked.

"Yes, right after his heart attack. I was twelve years old, and my parents brought me here to live with my grandparents while Dad recuperated from open heart surgery."

Bryn squinted against the bright sun. She could make out a figure sitting atop the corral fence and wondered what Micah would be like now. Micah was two years older than she, and Bryn had worshipped her that summer. Camille would pack her a lunch, and then Bryn and Micah would ride horses or swim during the day, and darkness would fall before she returned home for dinner.

"How is Micah doing?" Bryn asked curiously.

"She's doing fine as far as I can tell," Camille said. "She had an accident a few years ago, which left her unable to ride as much as she would like, but she immerses herself in the management of the farm."

Bryn could tell that Camille was impressed with Micah, too.

"Too much so, sometimes I fear," Camille added.

"Why do you say that?"

"She has a mile-long waiting list for her horses and doesn't take time out for herself at all. It's just work, work, work," Camille chided. "Just like someone else I know will probably do."

Bryn smiled, knowing that, at least at first, she would work long hours until she had fully assessed her grandfather's practice to determine their needs. "Once I get into the swing of things, I promise I will try to take it easy."

"Boy, have I heard that song and dance before," Camille said with a deep chuckle.

"Is Sullivan's Trace still the major customer for Grandfather?" she asked.

"Most definitely, he spends most of his time over there," she said as she looked toward the neighboring farm.

"Good, at least I will be close to home."

"That you will," Camille said. "Why don't you bring your bags in while I tend to dinner," she suggested. "I expect your grandfather to be home in an hour or so, and I usually try to have dinner ready for him."

"No wonder he's so spoiled if you treat him like that," Bryn teased.

"Your family has been very good to me. After my Herbert passed and I moved out here, they treated me like family," she said with a tone of appreciation.

"You have always been family," Bryn said as she stood and hugged Camille. "As soon as I finish unpacking, I will come down to check on you," she promised.

"Child, I have been cooking for that old man since before you were born," Camille said with a laugh. "I know exactly how he likes his food, but you can come and keep me company."

"As long as I stay out of your way in the kitchen, is that what you are saying?" Bryn asked with a grin.

"Exactly," Camille answered and disappeared into the house.

Bryn walked to the truck and filled her arms with luggage to carry into the house. It was a two-story home, much too large for such a small family, but her grandfather would not even discuss moving into something smaller. He could not bear to leave the home of so many beautiful memories behind. Bryn climbed the steps and pushed open the door to her old room.

Camille had placed fresh linens on the bed, and Bryn walked across the room to put the luggage down at the foot of the bed. She looked at the double French doors and walked over to them. With a quick twist of the knobs, Bryn opened the door to a small private balcony that looked out toward the Trace. Just as she had remembered, Bryn smiled to herself. So many mornings were spent sitting in the rocker, waiting until the sun rose so she could begin the next grand adventure with Micah.

The thought of her old friend sent a strange sensation of warmth through her body. Surprised by her body's reaction, she shook her shoulders and returned inside to put away her clothing.

†

Sully stepped gingerly off the fence and followed Glen into the stables. "Be sure to give him a good rubdown after you remove his tack," she said as she turned to leave the barn.

"Yes, ma'am," he said as he walked the young stallion into the stables.

Sully stopped and turned back toward Glen. "You did a good job today, Glen."

"Thanks, Sully, that means a lot coming from you," he said with pride.

She returned his smile as she started for the house.

# CHAPTER TWO

---

Bryn finished putting her clothes away and joined Camille in the kitchen.

"Is that your fried chicken I smell?" she asked as she stepped into the kitchen.

"Fried chicken, rice, gravy, fresh tomatoes, and corn I picked just today," Camille said.

"Dear Lord, how will I keep from gaining a ton of weight eating your cooking?" Bryn joked.

"You will be so busy you will burn off every calorie I can feed you," Camille promised. "Somehow, I still don't think you realize just how large your grandfather's practice really is," she added with a grin as she shook her head from side to side.

"You are beginning to scare me. I wonder now if I have bitten off more than I can chew," Bryn said, a worried frown furrowing her brow.

Camille chuckled softly. "If your grandfather can handle it at his age, I am sure you will be just fine, Bryn, so don't let my prattling worry you."

Bryn settled into a stool at the breakfast bar and picked up a fresh glass of tea. She was lost in her thoughts and did not hear her grandfather's approach up the drive.

†

Sully stepped onto her front porch just as she heard Doc Barton's old truck turn into his drive. Camille would have dinner waiting for him, and he would spend this night getting reacquainted with Bryn. She felt a twinge of jealousy as she stepped through her front door and walked to the kitchen to find it cold and empty. She thought how nice it would be to have someone to cook for her, then shook a painful memory from her mind.

Sully and Alisa had been lovers for three years before her father got sick, and she was called back home to run the family business. Alisa had been born and raised a city girl, and three months after Sully's father passed, Alisa decided she needed the city to be happy. One afternoon, Sully walked into the house to find Alisa's bags packed and her lover sitting at the desk to write her a note. When Sully realized what was happening, her anger rose quickly.

"Were you going to leave just like that, with nothing more than a note?" she demanded to know.

"I didn't know how or what to say to you, Sully," Alisa said, tears starting to fall. "I am withering away out here, and I must leave. I know you have responsibilities here, so I won't ask you to join me," she said as she balled the paper in her fist and dropped it into the trash.

Sully felt betrayed by Alisa after all they had shared together. "I thought all you wanted was to be with me," she said, her anger forcing the words from her throat.

"I've changed. I just cannot live with the isolation out here," Alisa said. "My heart yearns for the sounds of traffic and the rumble of train cars."

"Let me help you with your bags, and you can be out of my life then," Sully said with venom.

"Sully, please don't make this any harder than what it is for me already," Alisa begged.

"It can't be too hard if you can just walk out like this with no discussion and no chance of a compromise," Sully spat at her. Even as the words left her lips, Sully realized there would be no compromise. She would not leave the farm, even for a woman as beautiful as Alisa. She grabbed the last two bags, strode angrily to Alisa's car, and tossed them into the back seat.

Alisa followed Sully outside and stood frozen, her jaw hanging slack as Sully stormed past her without another word and slammed the front door behind her. Alisa turned for a final look, then walked to her car and drove away.

†

For several months, Sully had sunk into a well of bitterness and self-pity at the betrayal she felt. After she had drowned her sorrows in enough single malt scotch, Sully decided her life would go on, and she would never allow a woman to hurt her again like Alisa had. She focused all her energy on managing the farm and did her best to fight off the loneliness that, on some nights was almost unbearable.

Sully walked to the fridge, made a sandwich for her meal, and pulled a cold beer from the shelf. She sat at the small kitchen table and watched the sun disappear beneath the horizon. After finishing her sandwich, Sully took her beer to the front porch and sat in one of the heavy rockers. She sipped her beer and watched as the shore of the small lake came to life with the dancing of fireflies.

Glittering bright green and yellow, the tiny insects floated across the warm night as they danced to entice their mates. Sully could not resist joining them on the lake's shore, and she walked down to sit at the water's edge. She had not thought of Alisa in months and shook her head, trying to erase the memories from her mind. The hurt stung anew as she thought back to the last day.

Alisa had taken her breath away the first time they had met with her incredible beauty. Sully had been instantly smitten with her and gave her heart away so quickly, the same heart Alisa crushed when she left abruptly. It had always come down to Alisa's needs over hers, and until then, Sully had always compromised her needs for Alisa's, but when she took a stand for her own needs, Alisa took the opportunity to flee.

Sully shook her head again. "Get a hold of your heart, girl," she said aloud. "She is gone, and you are better off without her dominating your life."

She drained the beer and sat in the deep chair by the lake. The moon had risen full and shone brightly down upon the rippling water. A slight breeze had come up in the early evening but did little to ease the oppressive heat. A sudden flash of lightning in the distance caught her attention. Mother Nature would tease them with a distant electrical storm but refused to send the rain they desperately needed. Crops would continue to wither while animals and humans wilted in the deadly heat.

Sully closed her eyes and laid her head back against the chair, her ears full of the sounds of the night.

†

After sharing a delicious meal with Bryn and Camille, Doc suggested he and Bryn step out to the porch for a chat.

"It is so good to have you here finally," he said as they took seats in two rockers on the porch.

"It feels good to be here," Bryn replied. "I look forward to beginning to work with you," she added.

"There is so much to share with you in the next few weeks," Doc said. "If you are ready, we will get a start at the office tomorrow morning and check the schedule."

"That sounds great," Bryn said as she studied her grandfather's weathered face.

Doc stared out across the lawn at the lightning flashing in the distance. "Damn, I wish we could get some rain around here."

"Should I go out and dance a rain dance?" Bryn teased.

"I am almost to the point where I would be willing to do one myself," Doc answered. "Even the lakes are beginning to dry up around here," he said as his eyes stretched across the darkness toward Sullivan's Trace.

"We should visit to see Sully tomorrow," Doc said.

"Sully?" Bryn asked.

"Micah hasn't been called by her first name in years. She was nicknamed Sully late in high school, and the name has stuck," her grandfather explained.

"That is good information to know. What else should I be aware of?"

Doc cocked his head at his granddaughter. "Well, I guess that depends. Sullivan's Trace is still my largest client, giving me at least seventy-five percent of my business," he said.

"What's she like? That summer of our friendship was so many years ago, I can hardly remember what she looks like," Bryn said.

Doc's eyes glistened as he spoke of Sully. Bryn quickly picked up on her grandfather's admiration for her old friend.

"She is incredible with the horses, and her steeds are the most desired cutting horses in North America," he explained. "She learned well about breeding and training from her father and has lifted the farm beyond what her father had ever dreamed it would be."

"Married? Children?" Bryn asked.

Doc looked directly into Bryn's eyes. "No, she has never married. There was a woman with her when she first moved back, but her longing for city life got the better of her," he said with a grin. "I can't honestly say I was sad to see her go," he admitted, "but I hate that Sully lives a lonely life.

Bryn sat quietly as she waited for her grandfather to expand on his comment, but Doc remained quiet. She found her eyes drifting over to the large barn that blocked the house where Sully lived, apparently alone.

"Funny, though," Doc said. "When I told Sully you were coming out to take over, she asked the same questions about you."

Bryn was stunned by her grandfather's revelation. She had doubted that Sully would even remember her after all these years. She had assumed Sully, several years older, would have quickly forgotten the long-legged, ponytailed girl who worshipped her that summer.

"So, what did you tell her?" she asked curiously.

"Oh, I just said you were concentrating on work and waiting for your soul mate," Doc said with a grin.

Bryn felt her cheeks flush under the dim porch light. She had never shared her brief, limited experience with Rose right after she finished college, but she knew her grandfather was very perceptive and read her expressions perfectly. Was her sly fox of a grandfather attempting to play matchmaker here, Bryn wondered. He did appear to think very highly of Sully, but how could he know both women were attracted to other women?

"Nice answer," Bryn said as the clock in the foyer chimed loudly.

Doc glanced at the watch on his wrist. "We have a long day ahead of us tomorrow, and you must be tired from your travels. Why don't we call it a night and get an early start in the morning," he suggested.

"That sounds like a good plan," Bryn said as she stood and stretched before she reached to pick up their glasses.

"I'll get those," Doc said. "Go on, and I will see you in the morning."

Bryn leaned over and kissed her grandfather on the cheek. "It's good to be home," she said.

"It's great to have you here," he said as he picked up the glasses and moved to hold the door open for his granddaughter. "Camille has breakfast ready by six," he said as Bryn walked past him.

"I will see you in the morning then," Bryn said as she started up the stairs.

"Good night," Doc said before he watched her disappear up the stairway.

†

Camille had turned on a small lamp beside the bed in Bryn's room, and she was met by a cool breeze as she closed the door behind her. The entrance to the balcony was open, and a breeze flowed softly into the bedroom. Bryn felt herself drawn to the balcony which faced Sullivan's Trace. The moon had risen fully and was shining down onto the small lake.

†

Sully had drifted off to sleep sitting at the lake, and the cool breeze that had come up chilled her awake. She stood and stretched before turning toward the house. As she made her way to the house, she thought a hot shower and clean sheets would be welcome to her body.

†

Bryn strained her eyes in the darkness. Maybe it was her imagination, but she thought she saw a figure moving through the dark at the lake's edge. She relaxed and allowed her eyes to adjust to the darkness. They confirmed that someone, presumably Sully, was walking from the lake toward the house. She was excited to meet Sully again tomorrow and watched her until she was hidden by the barn.

†

Sully's eyes were drawn to Doc's house, and she saw the silhouette of a figure standing on the second-floor balcony. That was Bryn's room during the summer of her visit, and Sully wondered what it would be like to meet her as an adult. She took that thought with her as she climbed the steps to the house in search of a hot shower.

†

Bryn changed into a light pair of pajamas and selected clothing for the next day before climbing into the bed and turning out the light. She was asleep almost as soon as her head hit the pillow, and her dreams were quick to arrive.

†

Sully lingered in the hot shower, enjoying the water against her skin as it erased the weariness of the day from her muscles. She dried her body and slipped into a light robe as she walked through the house to turn off the lights. In her bedroom, Sully pulled the covers back on her king-sized bed and draped her robe over the end. Her naked skin welcomed the feel of cool sheets as she lowered her body onto the bed. The soft thumping of the ceiling fan lulled her into sleep, her mind still thinking of Bryn with a smile playing on her face.

# CHAPTER THREE

---

Sully woke with the first rays of sunlight peeking through her window. She dressed and went to the kitchen to fix a light breakfast before walking to the barn, where her four-wheeler sat waiting. Sully picked up a small bag of dry dog food, dropped it into the passenger seat, and climbed behind the wheel. She pulled out of the barn and drove past the corral down a path leading to a back pasture where the mares and young foals were kept. Sully turned off the trail into a wooded section of land and followed the track for several minutes before it opened into a clearing. She pulled the vehicle next to an ancient oak stump, took the bag of dog food, and dumped it into a small metal tub. She stepped back into the ATV, drove forward a hundred feet, and parked beneath a tree to wait.

As anticipated, her wait was not long. Sully propped her feet on the dash as she listened for the slight sound of tiny feet on the dry sticks of the forest floor. The morning breeze was still cool, and the forest sounds were carried along the air. She smiled with delight as she watched the mother fox appear in the clearing, her nose lifted to smell the offering Sully had left for her. She cautiously left the protection of the forest and was followed by a pair of fox pups jostling along behind her. She quickly trotted to the tub and began to eat the food Sully had left for her.

Sully had spotted the female fox nearly a year before and, after seeing her numerous times, began to supplement her diet with dry dog food. Slowly, the fox became used to seeing Sully and would allow her to remain in the area while she came out to feed. Several months ago, the female was nowhere to be seen when Sully came out to bring food, but each time she visited, the food had disappeared. Sully breathed a sigh of relief once she saw the fox carefully herding two small pups ahead of her. She had grown thin, the strain of the feeding pups draining her strength, so Sully began bringing a larger bag of food for her more often.

The mother ate greedily while the pups romped around the stump. Sully enjoyed watching them play and was amazed at how quickly they grew. She leaned forward, and her foot slipped on the dash, creating a sound the pups heard. They stopped dead in their tracks, their bodies falling flat to the ground, and the mother lifted her head to look at the source of the sound. She spotted Sully sitting quietly in the small vehicle and made a soft woofing sound to her pups. They were reassured by their mother's communication and resumed their playing.

Sully smiled. The mother fox had made her day by giving her the sign that she trusted her caretaker enough not to send her pups scrambling for safety. Sully watched the fox eat her fill and then lift her head to look directly at her and, for a moment, she locked gazes with the animal who appeared to smile at Sully. With another quick bark to her pups, the fox spun on her hind legs and trotted back into the woods.

She stuffed the sack into a pocket in the dash and turned the key to start the engine. Sully drove down the small trail and continued to the foal pasture. She pulled into the middle of the field and parked as a herd of golden animals approached. Two dozen mares with foals of varying ages circled the vehicle, and Sully admired the beautiful animals that surrounded her. The sun playing on their golden coats brightened the morning as Sully reached into her pocket and drew out a knife. She walked to the rear of the vehicle, cut open a bag of apples, and began slicing the ripened fruit to indulge the young horses with a sweet treat. The foals surrounded her as they crowded in close for a sampling of the gifts she had to offer. Sully found great joy in working with the animals from birth to mold their temperament and bond them to the human touch. She fed them sliced apples and then ran her hands over their shoulders and down their legs, and for the older foals, Sully began leaning across their backs to get them used to bearing a human weight. She quickly found herself lost among the horses.

†

Bryn joined her grandfather and Camille in the kitchen for breakfast as promised. Doc looked up and smiled when she entered the room.

"Good morning. I hope you slept well," he said.

Bryn returned his smile. "I haven't slept that well in ages," she admitted.

"There is nothing like fresh country air to help you sleep at night," Camille added. "Would you like coffee?"

"I would love a cup."

"I'll take a refill, too," Doc said.

Camille picked up his empty cup and shook her head. "It's a good thing you got here when you did, or he would have drained the pot," she said.

"I am just a one-cup person, sometimes two, and then I switch to juice or water," Bryn said.

"Is apple still your favorite?" Camille asked.

Bryn smiled at the thought of Camille remembering that fact. "Yes, it is," she said, smiling with Camille.

"What would you like for breakfast? I think a few slices of bacon are left, and I can have toast and eggs ready in a few minutes," Camille offered.

"Some toast and bacon will be just fine," Bryn said.

"You better eat up. It will be a long time until lunch," Doc said.

"Very well, I will have some soft scrambled eggs," Bryn said, much to Camille's delight.

"That's better. I thought we would stop for you to meet Sully and check on her mare before heading off to make other rounds today," Doc said.

Bryn sipped her coffee as her grandfather spoke. "That sounds like a good start."

Camille delivered a plate of eggs, toast, and bacon with a glass of chilled apple juice.

"Thanks, Camille," she said.

"You are very welcome," Camille said as she sat at the table.

"Are we still headed to the office this morning?" Bryn asked.

"I thought we would run by and check to see if we have appointments and then drop by next door to check on Sully's mare and the rest of the stock." Bryn noticed a scowl on Doc's brow. "That colt she is expecting has me worried."

"Why is that?"

"Because he is going to be large at birth, especially if the mare goes full term in another few weeks," Doc said.

"Will he be too large for a natural birth?" Bryn asked.

"That's what I am not sure of. The mare is from good breeding stock, and this will be her third foal, but I still can't help but worry."

Bryn took the last bite of breakfast and washed it down with juice. "Well, let's go to the office, and then we can check on the mare," she said as she rose to carry her dishes to the sink.

"Leave those, and I will get them," Camille said.

"Thanks for a great breakfast. Let me brush my teeth, and I will be ready to go," Bryn said as she passed her grandfather.

"I will get the truck warmed up," Doc said as he walked toward the front door.

†

Doc and Bryn made a quick stop at the office to check the calendar and found no appointments for the day. This would allow them to spend time acquainting Bryn with customers. She smiled as they turned down the drive to Sullivan's Trace.

Her excitement faded quickly when no one was present to meet them as they drove up to the barn. Doc parked and stepped out of the truck. "Let's go check on the mare, and then we can track down Sully."

Bryn followed him inside a large open barn with stalls kept immaculately prepared. They passed stalls filled with beautiful golden palominos that lifted their heads to watch her and Doc pass by. The stall at the end was the largest by far, occupied by a bright-eyed mare. Bryn breathed in the clean smell of fresh wood shavings that covered the stall floor. Doc stepped into the stall, followed by Bryn, and ran his hand down the mare's neck.

"How are you feeling today, my beauty?" he asked softly.

The mare turned to look at Doc and watched him curiously as he inspected her expansive belly and swollen udder. He softly pinched a teat, and a warm stream of milk oozed from the nipple. His hand smoothed down her rear haunch and pushed her tail aside.

"She hasn't begun to dilate yet, but her time is growing close," he instructed.

Bryn had placed her hand on the mare's swollen belly, and she could feel the colt's movement deep inside. "He seems anxious to come out," she said as her fingers traced the movement.

They turned at the sound of footprints approaching from behind them. Bryn turned around and was disappointed again. She had hoped Sully would join them in the barn, but a young man approached instead.

"Good morning, Glen," Doc said.

"Morning Doc, is this your granddaughter?" Glen asked, eyeing Bryn closely.

"That would be Dr. Bryn Barton," he said proudly.

Bryn smiled and offered the man her hand, "Nice to meet you, Glen."

"Likewise, ma'am," Glen said as he softly shook her hand.

"Where is the boss lady this morning?"

Glen looked back to the front of the barn. "One of the Gators is gone, so I would assume she is paying a visit to the foal pasture," he said. "She can't seem to get enough of the young ones," he said with a chuckle.

"Let's take a ride out and visit Sully in her haven then," Doc said to Bryn.

"The keys are in the other Gator," Glen said as he began filling buckets with sweet feed for the horses in the barn. "You know the way, don't you, Doc?"

"I have been there a few times," Doc said with a wry smile.

"You can drive," Doc said as he slipped into the passenger seat.

Bryn walked around, climbed behind the wheel, and then turned the key to start the engine. She pulled out of the barn and headed in the direction Doc was pointing. They passed field after field of clover and other grasses that would soon be turned into hay for winter feeding. Bryn sighed softly as she looked across areas of verdant green that seemed to go on forever. They drove for another five minutes before a tree line came into view. The path came to a junction, and Doc waved her to the right. The trees were dense for several minutes, and suddenly, a golden clearing appeared. The sun had risen a few hours earlier, but the glow coming from the clearing was amplified by the sun gleaming off the golden coats of several dozen horses.

Bryn's foot slipped off the gas pedal as she took in the sight before her. There, encircled by foals and their mothers, was Sully, oblivious to anything other than the animals she loved. It was apparent by the way the animals nuzzled into her and crowded near that they adored her just as much. Bryn found the gas once more and drove closer to the small herd.

Bryn saw Sully's head turn when she heard the approach of the Gator and turned to find Doc and Bryn. Sully began walking toward the approaching vehicle. Bryn stopped short of the herd and followed Doc from the Gator.

†

Doc spoke to Sully, giving Bryn a few seconds to examine Sully. Long legs were covered by dark jeans, and a navy pullover shirt revealed solid, tanned arms. As her eyes traveled up Sully's body, Bryn met the stare of crystal blue eyes as Sully looked at her.

"I think you remember Bryn," she heard her grandfather say.

Sully smiled at her as she reached her hand out. "It has been too many years, but she has grown into a beautiful woman," Sully said as her eyes smiled at Bryn.

Bryn felt her cheeks flushing as she slipped her hand into Sully's. "It is good to see you again," Bryn said. "From what grandfather says, we will be spending a bit of time together," Bryn managed to say.

"I look forward to that," Sully said with a firm squeeze of Bryn's hand.

A comfortable silence fell between them as their eyes were locked in an embrace. Doc suppressed a chuckle as he spoke to break the silence. "We checked on the mare before coming out."

Sully realized Doc was speaking, released Bryn's hand, and turned back to face him. "What was that, Doc?"

"I said we examined the mare before coming out," he repeated. "The mare doesn't look like she will make it to full term."

"I didn't think so either. We should keep a very close eye on her for the next week," Sully said as she turned to look at Bryn again.

†

Doc carefully viewed the exchange and walked into the gathering herd to give the two women a moment of privacy. He couldn't help but smile at how well the two women interacted together. Even an old man of his age could feel the spark of electricity in the air that connected them. He busied himself, examining the animals gathered around him. They were beautifully bred and would turn into prime animals for breeding and working stock under Sully's guidance and training.

†

Bryn was speechless, and the blue eyes held her transfixed as they searched deep into her soul. She felt a shiver of pleasure pass through her body as Sully's eyes devoured her completely.

Bryn forced herself to tear away from Sully's gaze and looked after her grandfather. "It looks like you have built quite a herd," she said.

"She has bred some of the best stock I have ever seen," Doc said as he slid his hand down one of the foal's backs. "Strong and sure-footed with excellent temperament to boot," he added as he turned and grinned at the two women.

"They are incredible animals. I hate letting go of even one of them," Sully admitted.

"Well, at least you are very selective of your buyers," Doc said. "Too many breeders don't bother to check into potential buyers, and good animals are ruined."

"That is sad but all too true," Bryn said. "I saw that too often at the tracks."

"I can only imagine the abuses you saw in the racing business," Sully said as she shook her head. "I swear some of those owners should be taken out and shot for what they do to their animals."

"Unlike you, who treats her animals like family, too many owners just look at their horses as another piece of investment property and not a living, breathing creature," Bryn said, with a note of sadness in her voice.

Sully turned toward an approaching colt and dug her hand into her pocket to pull out her knife. The colt stopped in front of her and waited patiently as she sliced a portion of the apple she had been hiding and placed it in the palm of Bryn's hand.

"He can't get enough of the apples," she said with a grin.

"Looks like you have him spoiled," Bryn said as she watched the colt gently take the apple from her with soft lips that tickled the palm of her hand.

"Every chance I get," Sully said.

Doc's cell phone rang. He answered the call and then turned back to Bryn and Sully. Bryn was disappointed that a call would pull her away from Sully so soon.

"I forgot I was supposed to drop some supplies off to Darren Green," Doc said.

To Bryn's delight, Doc suggested she stay with Sully, and they meet for lunch.

"I think I can handle the delivery. Why don't you and Sully discuss the herd and then meet me in town for lunch?" he suggested.

Bryn looked at Sully. "Do you have plans?"

"I do now," Sully answered with a smile.

"Meet me at the café at noon then," Doc said.

"We will be there," Sully promised.

"I will see you there," Doc said, returning to the Gator and driving away.

"Have you kept up with your riding?" Sully asked.

"Not as often as I should."

"We will have to change that then," Sully said. "If Doc finishes with you early today, why don't you come over for a ride," she suggested.

"I would like that," Bryn said.

"Good," Sully said as she turned her attention back to the horses.

"They really are beautiful," Bryn said. "I know you must really hate to sell any of them."

"I do, but they are born to work, and I can't keep them all busy here."

"Do you still do most of the training?"

"No, unfortunately, I had an accident a few years ago, and the injury to my back doesn't allow me to ride as much as I would like, so I supervise the training. Glen is currently the rider I use to train."

"Yes, I met him back at the barn," Bryn stated.

"He is a good rider but still needs some work," she said as she checked a halter on one of the mares.

"I know you will teach him well."

"I love your confidence in me," Sully said as they walked among the horses.

"I doubt you have ever lacked confidence," Bryn said boldly, causing Sully to look at her.

"Not often, but I have had my moments," she said.

Bryn saw a flicker of sadness pass over Sully's face, and she could kick herself for making that comment.

"I have a half dozen, two and three-year-olds that Glen is training, and hopefully, several will be ready for competition this fall," she said.

"So, you do still show?"

"Just enough to keep the name of the farm in the limelight and to market the horses to the best possible buyers," Sully said. "I usually go for three to six weeks over the fall months."

"That isn't too bad," Bryn said.

"No, not at all, and with the reputation the farm has developed over the years, I usually have every available horse sold after the first couple of shows," she said with great pride.

"High quality horses are hard to come by," Bryn said. "You have much to be proud of from what I have seen."

"If everything Doc is proposing comes true with the birth of the next colt, we will have a bloodline that will be even better than the original Sun Dancer," she said.

"Have you picked out a name yet?" Bryn asked.

"No, I usually wait until the foals start showing off personality traits before I name them," Sully said.

"That makes sense," Bryn said as a filly nuzzled into her side.

"This sweet little girl," Sully said as she stroked the filly's neck, "is going to be called Sun Dancer's Jewel." Sully planted a kiss on an upturned face. "She has a heart of gold and has the confirmation to be a great breeder."

"She is beautiful."

"How do you feel about returning after so many years?" Sully asked.

"I always hoped I could take over for grandfather," Bryn said. "Life in the city and working the racetracks wasn't my cup of tea. I miss the peacefulness and genuine people who live in farm country."

"We are a breed apart from city folk," Sully said with a smirk. "You aren't afraid of getting bored or not being challenged enough?"

"I think you will be challenging enough for me," Bryn said without thinking. She felt her face instantly heat up as she realized the sexual undertone of her comment.

Sully looked at her curiously, a smile playing on her lips. "I am not quite sure how to interpret that statement," she said.

Her smile broadened as Bryn fidgeted and tried to devise an explanation that would allow her to wiggle out of the uncomfortable situation she had caused.

"Grandfather says that Sullivan's Trace accounts for three-quarters of his business," Bryn said without looking up at Sully. Had she looked into Sully's eyes, she would have seen the amused gleam in her eyes.

"Well, I hope then that I will provide enough challenge for you," Sully said as she walked deeper into the herd's midst.

It was Bryn's turn to ponder an interpretation, and she held back from the group for a moment to collect her thoughts.

# CHAPTER FOUR

---

Bryn took a deep breath and followed Sully into the middle of the herd of horses. She immediately noted a frown on Sully's face as she looked over the herd.

"Is there something wrong?"

"Someone is missing," Sully replied, silently counting the herd.

Without speaking, Sully took off at a brisk pace across the field toward a small expanse of woods. Bryn hurried to catch up to her. "Have you figured out who it is yet?"

"A mare and a filly of about three weeks old," Sully said as her eyes scanned the distance before her.

As they approached the tree line, Bryn could hear a loud crashing sound and a muffled growl. Sully took off at a full run, stopping only long enough to grab a tree limb as a weapon. Bryn tried her best but could not keep up with Sully as she raced toward the sound. She watched Sully jump a small creek, her booted foot splashing in the water. The sounds grew louder and fiercer as they approached. Bryn's heart raced as she realized the growling emanated from some type of canine beast, and the crashing sound was soon discovered to be the mare's attempt to protect her foal from attack from a pair of wild dogs.

Sully screamed at the dogs and fearlessly began to swing the limb at the attacking animals, striking one in the chest as he lunged after the foal. The wild dog yelped and shrank back from Sully. She chased the second animal, swinging wildly as her rage burned through her muscles. Intimidated by the humans, the animals turned away and sprinted into the woods.

Bryn stood motionless in shock at the site of the foal. The beautiful golden coat was hidden by a layer of freshly spilled blood, and the mare did not look much different. She quickly assessed the mare and found there were no life-threatening injuries to her, but the foal was a much different story. Most of the muscles in her chest had been torn to shreds, and her wounds were bleeding profusely.

"We have got to get her back to the barn immediately," Bryn said.

"Run back to the field and get the Gator, please, Bryn," Sully said with tears running down her cheeks.

The sadness and distress in Sully's voice broke Bryn's heart. She pushed away her desire to wrap Sully in her arms and returned to retrieve the vehicle. She used her cell phone to call her grandfather.

Breathlessly, she spoke to her grandfather. "There has been an accident, and I need you to bring my medical bag back to Sully's," she told him. "A foal has been attacked, and it is going to take a large amount of stitching to sew her up," she told him.

"I will be there in ten minutes," Doc said.

"Please hurry, Grandfather," Bryn pleaded.

Doc quickly identified the worry in Bryn's voice, slammed the brakes to perform a U-turn, and headed back to Sully's.

†

Sully took off her shirt and placed it against the foal's bleeding chest as she tried to slow the bleeding. With each rapid beat of the terrified animal's heart, precious blood-soaked Sully's shirt, and she knew if the foal was to survive, she had to act quickly. Sully lifted the animal in her arms as gently as possible and began walking out of the woods. She ignored the throbbing in her back and allowed her adrenalin to push her forward.

She had cleared the woods by ten yards when Bryn arrived with the Gator. The mare followed closely as Sully stepped into the Gator with the foal still in her arms and trotted beside them as they began the journey back to the barn.

"Doc is on his way with supplies," Bryn said, trying to comfort Sully.

Sully looked up at her, and the fear of the foal's imminent death was written all over her face.

"We will do everything we can to help her survive," Bryn promised as she looked away from the pain in Sully's eyes.

The small animal no longer had the strength to struggle, and she lay quietly in Sully's arms. As they approached the herd, the smell of blood reached the horses' nostrils, and the mares called wildly to their foals to collect them in a defensive grouping.

When they reached the path, Bryn could drive faster, and they raced toward the barn, praying they would arrive in time to save the foal. She looked over at Sully, now covered in the foal's blood.

"Is the bleeding slowing at all?"

Sully carefully peeled the soaked shirt back from the significant chest wound and was slightly relieved to see the blood beginning to clot. "I think it is stopping," she croaked, her voice full of emotion.

As the barn came into sight, Sully sensed Bryn was relieved to see Doc's truck barreling down the driveway. It would take both their efforts to save the tiny foal.

†

Doc parked the truck and ran into the barn to find Glen. "There has been an accident, and Bryn and Sully are bringing in a filly. Make us a soft pallet of whatever you can find, and make it fast," he said to Glen.

Glen immediately began making a pallet of winter blankets they used to provide comfort from the elements during cold weather while Doc set out medical supplies on a small table. He quickly realized he would not have enough catgut to stitch up the foal and sent Glen scrambling from the barn to drive to his office for more supplies.

Glen was flying down the drive in Doc's truck when Sully and Bryn arrived.

The panic on Sully's face showed Doc how severe the injury was. She was usually a confident person, and he could see the heavy worry on her face as she stepped out of the vehicle carrying the foal.

"Glen has made us a pallet. Place her there, and let's get a good look at her," he said.

Sully carried the foal into the barn, knelt to place her on the soft pile of blankets, and stepped away to make room. Doc and Bryn knelt and carefully removed the shirt from the foal's chest. The raw flesh was laid open in a mixture of pink and red.

The mare who had caught up with them nudged Sully with a muffled sound. Doc looked up at the mare.

"Why don't you see if you can clean her up and inspect her for injuries while we work on the foal," he suggested. "I sent Glen for supplies."

"I will start cleaning her wounds if you will get an IV started so we can get some fluids and some pain medications into her," Bryn said.

Doc nodded and rose to start his project while Sully led the mare from the stall and gently cleaned the blood from her coat.

†

Sully found a few gashes and bites from her efforts to protect her foal, but nothing that would require immediate attention.

"You did your best, girl," Sully softly spoke to the mare as she stroked her coat. "We will do everything we can for your baby," she promised as she looked the mare straight in the eyes.

Sully watched Bryn gently brush betadine across the foal's shredded chest. As the blood was removed, she discovered there was little muscle tissue to work with. They would need to do their best to reconnect muscles and tendons to repair the foal's chest.

What had started out as a lazy, laid-back day had turned into a nightmare, Bryn thought as she stole a glance at Sully. The pain medicine was working as the foal closed her eyes and placed her life in Bryn's hands.

Glen returned at a gallop and brought a bag of supplies into the stall.

"Holy shit," he exclaimed when he saw the gaping wound in the small animal's chest. "What happened?"

"Apparently, a pair of wild dogs caught the mare and filly at the stream taking a drink and attacked," Bryn said. "They looked half-starved when we arrived, and Sully chased them off."

Glen looked at Doc, then at Bryn, and finally at Sully, stunned into silence.

"Why don't you take over for Sully and allow her to get cleaned up," Doc suggested to Glen, who walked over to Sully.

"Let me finish here, and you go clean up and change clothes," he said.

Sully nodded and walked over to the stall where Doc and Bryn were busily working on the foal. "Is there anything I can do?"

"This is going to take hours, so why don't you get cleaned up and dressed in fresh clothes," Doc said.

†

Sully looked down and found she was covered in blood and was bare from the waist up except for her sports bra. She was too shocked to be embarrassed and walked from the barn toward the house. She stripped the remainder of her clothing in the laundry room and walked to the shower.

Sully was mesmerized by the amount of blood that rinsed from her body to swirl down the shower drain. She shook the negative thoughts of the foal's possible death from her mind and quickly bathed. She dried and dressed in clean clothing before leaving her bedroom. As she passed the stone fireplace, her eyes fell upon her father's hunting rifle.

The hot, dry weather had forced the wild dogs to become desperate, and Sully feared there would be additional attacks if she did not take immediate action to protect the rest of her herd. She took the rifle down, loaded it, and took a box of ammunition before leaving the house. She walked directly to the Gator she and Bryn had used, and without a word to anyone, Sully drove back to the foal pasture.

The animals were still gathered in a tight group, the mares tense with fear as the foals remained close to their mothers.

She drove past the herd toward the stream and parked the Gator. She took the loaded rifle and poured a handful of shells into her hand to place them in her pocket. She left the vehicle and began tracking the wild dogs on foot through the dense forest. She walked silently, her eyes and ears straining for a glimpse or sound of her prey.

Sully despised killing any animal, but she knew that once the wild dogs tasted blood, they would return until they were successful in their hunt. She stalked the pair for over an hour before she reached a high ridge that would allow her to see from a distance. She climbed to the peak and lay down on her belly to look across the ridge. Her ears were first to detect the presence of the dogs growling at one another.

She lifted the rifle and brought the larger of the two animals into the sight of the rifle's scope. They were safely in range, and before her resolve faltered, Sully squeezed the trigger, sending a speeding bullet into the body of the targeted dog. Before the first animal fell to the ground, Sully searched for the second one. She located it and tracked it as the animal bolted in fear. Sully squeezed off another shot, but her aim was off, and it sailed dangerously high above the dog's head. She steadied her aim and fired again, dropping the animal in his tracks. Sully placed the rifle on the ground and watched for signs of movement for several minutes. As she sat up and leaned against a rock, both animals remained motionless. The tears began to fall down Sully's cheeks as she confirmed her prey was dead.

†

In the stillness of the day, Bryn lifted her head as the sound of rifle shots resounded from deep in the forest. She turned back to catch her grandfather's eyes. "I guess we don't have to worry about attacks from those two anymore."

"No, I would imagine Sully has dispatched the culprits of this mess," Doc said as he resumed the tedious work of sewing muscle and tendons.

"Glen, this is going to take several more hours. Can you rig us some extra lighting?" Doc asked.

"Sure thing, Doc," Glen said, then disappeared into the barn to return several minutes later with a halogen lamp that he hung on the stall walls.

"That's perfect, thanks," Doc said. "How is the mare?"

"She has a few bites and gashes that could use some of your stitch work, but she is resting quietly and watching patiently from the stall next door," Glen said.

Bryn looked up to find a pair of deep brown eyes peeking through the top rails of the stall, looking down upon them with concern for her baby. "No pressure here," she said with a grin to her grandfather.

"Let's take a stretch break and change the IV bottle," Doc suggested.

Bryn stood and raised her arms above her head. It did feel good to stretch after over an hour of kneeling to work on the foal's wounds. She walked over to find Doc searching through his bag to load a syringe with a powerful antibiotic. "We will need to administer the antibiotics and pain medicine every four hours today and into tomorrow to ward off the infection and keep the foal sedated if we have any hope of saving her," he said.

"I will stay today and tonight, and you can relieve me tomorrow morning," Bryn said.

"Are you sure you are ready for that?" Doc asked.

"I might as well jump in with both feet," she said as she picked up a stethoscope and checked the foal's vital signs. "She is young to be so strong."

"If she can survive the night, I think her chances are good," Doc said. "I can't guarantee how well she will walk or run, but hopefully, she is young enough to adapt and heal."

Glen returned to the stall. "Is there anything I can do?"

"Call my house and ask Camille to prepare sandwiches and lots of coffee, and then you can go pick them up," Doc said. "It is going to be a long day, and we still have several more hours before we are finished tending to her injuries."

"I will take care of it," Glen said, leaving the stall.

Bryn heard the rumbling of the Gator's motor and looked out to see Sully returning from the pasture. She watched as Sully parked the vehicle and disappeared into the house carrying the rifle. "I will start back on the foal if you want to tend to the mare," she told her grandfather.

"I could use a few more minutes of stretching," Doc admitted, then picked up his bag and walked to the next stall to begin tending to the mare's injuries.

Bryn resumed stitching the foal's chest, concentrating so intensely that she did not hear Sully's approach.

"I thought this might help," Sully said as she placed a portable massage table inside the stall. "It can't be comfortable kneeling down on the ground to work on the foal."

"That would make it much easier. Can you help me get the filly on the table?"

Sully leaned down and grabbed two corners of the pallet of blankets, and with Bryn's help, they lifted the foal gently onto the table. Despite their care, the filly groaned in pain.

"Will she make it?" Sully asked.

Bryn took a deep breath and looked up to find Sully's eyes wet with tears. "Her vital signs are strong, and she is young and healthy, so I will say her chances are good if she survives the night."

†

Sully was relieved by the glimmer of hope Bryn had given her. "Is there anything I can do?"

"Yes, as a matter of fact, you can pull up a chair, keep me company, and help me finish tending her wounds," Bryn said. "Start by hanging the IV bag on the stall next to the light."

As Bryn instructed, Sully placed the bag on the stall wall and turned back toward her.

Bryn looked up and checked the level on the bag. "Grandfather, we will need more fluid before the night is out. How many more bags do you have at the office?" she asked.

"I have one more bag with me and several cases at the office," he answered. "When I have finished with the mare, I will go to the office and bring a case here. Sully has a refrigerator in the barn office we can use for storage."

"That should work. Will you also bring out extra medications that I can use tonight?" Bryn asked.

"Of course I will," he answered. "Especially since I will be the one sleeping in a comfortable bed tonight," he added with a grin.

"It's not a bed, but I have a very comfortable queen-sized air mattress," Sully said. "I will bring it out, and you can rest on it," she said as she sat on a rolling stool near the foal's head.

"That would be nice," Bryn said. "I must be up at least every four hours to administer the medications and check on the foal."

"I will be sure to wake you then," Sully said.

Doc silently treated the mare's wounds as Sully stroked the foal's head while she watched Bryn work.

"Your stitches are very tight and clean," Sully remarked.

"It is not uncommon for a horse to get cut in a starting chute, so I have had plenty of experience stitching horse flesh," Bryn said. "Will you hand me another length of catgut?" she asked.

Sully reached into the bag of supplies and handed her a length of the fine material.

"Thanks," Bryn said as she continued the intricate work of her stitching.

Sully watched as each movement of Bryn's hands made the foal's chest a little more recognizable. She tediously reconnected muscle tissue with tendons and used available skin to cover the wounds.

Hours passed before Bryn made the final stitch and cut the remaining thread. She looked up at Sully. "That is all I can do for now. The rest depends on the foal's will to survive."

"Thank you for everything you have done," Sully said.

"Don't worry, you will get a hefty bill," Bryn said with a wink. "I just wish this would never have happened."

"Me, too, but hopefully, it won't happen again," Sully said.

"Why don't you two wash up and come eat a sandwich," Doc said from the office.

"I am hungry," Bryn said.

"You did work up an appetite. There is a small bathroom in the office where you can wash up," she said as she led Bryn out of the stall.

Sully was surprised that it was nearly six in the evening when she took a hot mug of coffee from Doc. Bryn walked past them into the bathroom and returned a few minutes later.

"All yours," she said to Sully as she sat by her grandfather and looked over the plate of sandwiches Camille had made. "You better hurry before I eat all of these," she teased.

†

Sully walked to the bathroom to wash her hands, and when she looked into the mirror, tired eyes stared back at her. It had been a very long day, and the night promised to be lengthy as well.

Sully walked back to the table and returned to her seat.

"Would you like me to stay the night?" Glen asked.

"No, Glen, I don't know what else you can do tonight, but thank you," Sully said.

"All you have to do is call if you need anything," he said, standing to leave.

"I will," Sully promised.

"See you tomorrow then," he said and left the room.

"Camille has sent over plenty of sandwiches and coffee," Doc said, "and I am sure she is working on a hot meal now, so go easy on the sandwiches."

"I will still have room for Camille's cooking," Sully said as she finished a sandwich.

"The filly should be fine for a little while. Why don't you drive me back to the house to shower and dress in clean clothes," he suggested. "I will help Camille finish dinner and bring you a hot meal for two."

"Let me hang another bag of fluids and push some pain medicine, then we will go if Sully is comfortable with that," Bryn said.

"I can hold down the fort for a short time," Sully said as she followed Bryn. She stopped and turned toward Doc. "Thanks for everything, Doc."

"I am glad we were here to help out," Doc said, reaching for Sully and giving her a warm hug. "Call if you need anything tonight."

"I will," she said, turning to follow Bryn.

## CHAPTER FIVE

---

Sully followed Bryn back into the stall where the filly was resting. Bryn took her vitals and was pleased that the young animal slept peacefully. It was still too early to tell, but she felt the filly would pull through.

"Will you help me move her back to the pallet?" Bryn asked. "I think she will rest better there."

"Sure," Sully said, lifting one end of the blanket as she and Bryn moved the animal to the stall floor. "Mom can see her better here, too," she said, noticing the mare watching them closely.

Bryn smiled at Sully. She really loved her animals, and they seemed to be the focus of her every thought. Bryn hung another bag of fluids and injected another round of antibiotics. "That will hold her until I get back." She turned away from the filly to find Sully standing right behind her. Sully was close enough that Bryn could smell the fragrance of the soap she had used to shower. Bryn's mind skipped wildly at the thought of Sully in the shower, and her cheeks flushed.

Sully did not miss the blush and stepped back to look at Bryn. She looked into Bryn's eyes. "Is everything all right?" she asked.

"Yes, I'm fine, everything's fine," Bryn stammered. "I will be back soon," she said, stepping around Sully and joining Doc in the truck.

†

Sully leaned back against the massage table and smiled, remembering Bryn's blush. She wondered what she had thought to make her cheeks flush like that. Sully listened until the sound of Doc's truck disappeared into the night and then walked back to her house. She dug out the air mattress, a pillow, and a blanket to carry back to the barn. In the office, Sully used a pump to blow up the bed and placed it in the walkway between the stalls. She put the blanket and pillow on the mattress and then walked in to check on the filly.

†

"You did a fine job today," Doc said to Bryn as they drove home. "I haven't been able to stitch like that in years," he added.

"Thanks, I was pleased with the job, too. Do you think the filly will survive?"

"If the blood loss wasn't too great and infection doesn't set in, I think she has a good chance. I worry about her ability to stand and walk, though," he answered honestly. "She took a lot of damage to her muscles."

"Hopefully, she is young enough to regenerate those muscles," Bryn said.

"It is not unheard of by any means, but don't get your hopes too high," Doc said.

"Is there anything I need to watch out for tonight?"

"Keep her hydrated and be alert to a spiking temperature. If the wound is infected, we will know quickly enough."

Bryn nodded as Doc placed the truck in park and shut off the engine. "Are you in doubt about something?" he asked. "You seem distracted."

"I feel like saving this filly for Sully is crucial, and I don't want to make any mistakes."

Doc turned in the seat to look at his granddaughter. "The filly is in God's hands now. Sully knows you are doing your best to help her little girl survive and understands that, sometimes, you can't save them all, no matter how hard you try."

"But I feel it will be such a disappointment to her, and she will lose her confidence in me if the filly doesn't pull through," Bryn said with emotion trembling in her voice.

"You should know one thing about Micah Sullivan," Doc said. "If she did not have confidence in you, she would have never allowed you to touch her animals."

Bryn realized this was true and began to relax a little.

"Go ahead and shower while I help Camille finish dinner, and then I will take you back. It will be a long night, so get a good meal in your belly and get as much sleep as possible."

"I will try to hurry," Bryn said as she stepped from the truck.

†

Doc smiled with pride and followed his granddaughter into the house. He walked into the kitchen to find Camille adding the finishing touches to a pot roast.

"My, that smells heavenly."

"I will have dinner ready in just a few more minutes," Camille said. "How is the filly?"

"She's holding her own for now," Doc said. "Tonight will tell it all."

Camille looked at him with a wry grin. "And you don't plan on spending the night over there?" she asked.

"Nope, Bryn has eagerly volunteered for duty, and I am not about to try to convince her otherwise," Doc said. "Besides, she can tolerate sleeping on the ground much better than I."

Camille chuckled. "Well, you do have a point there. You aren't as young as you used to be," she teased.

"No need to remind me of that," Doc said as he reached for a biscuit and had his hand promptly slapped away.

"You can wait a few minutes."

Doc grumbled and turned toward the refrigerator to get a cool drink. "Can I at least have a glass of tea?"

"Yes, you can. If you want to speed things up, you can set the table," Camille said.

Doc took a sip and then went to the cupboard for dishes as he helped Camille with dinner.

†

Upstairs, Bryn shed her clothing and started the shower. She stopped at the sink to brush her teeth and looked at her image in the mirror. Bryn felt that she didn't have the glamorous looks some women had, but she was attractive in a natural way. Her skin was pure, and she never needed to cover it with makeup or other beauty products. Bryn wondered if it would be enough to attract the attention of a woman like Sully. *It would have to be*, she thought to herself. There was no time to change now. Still grinning, she stepped into the shower.

As she lathered her body, she thought of the fresh smell of Sully, and she felt her body burning again. Bryn felt giddy as she thought of Sully, and her body responded to those thoughts with anticipation as her hands roamed across her chest. Bryn closed her eyes and imagined Sully's hands on her body instead of hers. Deep inside, Bryn felt her body shudder with desire for the woman who had been her childhood hero and had grown into the woman who made her heart catch in her throat.

†

Sully sat beside the filly's head on the stall floor and leaned against the wall. Sully's hand softly stroked the filly's head and neck as she watched over the small animal. The filly stirred long enough to lift her head and look at Sully with pain-filled brown eyes. She moaned softly and placed her head in Sully's lap, closing her eyes against the pain.

Tears ran down Sully's cheeks as she imagined the pain the young animal must be feeling, and she contemplated her actions for only a moment. There was no way Sully wanted one of her babies in pain, but she would also not give up on them if they had the will to fight.

"Try to be strong, little one. The pain will ease up soon," Sully promised. Her fingers scratched the soft coat behind the filly's head, and she fell into a deep sleep. Sully leaned against the wall and looked up at the ceiling. She had forgotten the barn roof had skylights, and she looked through the transparent covering to see a sky brilliantly lit with stars. The rhythmic breathing of the filly filled Sully's ears, and when she allowed her eyes to close, she drifted off to sleep.

†

Bryn picked up the picnic basket Camille had filled for them from the truck seat and closed the door softly behind her. She entered the barn and placed the basket on the table before entering the stall area to check on the filly. Bryn was surprised Sully was nowhere in sight as she walked through the barn. She walked past the mattress and then turned to step into the stall and stopped.

Sully was utterly relaxed in her sleep, and her face was filled with peace as her fingers lay entwined in the filly's mane. It had been a horrible day, and Bryn was sure Sully had been awake for many hours before she and her grandfather joined her in the pasture. She must be exhausted from the emotional trauma that had occurred today. Bryn was also tired. The enjoyment she had experienced in the shower did little to revive her as she had hoped. For a fleeting second, Bryn envied the foal with its head lying in Sully's lap. She would love to be curled up against Sully now.

†

Sully's subconscious sensed another presence in the room, and she quietly stirred from her nap to find Bryn leaning against the stall door, smiling at her while she slept.

"I guess I drifted off for a while," she said as she wiped her face.

"It has been a long day," Bryn said. "You have to be exhausted with everything that has gone on today."

"Nothing that a quick cat nap won't cure," Sully said.

"How about a nice hot meal to add to that?" she asked.

"That sounds good." Sully gently lifted the filly's head and returned it to the blanket. "Is it too early for another pain shot?"

Bryn glanced at her wrist. "No, I think it would be fine. Has she been showing signs of pain?"

"Yes, before I fell asleep."

"I will go ahead and give her another dose. It is a little early, but it won't hurt her," Bryn said as she turned and opened her bag.

Sully watched as Bryn administered the medicine into the IV line and rechecked the filly's vital signs. "Still going strong," she said to a watchful Sully. "Now come with me, and we will share Camille's good cooking," Bryn said with a grin.

Sully followed Bryn back into the office to the table where she had spread out the meal Camille had prepared.

"Oh, dear Lord, you didn't tell me she baked biscuits. I would do anything for one of Camille's biscuits," she raved.

"Oh really," Bryn said as she picked up a biscuit and waved it before Sully. "I will have to keep that in mind," she added with a devilish grin.

Sully took the biscuit from Bryn and took a bite from it. "You do that," Sully said, challenging Bryn.

Bryn ignored the remark and sat down to begin serving their meals. She dipped out large slices of the pot roast, vegetables, and gravy onto the plates Camille had packed and unwrapped a half dozen biscuits. "Would you like honey or butter for your biscuits? Camille packed both."

"Both. I swear that woman must have been sent from heaven," Sully said. "She cooks the most amazing meals."

"Yes, she does. I can see that I will have to start an exercise program if I continue to eat her cooking."

"You can just come over and work with me daily," Sully offered. "Mucking stalls or baling hay will work those calories off you," she teased.

"Will you let me drive the tractor?" Bryn teased back.

"Heck no, that's my job," Sully said. "You can load all the hay bales you want, though."

"Gee, thanks," Bryn said. "With your back in the shape it's in, how do you get all that hay to the barn?"

"Well, it helps to have connections. I buy new equipment for the high school football program for a week's work of muscle," she said.

"That's a good deal for both you and the school."

"I will cut, rake, and bale the hay, and when I get enough of a head start, Coach brings out trucks and the team. They load, haul, and store about ten thousand bales for the farm."

"That's a lot of hay," Bryn said.

"I use most of it during the winter and sell a couple thousand bales to some of the local farmers. Usually, those are the funds I use to buy equipment, so it all works out well."

"Such a clever woman," Bryn teased.

Sully found herself chuckling, which surprised her. It felt good to laugh. She could not remember how long it had been since she had done so and was surprised after the hectic day they had shared that she could find anything humorous. Bryn was easy to be around, and she seemed to be comfortable, too.

Sully poured glasses of tea, and they shared the hearty meal. "I have an alarm on my watch if you want to nap while I watch over the filly," Sully offered.

"That would be nice, but are you sure you wouldn't like a nap first?"

"I already had a power nap, remember?" she said.

"That's right, how could I forget?" she said with a warm smile.

They cleaned up the dishes from their meal together and walked in to check on the filly. She seemed to be resting well.

"It's almost eight. I will wake you at midnight," Sully said, setting the alarm as Bryn put away her instruments.

"Promise me you will wake me if she shows any signs of distress," Bryn said.

"I promise," Sully said as she dimmed the barn lights, leaving just enough to softly illuminate the filly's stall. She watched Bryn until she was sure she was comfortable and stepped back inside the stall.

She carefully lay down beside the filly and stroked down the length of her body. As her hands sifted through the soft coat, Sully noticed something for the first time. She strained her eyes to look closer and confirmed her original findings.

The filly's coat was splotched with a faint dappling where her coat was a lighter shade.

"That's it," Sully whispered. "I will call you Sunspot for your dappled coat," she told the sleeping filly. "Yes, Sunspot it will be," she repeated, proud of herself.

In the quiet of the barn, Sully could hear the soft breathing of the filly, and with her hand next to Sunspot's shoulder, she could feel the vigorous pounding of her heart.

Just outside the stall, she could hear Bryn breathing softly as she drifted off to sleep. Sully continued to run her hand down the filly's body, stroking it softly as she whispered words of comfort to her. The warmth of the filly's body began to seep into Sully's body, and she began to relax. When she could no longer keep her eyes open, she laid her head on Sunspot's neck and fell asleep.

# CHAPTER SIX

---

Sully was awakened by a gentle shaking movement. She struggled to open her eyes and focus on her surroundings. As the reality of where she was sunk in, Sully realized what had caused her to wake.

Sunspot's body was convulsing and soaked with sweat. The fog in Sully's brain lifted, and she called out for Bryn.

"Bryn, please wake up. I need you now," Sully pleaded.

†

Bryn heard the distress in Sully's voice and flew from the mattress to enter the stall. Her eyes immediately fell on the filly, and she rushed to her bag. Bryn pulled out a tympanic thermometer and lifted it to the filly's ear. She watched in horror as the LED numbers climbed rapidly, and Bryn knew she must act immediately to reduce the filly's fever and attack the infection.

"I need to insert a catheter into the filly's jugular vein to start a stronger antibiotic," Bryn said as she took supplies from her bag. "Can you find more blankets to keep her covered?"

"I will be right back with more," Sully said.

Bryn quickly located the best entry point to insert the catheter and placed it before Sully returned. She was busy taping the tubing in place when Sully returned. "Cover her body," she instructed as she upturned a bottle and filled a hypodermic with oxytetracycline.

"This is a potent antibiotic, and it may take up to five doses to extinguish the infection, but it should help reduce the fever," Bryn explained.

"Are we going to lose her?" Sully asked.

"Not without one hell of a fight," Bryn said, trying to sound confident as she began administering the medications. "I will also add an anti-inflammatory to her regular IV, and we will continue to push fluids to keep her hydrated."

Sully covered the filly and watched Bryn work. "You are going to be just fine, Sunspot," she promised the small animal.

"Sunspot," Bryn said.

"Yeah," Sully said. "She has a dappled coat, I never realized until tonight."

Bryn smiled at Sully. "That is a perfect name for her."

Sully returned her smile, but a soft groan made the smile disappear instantly.

Bryn reached over and covered Sully's hand with her own. "We are going to bring her through this together."

Tears slid down Sully's cheeks, and she lowered her head to hide them. Bryn let go of her hand and lifted Sully's chin. "It's okay to cry," she said, reaching out to hold Sully.

Sully collapsed into Bryn's embrace, and the tears fell in earnest. They remained silent until her tears began to subside, and Sully pulled away from Bryn.

"I'm sorry," she said, looking embarrassed.

"There is nothing to apologize for," Bryn said. "I know how important each of these animals is to you." She searched Sully's eyes for a sign of relief. "Why don't you wash your face and prepare a pot of coffee? We can sit up together and watch over Sunspot."

Sully stood and left the stall. Bryn took a deep breath and checked the filly's vitals. The convulsions had stopped, and she appeared to be resting once more. At one hundred five degrees, her temperature had grown dangerously high and would have to be monitored closely. If the antibiotics were not successful in reducing the fever, the filly would have to be transported to the office so they could attempt an ice bath, but that would only be a last resort. Bryn prayed the drugs would be effective.

She sat down beside the filly and leaned back against the stall wall. Bryn could feel the mare's soft muzzle and warm breath puffing through the rails, and she turned to look at her. "She's a tough little girl, Mama," she said. "She's going to be okay."

Bryn heard Sully approaching the stall and turned to watch her step back inside and join her beside Sunspot. Sully handed her a steaming mug of coffee.

"Thanks," Bryn said as she took the coffee from Sully and took a sip.

"I didn't know how you like your coffee, so I took a wild guess," Sully said.

"Just perfect, light and sweet, just like I would have fixed it," Bryn said.

Sully reached down and stroked Sunspot's neck, and the filly raised her head and stretched to reach Sully's lap. Sully moved closer and took the filly's head in her lap.

"It looks like you have a new best friend," Bryn said.

"A lifelong one if she survives," Sully said.

"Why is that?"

"As much damage as she has, her conformation will be ruined. Hopefully, she will become strong enough to walk, but her future as a working horse is gone," she said as she stroked down the filly's face. "She may make a nice pleasure horse and possibly breeding stock, but she will stay with me regardless."

"I hope we will be surprised at how well she heals," Bryn said. "She has a lot of fight, which can only work in her favor."

"They are tough stock, and if there is a chance to survive, this little one will do it. I can feel it," Sully said.

Sunspot made a soft sound as if to agree with Sully's statement.

"I wouldn't mind a nice saddle horse to have to ride," Bryn said. "That is if you would consider selling her to me."

"Selling her, no, but if she can bear a rider, she will be yours anytime you want to ride. I just can't see me letting her go completely after what she is going through, but if she survives, it will largely be in part to your efforts, so you will be part owner," Sully said.

Bryn really liked the sound of that. "So we would have joint custody?" she teased.

Sully chuckled. "Yes, I guess you could think of it like that."

Bryn sat back against the wall to drink her coffee and study Sully. Her large hands gently stroked the filly's head, soothing the young animal. In her years of practice, Bryn had seen many people with a unique way with animals, but Sully's touch and the way she spoke to the animals comforted them even when their bodies were filled with pain.

Stroking the animal also seemed to help Sully relax. Bryn watched as the tension in Sully's upper body seemed to flow out of her, and her hand moved down the filly's neck. Sully leaned forward, bending over Sunspot's body, stretching her lower back muscles.

"How is your back feeling?"

"I can definitely feel today's exertion," Sully said with a slight grimace as she straightened.

"You do have a massage table over there. If you want to stretch out, I will see if I can loosen those muscles for you," Bryn offered.

Sully smiled very sweetly at Bryn. "I may take you up on that later."

"The offer stands whenever you are ready."

†

Sully nodded her head and lifted the coffee to her lips. They sat silently until they finished their coffee, and Bryn returned to the kitchen for refills. When she walked back into the stall, Sully noted the exhaustion in her body. She had barely fallen asleep when Sully had awakened her earlier.

“Thanks,” she said, taking a fresh cup of coffee. “You didn’t get much sleep earlier, so you can try again when you finish your coffee,” she suggested.

“I think I am too wired to sleep right now,” Bryn admitted. “Why don’t you try to catch some sleep?”

“I’m too wired, too,” Sully said with a grin.

The alarm on Sully’s wrist went off, and she reached down to reset it as Bryn gathered her equipment to check the filly’s vital signs.

Sully held her breath as Bryn lifted the thermometer to Sunspot’s ear.

†

Bryn watched the reading climb quickly and let out a sigh of relief when the escalation slowed. She turned the instrument to face Sully. “It’s still higher than I am comfortable with, but at least it is coming down.”

“One hundred three,” Sully said aloud.

“It dropped a little over two degrees after the first dose,” Bryn said, standing and walking to her bag to draw up the next dose. “I hope we can get another two degrees out of the next dosage.”

“Me too,” Sully said as she watched Bryn slowly press the plunger on the syringe to administer the medication into the catheter.

Sunspot struggled slightly in Sully’s lap. “Does that hurt her?”

“The medicine is powerful. Sunspot is possibly reacting to a burning sensation as it hits her bloodstream.” She noted the worried look on Sully’s face. “It should pass very quickly.”

Sunspot settled down and rested quietly again, much to Sully's relief. Bryn, too, settled back in, sitting shoulder to shoulder with Sully.

They sat in comfortable silence as they listened to the filly's relaxed breathing and the soft moaning of the breeze outside.

†

Sully watched over Sunspot and listened to Bryn's breathing start to deepen. She quietly slipped an arm around Bryn's shoulder to brace her head as it rested softly on her shoulder. The warmth of Bryn's body on her own comforted Sully as she watched her sleep soundly.

Sully sat her coffee cup in the wood shavings and rested her head against the stall. Bryn turned slowly in her sleep until her hand rested comfortably on Sully's thigh. With great restraint, Sully fought the urge to run her fingers through Bryn's curls as she slept. She closed her eyes to allow her body to relax as her mind spun wildly with thoughts of Bryn.

# Chapter Seven

---

Bryn woke two hours later with Sully's arm still wrapped around her shoulder. The harder she tried to remain still and not disturb Sully's rest, the more she squirmed. Even Sunspot, who was alert, tried to stay still, but despite their efforts, Sully woke to two pairs of soft brown eyes watching her.

"Am I missing out on something here?" she asked, not moving her arm from around Bryn's shoulder.

"No, we were trying to be quiet to prevent waking you," Bryn answered as she looked up at Sully.

She hated to move, but she was beginning to get a crick in her neck. Sully moved her arm as she sat straight and turned her attention to Sunspot.

"How are you feeling, little one?"

Sully seemed relieved by the brightness in the filly's eyes. They had been clouded with pain earlier, but now they were shining brightly and with curiosity as the filly studied her.

†

Bryn climbed to her feet and completed checking on her patient. Sunspot's fever had broken during the night, and Bryn's heart was filled with renewed hope that the young animal would survive her trauma. As she read the thermometer, the smile on her face relayed the good news to Sully without a word.

"The worst has passed," Bryn finally spoke.

"That's the best news I have heard all night," Sully said.

"I think she will rest quietly for the remainder of the night," Bryn said as she administered the next dosage of medications.

"I hope so," Sully said as she stood and lifted the soft blanket over the filly's shoulder. "I will be right back," she said, leaving the stall.

Bryn finished her examination of Sunspot and put her instruments away.

†

Sully entered the office and used the restroom before searching the refrigerator for a bottle of cold water. She opened it and took a long drink before replacing the cap. Sully checked the clock to see that it was four in the morning. Her body was exhausted; she knew Bryn also had to be beyond tired. She walked back into the stall and handed Bryn the water.

"Thanks," Bryn said as she took a long drink.

"Do you think she will be okay without us for a few hours?" Sully asked.

Bryn seemed puzzled by Sully's question. "Yes, I think she will be fine."

"Good, come with me then," Sully said as she offered Bryn her hand. "I know we could both use some sleep," she said with a smile. "I am a light sleeper and will hear Sunspot if she becomes distressed," Sully said as she took Bryn's hand and led her out of the stall to the air mattress. "I have my alarm set for the next medication time, so if we are lucky, we can get a few hours in."

†

"Sounds wonderful," Bryn said. She was exhausted and welcomed the opportunity to stretch out, especially next to Sully. Bryn took her shoes off and lay down next to a bootless Sully. "If you wake early, get me up, too," she said.

"If I need you, I will. Otherwise, I will let you sleep as long as possible," Sully said as she turned toward Bryn. Her eyes searched Bryn's. "I feel I must warn you I like to snuggle in my sleep."

"No warning is necessary," Bryn said as she took Sully's hand in hers, turned on her side away from Sully, and pulled her arm around her waist.

Bryn heard Sully chuckle softly as she allowed her body to be pulled closer to Bryn. She felt Sully press in close until she could feel Bryn's heat caress the front of her body. Her head rested on a pillow, and she breathed in the clean scent of Bryn's hair. Content, Sully sighed gently and closed her eyes to sleep.

†

Bryn's heart pounded as she felt Sully's body press close to hers. She thought her heart would stop beating when she felt Sully's hand slide under her shirt to rest on her warm skin. With great restraint, she stifled a moan and willed her body to relax enough for her to fall asleep. Bryn felt the warm puff of air as Sully's breathing deepened as she drifted.

†

Doc stretched in his bed and turned to check the clock. Bryn had not called, so he assumed the night was going well. He turned onto his side and decided to get another hour's sleep before climbing from his bed to begin what he knew would be a long day.

When he awoke an hour later, the dark had faded as the sun slowly approached to welcome a new day. He climbed from the bed and looked out his bedroom window at the stars during the last few minutes of darkness. Before showering, he walked to his closet and pulled out freshly pressed jeans and a work shirt. Doc could hear Camille stirring in the house as she entered the kitchen to start the coffee and breakfast.

He showered and dressed before rechecking the clock. He had time for a quick breakfast before driving over to check on the filly and relieve Bryn and Sully for some much-needed rest. He walked into the kitchen just as Camille finished a skillet of gravy.

"Good morning. I trust you slept well."

"Like a rock," Doc answered.

"Grab some coffee, and breakfast will be ready in a minute."

"Biscuits and gravy?" he asked.

"Yes, I thought you would like something to stick to your ribs this morning," she teased.

"What a perfect way to start the morning," Doc said.

"I assume you are headed next door when you finish," Camille said.

"Yes, I thought I would relieve Bryn and Sully."

"Send them over for a hot breakfast," Camille instructed as she served Doc a platter of gravy-covered biscuits.

"I will try, but convincing Sully to leave the barn may be hard. You know how she is about her animals."

"You just tell her I am expecting her and remind her how I hate to be disappointed," Camille said sternly.

"Yes, ma'am, I will," Doc answered as he cut into the biscuit. "When I tell her you have fresh biscuits and gravy waiting for her, she may not fight much," he teased.

"Not if she knows what is good for her," Camille said as she returned to the stove to prepare a plate for herself.

Doc finished his breakfast and poured a fresh cup of coffee. "That was another perfect breakfast, Camille," he said.

"I am glad you enjoyed it. Send those girls over soon," she said as he walked toward the door.

"Will do," he said as he slipped out the front door.

†

Doc drove the short distance to Sullivan's Trace and parked in front of the barn. The sun had barely crept above the horizon when he stepped from his truck into a crisp, clear morning. Silence surrounded him as he approached the barn and padded into the office. He walked into the stable and smiled when he saw Bryn and Sully still asleep on the mattress. They were snuggled together with Sully's arm draped protectively over Bryn's body. He walked past them into the stall and quietly examined the filly. The young animal was covered in a pile of blankets, and when he checked the bottles of medicine and found the strong antibiotic, he deduced she had spiked a fever during the night. He took the thermometer and checked the filly's temperature. A few tenths above normal. The treatment Bryn had chosen worked well. He was very proud of his granddaughter's skills. He pulled the blanket back to check the filly's wounds. All the stitches were intact and dry, which would help them heal correctly.

He stood up and stretched, then checked his watch. It was time to wake the girls and send them off for breakfast. He picked up his coffee and walked out of the stall. He leaned down and gently shook Sully and Bryn awake.

"Good morning, you two," he said.

"Good morning, Doc," Sully said.

"Morning, Grandfather," Bryn added as she sleepily wiped her face.

"It looks like you two had a busy night," he said. "Her temperature is almost back to normal," he added when he saw Sully's worried look.

"The filly spiked a high fever, and it took several doses to bring it down," Bryn said.

"She looks good," Doc said. "Sutures are dry and intact."

"That coffee smells good," Sully said. "Would you like some?" she asked Bryn.

"I have strict orders to send you two next door," Doc said. "Camille has fresh biscuits and gravy waiting for you."

"Mmm, biscuits," Bryn teased Sully.

"I guess there is no arguing then," Sully said.

"Not if you don't want to suffer the wrath of Camille," Doc answered.

"I would rather face the devil himself," Sully teased.

"You are such a smart woman." He watched the two women rise and stretch. "Go eat and get some rest. You two look like you could use some food and sleep. I will take over from here."

"I won't be long," Sully said.

"You need food and rest. Glen will be here soon, and he and I can handle things until later today, so I order both of you to get some rest."

"Okay, but I will check in when I return," Sully said.

"Fine, but then I will send you off to the house," Doc promised.

"Very well, you have a deal," Sully submitted.

"I don't expect to see you either until late afternoon," he said to Bryn.

"Yes, Grandfather," Bryn said.

"I will call you both if I need you," he promised. "Now go before Camille starts calling."

Sully grinned at Bryn. "Are you ready?"

"Do we have any choice?"

"Not really," Sully said. "Besides, all this talk of food is making me hungry," she said, pulling on her boots.

Doc watched them leave and then turned to check on the mare's injuries and examined the pregnant mare. After finishing his examinations, he searched the barn until he found the equipment he hoped would be there. He made a mental note to have Glen bring the equipment to the filly's stall as soon as he arrived. Doc knew the best medicine the filly could get right now was a meal of her mother's milk, and he felt the filly would be strong enough to stand with the support to nurse. He smiled, pleased with his idea, and patiently waited for Glen.

†

Camille heard the girls pull up in the drive and was pouring apple juice and coffee when they walked into the kitchen.

"Good morning, ladies," she said. "How was the night?"

"Long, but I think the filly is going to pull through," Bryn said.

"Of course she is. She had the best vet and owner pulling for her all night long," Camille said. She eyed Sully carefully. "And you, young lady, need to start visiting more. You are way too skinny these days."

Sully chuckled and grinned at Camille. "If I eat too much of your cooking, I will become lazy," she teased.

"No way, not as hard as you work. You will burn the calories off in no time. It is still good to see you," she added.

"It's good to see you too, Camille," Sully said as she bent down to kiss her on the cheek. "When Doc said you had biscuits and gravy, there was no way I would turn down your breakfast offer."

"Well, make yourself at home, and I will bring over some food," Camille said as she took two plates down, filled them with biscuits, and smothered them with sausage gravy. When she carried the heaping plates to the table, Sully's eyes sparkled with delight. "This should help you both get some rest. Get your bellies full and crawl into bed," Camille said.

"We didn't get much rest last night, so I bet we both drop off to sleep quickly," Bryn said.

"No doubt," Sully said as she filled her mouth with a bite of biscuit. "I feel like I could sleep for days, but I know my body will not allow me to sleep beyond six hours."

"You just make sure you get every minute of it then," Camille said. "The filly is in good hands with Doc, so there is no need to worry about her."

"I know, but I don't want her to think I have abandoned her."

"Trust me, she will know better, and you need to take care of yourself so you can help her heal," Camille reminded her.

"Don't forget we have joint custody, so I will be there to help, too," Bryn added.

"Joint custody, what's this all about?"

"Last night, Sully promised me part ownership of Sunspot and said I could ride her whenever I wanted if she became strong enough to bear a rider," Bryn said.

"Sunspot is a cute name," Camille said with a soft chuckle. "You come up with some of the best names I have heard," she told Sully.

"She has a faint dapple to her golden coat, so I thought the name was appropriate," she explained.

"Clever girl," Camille said as she walked to the coffee pot to refill their cups.

†

While Bryn and Sully ate breakfast, Glen arrived at the barn and was quickly put to work by Doc.

"Good morning, Glen," Doc said. "I have a few chores for you this morning."

"Great, what can I do for you, Doc?" he asked.

"There is a hay lift in the back of the barn with a sling attached. I want to use this to lift the filly to her feet so we can bring the mare in and let her nurse," Doc explained. "I think the comfort feature and the nutrients in her mother's milk are the best medicine for her at this point."

"I'm on it, Doc," Glen said and disappeared.

Ten minutes later, Glen had the lift inside the stall, and they worked carefully to place the sling beneath Sunspot's body. Once Doc was satisfied with the placement, he turned to Glen. "Will you bring the mare in?"

Glen smiled with excitement. "I will be right back."

Doc leaned down to Sunspot's head. "Are you ready for some breakfast?" he asked, stroking her neck.

Glen led the mare into the stall, and they allowed her a few minutes to smell her foal and lick her face with tender kisses.

"I'm sure your baby is hungry," Doc said to the mare. "Are we ready?" he asked Glen.

"Let's give it a try. I will pump the hydraulics to take the slack out and then help you get the filly to her feet," Glen suggested.

"That sounds like a good plan," Doc said. "Let's take it slow, so we don't damage the stitches."

"Got it," Glen said as he began slowly pumping the lever until all the slack was removed from the sling.

"A few more," Doc said as he watched the lift raise the filly's body gently off the pile of blankets. He moved in to support the filly and guided her legs beneath her body to test her ability to bear weight. "Just high enough to support her feet to stand flat on the ground," he instructed Glen.

They watched as the filly briefly struggled with the awkwardness of the sling and then relaxed as her legs regained the strength to hold her up. When Doc let go of her, the filly stood firmly with the support of the lift. He pulled the mare forward, and the filly instinctively moved her head and began suckling. Doc looked at Glen, smiling broadly as he watched the filly nurse.

†

Sully finished her meal and thanked Camille again before she left the house, eager to return to check on Sunspot. Bryn walked out to the truck with her. "Try to get some rest, and I will see you later today," she said as Sully stopped to open the door.

"Thanks again for all you have done for her," Sully said.

"My pleasure," Bryn said with a smile. "Sleep well," she said as Sully climbed behind the wheel.

Bryn closed the door of the truck.

"You too, Bryn. I will see you soon."

"Later," Bryn answered as she turned to walk back into the house.

Sully watched her walk for a few seconds and then reached down to start the engine. Bryn turned and waved as she reached the front door. Sully returned her wave and put the truck in gear.

Sully was shocked when she walked back into the barn and found Sunspot up and nursing. "That is amazing, Doc," she exclaimed as she watched with excitement.

"Her mother's milk is what she needs right now," Doc said, turning and smiling at her.

"I can't believe she is strong enough to support her weight," she said.

"Not one hundred percent, but it will be good for her to be up for short periods until she is ready to stand alone," he explained.

Sully watched as Sunspot ate hungrily with a renewed hope that she would survive adversity and thrive.

"Okay, now that you see her doing well, it's time for you to go and take care of yourself," Doc said.

"Aww, just five more minutes," Sully playfully teased.

"No, off with you now," Doc teased back.

"I will see you guys later then," Sully said as she turned and walked toward the house.

In her bedroom, she quickly stripped out of her clothes and walked to the bathroom to rinse off before crawling between her sheets. Sully had barely placed her head on the pillow and closed her eyes when sleep arrived to consume her, and she slept soundly.

†

Bryn, too, found that sleep came quickly to her as she snuggled into a pillow with thoughts of Sully's hand resting on her stomach and playing through her memory.

# CHAPTER EIGHT

---

Sully surprised herself by sleeping beyond her normal six hours and found she had slept for eight hours when she woke. She felt the extra sleep in her body as she woke up stiff and sore, especially in her lower back. She slowly crept from the bed and painfully walked into the bathroom to begin drawing a bath in her whirlpool tub. Sully hoped the swirling hot water would help to relax her muscles and allow her to stand fully erect.

While the tub filled, she walked into a large closet and selected clothes for the day. Soon, she would have to begin cutting the hay, but today, and maybe another day or two, she would spend in the barn monitoring Sunspot and assisting with her healthcare.

Sully carefully climbed into the tub and pressed the button to start the jets. She leaned back on a pillow and closed her eyes as the hot water began working magic on her body. She could feel the knotted muscles in her back begin to loosen, which eased the pain she had awakened with. Her doctor had prescribed medications, but Sully refused to take them. They made her feel lethargic when she took them, and she would rather struggle against the pain than feel that way. The relief from the medications was also short-lived, and Sully did not want to become dependent on increasingly higher dosages.

After ten minutes of treatment, Sully sat forward and stretched the muscles of her lower back. When she could move from side to side, relatively free of debilitating pain, she stopped the jets and walked to the shower. Sully finished bathing and dressing before walking to the kitchen for a cold drink. She shook her head when she looked at the kitchen clock to see it was already six in the evening. She stepped outside to find the sun was on its journey beyond the horizon. As she walked across the yard, she saw Doc's truck was gone, along with Glen's.

†

Bryn looked up from the stall and watched Sully gingerly walk across the yard toward the barn. It was painfully evident that Sully was paying dearly for her overexertion from yesterday, and Bryn wished she could do something to relieve her friend's pain.

†

Sully entered the barn and breathed in the rich smells of freshly mucked stalls. No matter where she would travel in her lifetime, Sully knew that it was this smell that she would always associate with home.

The barn was virtually silent, making Sully wonder if it was without human presence, but as she walked toward Sunspot's stall, she found she was not alone. As she approached, she could hear Bryn speaking to Sunspot.

"That's a good girl," she heard her say as she stepped into the stall.

Sunspot was once again standing to nurse from her mother. She appeared much stronger than she had earlier in the day.

"She's looking good," Sully said as she entered the stall.

"She has been eating well this afternoon," Bryn said.

"How long have you been here?"

"I came over and relieved grandfather about four; she has nursed twice since then."

"I can't believe I slept so late," Sully said.

"I think your body was sending you a message," Bryn said.

"Maybe so, but it also let me know I lay still too long when I woke."

"Woke up stiff and sore, did you?" she asked.

"Like a board," Sully said. "I had to use the whirlpool just to stand straight up."

"How did you injure your back?"

"My foot slipped off a wet platform when we were moving hay several years ago, and I ruptured a disc. I had surgery to repair the rupture, but my body lets me know in a hurry when I move wrong or overdo things."

"I think yesterday would qualify for overdoing things," Bryn said. "Your adrenalin kicked in, and you weren't even aware of what you were doing," she added. "Do you have any medications?"

"I do, but I don't like the after-effects when I take them, so I suffer through the pain as long as I can," she said.

"Stubborn, too, I see," Bryn teased.

"A bit, yes, but I don't like feeling hung over all the time either."

"Camille sent dinner with me, so let me know when you are hungry," Bryn said.

"I do love that woman," Sully said with a smile.

"I think she is a little attached to you as well," Bryn said.

"She has been my second mother for years," Sully said. "When my mom passed, Camille was there to keep me from drowning in my grief."

"Camille is an amazing woman. I don't know what grandfather would do without her."

"Starve to death for one thing," Sully said. "I don't think he has cooked as much as a slice of toast in twenty years."

"That could be why the house is still standing," Bryn joked.

"Doc is an excellent vet, but he is one horrible cook," Sully said as she sat atop the massage table to watch Bryn and Sunspot. She leaned back against the wall to support her back.

"When I finish with Sunspot, why don't you let me give you that massage I promised?" Bryn said.

"I would like that very much. I will get some supplies together while you finish," Sully said.

"I shouldn't be much longer. I think Sunspot has gotten her belly full and is getting sleepy."

Sully climbed from the table and returned to the house for a sheet and massage oil. She stopped in the office and placed the bottle in the microwave for warming as she covered the table with a clean sheet. When she returned from retrieving the oil, Bryn finished lowering Sunspot back to the floor.

"Let me wash my hands, and I will be right back," she said.

Sully stripped off her clothes except for her panties and climbed onto the table, lying face down on the heavily padded table.

†

When she returned to the stall, Bryn was surprised to find Sully nearly naked. She was thankful that Sully's head was turned in the opposite direction as she entered the stall. Bryn could feel her face burning red as her eyes took in Sully's nakedness. Her body was long and lean, nicely tanned, and there did not appear to be any tan lines as she approached the table. She noticed a six-inch line of noticeably lighter skin running along Sully's spine, which was revealed as a surgical scar upon closer inspection.

"Are you comfortable?" she asked softly.

"Yes. It sounds crazy, but I could almost fall asleep here."

"By all means, go right ahead if you can," Bryn said. "The extra sleep won't hurt you."

"I know, but I want to stay up and help with Sunspot."

"I can handle Sunspot. Relax, and if you fall asleep, that's fine," Bryn said, pouring the warm oil into her hands and rubbing them together. She placed her hands together on

Sully's back at the base of her neck and slowly spread the oil across her skin. Bryn could feel the ripple of Sully's muscles beneath her hands as she concentrated her movements down Sully's spine.

"That feels really good," Sully whispered.

Bryn had worked as a massage therapist during her undergraduate years, but she had never felt someone's skin affecting her like Sully's. Her fingers glided across liquid silk as they stroked down her back, and her tongue was left speechless. The warmth of Sully's skin traveled up Bryn's hands and into her body and spread quickly, igniting desires she had not felt in a long time. She closed her eyes and let her mind get lost in Sully's body.

†

Sully felt the deep kneading of Bryn's fingers as she slowly worked the tension and pain from her muscles. "You are not only a great vet, but you have magic hands, too," Sully said.

"Are you feeling better?"

"Much. I may have to fire my normal therapist and hire you," Sully teased.

"Don't fire her, but I will give you a massage anytime you need one," Bryn said with a soft chuckle. "I would say you need one more often from the condition of these muscles," she added.

"It has been a while," she admitted. "Sometimes it is so hard just to find the time."

"You have to make the time and take better care of yourself."

"Yes, Mom," Sully jibed.

"That's right, smarty pants, your mom would have told you that," Bryn said as she smacked Sully's bottom.

"Ouch, that hurt," Sully said, with a pouty tone as Bryn poured more oil into her hand.

"I never would have thought you were such a cupcake," Bryn said as she resumed massaging Sully's back.

"Just be careful you don't displace my sprinkles," Sully said as she turned her face to look at Bryn.

†

Bryn couldn't help but laugh at Sully's remark. It was refreshing to see the smile on her face. "You know you should do that more often."

"What?" she asked.

"Smile," Bryn said. "You have a beautiful one."

"Doc, are you flirting with me?"

"Maybe," Bryn answered. "What if I am?"

"If you are, keep doing it. I like it," Sully answered.

Bryn's fingers traced the scar. "That looks like it was painful."

"I was flat on my back for a week in the hospital," she said. "I thought I would die before they would let me up."

"Did they have to restrain you to keep you still?"

"Well, no, but they did threaten to a few times."

"I bet you make a horrible patient."

"Well, thanks, Doc," Sully said.

"You are welcome. I just meant that you are very active, and it must have been miserable to be stuck in a bed for a week."

"I see, and yes, it was."

Bryn's hands worked down to massage Sully's side, her fingers brushing across her exposed breast as she worked her hands up to the shoulder. Her hands caressed the oil deeply into the long muscles of Sully's solid arms and down to the delicate bones in her wrists. Bryn added more oil to her hands as she massaged Sully's palm before stretching each finger individually.

"You have very nice hands," Bryn stated. "Strong muscles and yet soft to the touch."

"The hard work around here keeps them strong, and good gloves keep them soft," Sully said.

"Have you ever considered hiring more help around here?"

"Yes, but there are certain things I would rather do myself."

"I can understand that," Bryn said as she moved between Sully's feet. She started at the top of her thighs and stroked down to each heel with her supple hands. Her legs were lean but very well-muscled from years of riding and working on the farm. Even though her hips remained covered with panties, Bryn could see the muscles forming nicely rounded, firm buttocks that she ached to get her hands on. To tease Sully as much as herself, Bryn allowed her fingers to slip subtly beneath the edge of the panties as they glided down the inside of Sully's thighs.

Sully's body reacted to Bryn's touch. Her buttocks flexed as Bryn's fingers worked down between her thighs. The massage that had started so innocently was rapidly becoming much more as Bryn's touch ignited a passion that had presumably long lay dormant. Bryn's hands worked down her body, and then she massaged Sully's feet to finish the back side of her massage.

"Do we continue?"

"If you would like, I will never pass on a massage." Sully rolled onto her back, exposing the bareness of her body to Bryn as she watched her for a reaction.

Bryn's eyes slowly caressed Sully's body, and she was not surprised at what she saw. Sully had well-defined stomach muscles and small but firm breasts. Her nipples swelled as Bryn's eyes washed over them, and Sully caught a glimpse of Bryn's tongue darting quickly from her mouth to wet her lips. That action alone was enough to send a rush of pleasure between Sully's legs, and when Bryn leaned slightly and placed her hands on her stomach, Sully held her breath to stifle a moan.

Bryn felt Sully's muscles tense and then relax as she slowly swirled the oil into her skin. She looked up her body and met Sully's eyes, which she found a sparkling crystal blue. They danced with excitement as Bryn's hands moved together between her breasts to come to rest beneath her chin. Bryn massaged her chest muscles, the backs of her oiled hands brushing Sully's breasts as they moved on her body.

Sully slowly released the breath, letting out a soft hiss. "That feels really good," she said as Bryn's hands moved from her neck to her waist in one long movement.

"Relax and enjoy then," Bryn said as she repeated the movement.

†

Sully closed her eyes and focused on the pleasure of Bryn's hands on her body. Her nipples grew so hard they ached to be touched. Bryn's hands stroked all over the front of her body, grazing her breasts but never touching her overly sensitive nipples, driving Sully's body crazy with need.

†

Bryn's face glowed with a devilish grin as she covered Sully's breasts with the warming oil, slowly circling around her erect nipples. She heard a sharp gasp from Sully as the tips of her fingers grazed lightly over the top of Sully's nipples.

Sully's eyes shot open, and Bryn saw the color had quickly changed from sparkling with excitement to dark blue filled with desire. Bryn was utterly shocked by what happened next.

Sully trapped Bryn's hands with her own as she sat up quickly and spun on the massage table. She wrapped her legs around Bryn and pulled her into the table as a hand pulled Bryn's face forward. Sully leaned into Bryn as their lips met, and her tongue pressed between her lips with a passionate swirl. Sully moaned deeply into her mouth, the vibrations stirring both women. Bryn's fingers gently squeezed Sully's nipples, which broke the passion of the kiss.

Sully's eyes flew open, and her legs released Bryn as she gently pushed her away. "I'm sorry, I can't," Sully said as she lunged from the table, grabbed her clothes, and rushed from the stall.

Darkness had fallen around them, but Bryn could see Sully's figure as she dashed across the yard and disappeared into the house. She stood in the middle of the stall, more confused than ever, trying to understand what had occurred between her and Sully. Her tears fell freely down her cheeks as Bryn blamed herself for hurting Sully somehow, even though she could not fathom what she had done wrong. The reminder of the anguish on Sully's face as she rushed from the stall was enough to keep the tears flowing as Bryn's knees buckled, and she sank into the stall floor.

†

Sully closed the door behind her and leaned against it as the tears continued down her face. Clutching her clothes to her chest to hide her nakedness, Sully tried to determine why she had panicked and bolted away from Bryn. Her body welcomed Bryn's attention, and the kiss felt so right. So why had she run away, she asked herself?

Unable to come up with an answer, Sully walked into her bedroom and dropped her clothes on the floor. Her skin shone in the moonlight, glistening with the massage oil, and her nipples grew hard thinking of Bryn's hands teasing them. Frustrated by her lack of control and failure to find the answers she sought, Sully walked to the shower to rinse the oil and tears down the drain.

†

When Bryn managed to quiet her tears, she walked to the bathroom and washed her hands before rinsing the tears from her face. Her eyes had grown red and swollen. Her image stared back at her, confused about what had happened between them. Fearful of starting to cry again, Bryn dried her face and walked back into the barn. She was here to take care of the filly, and that is what she must focus on, she told herself as she walked past the massage table to check on Sunspot, who was still resting peacefully. She sat beside her and rested her head against the stall, completely confused.

†

The hot water and soap rinsed the oil from Sully's body but did nothing to ease the ache of desire for Bryn's touch. No matter how hard she tried, Sully could not erase the memory of how good it felt to have Bryn's hands all over her body. She turned off the water, dried, and dressed in a T-shirt and baggy sweatpants before collapsing onto the bed.

She felt horrible for treating Bryn the way she had but was at a loss for words to explain how she felt. Sully squeezed her eyes shut but still saw the shocked look on Bryn's face as she pushed her away.

Sully cried herself to sleep and slept for two hours.

# CHAPTER NINE

---

Bryn had kept herself busy caring for Sunspot but failed to keep Sully off her mind. It had been over two hours since Sully disappeared into the house, and Bryn feared she had hurt her so badly she didn't want anything else to do with her. That would be a devastating blow, personally and professionally. She had moved here to take over her grandfather's practice; Sullivan's trace was a significant account of that practice. Without Sully's business, the practice would struggle, if not fail outright.

She chastised herself for allowing her hormones to ruin something so critical to not only herself but to her grandfather. There were also her feelings for Sully, which had grown so deep and quickly. She thought that Sully had similar feelings, but her behavior tonight proved her wrong on that account.

Sunspot moved to lay her head in Bryn's lap, looking up at her with soft brown eyes. Bryn forced a smile and stroked down the filly's face. "You are dealing really well. I bet you are up on your own tomorrow at this rate."

Sunspot's warm tongue flicked out of her mouth to lick Bryn's hand to show her appreciation for all Bryn had done for her. Bryn was so profoundly touched by the filly's expression of thanks that she felt her eyes tearing up again.

Bryn sat with Sunspot until the filly drifted to sleep, and then she slipped out of the stall. She couldn't sit and look at the massage table anymore, or her tears would get the best of her. Bryn was emotionally exhausted and needed to step out for some fresh air. She knew Sully had several chairs at the lake, and Bryn started in that direction.

†

Sully startled herself awake and realized she had fallen asleep. The rest had brought no answers to the dilemma she found herself in, but she knew she must apologize to Bryn. She slipped on some shoes and walked through the darkened house.

Sully was about to step out her door when she saw Bryn walk from the barn and head toward the lake. She watched as Bryn faded into the darkness and stepped out the door. After gathering her courage, she would check on the animals and seek out Bryn to apologize for her behavior.

All of the animals were resting quietly in the barn. Sully returned to the kitchen and took out two beers. She stepped back into the night and began the walk down to the lake to see if that was where Bryn had gone. She looked at the heavens and the brilliant stars shining down upon them as she walked.

The night air had turned cool, and Sully walked toward the water. She could see the outline of Bryn's form as she sat huddled in one of the chairs. Sully could hear Bryn crying softly as she approached and knelt before her.

Bryn had covered her face with her hands to hide her tears and did not hear Sully's approach. Sully's heart ached at the sight of Bryn. She was so upset, and she reached up to take her hands from her face. Bryn jumped at Sully's touch and looked at her with a startled expression as Sully lowered her hands from her face and kissed each one.

"Will you forgive me for being such an ass?" she asked softly.

Bryn shook her head. "I am the one who is sorry for hurting you," Bryn said.

"For hurting me," Sully said. "You did nothing to hurt me, Bryn. Let's get that straight first. You made me feel things I haven't felt in a long time, and I panicked, but you did not hurt me."

†

Bryn looked into Sully's eyes and saw the sincerity in her words. "I thought I had done something to hurt you."

"No, Bryn, what you were doing felt incredible. My body wanted so much for you to continue, but I am not sure my heart is ready," she admitted. Sully handed her a beer and sat beside her.

Bryn leaned forward in the chair, relieved that she had not hurt Sully but also concerned with her words. She turned and placed her hands on either side of Sully's face and looked directly into her eyes. "I am not the woman that broke your heart, Micah. The least you can do is let me have a chance to love you," she said.

†

It had been years since anyone had called her by her given name, and that surprised her almost as much as the words Bryn spoke. "What did you say?" she asked, unsure what she had heard.

"I said I am not the woman who broke your heart."

"After that," Sully said.

"That the least you could do is let me have a chance to love you," Bryn repeated. "I had a crush on you when we were children, and all those feelings came rushing back when I saw you again," she admitted, searching Sully's eyes for acknowledgment.

The frown on Sully's face lifted to a smile. "I never realized that," she said. "I don't want our relationship, if we have one, to be based on a crush," she said. "It needs to be real and not some little fantasy game. Alisa broke my heart, and I don't think I can handle that again."

†

Bryn watched the tears sparkle in Sully's eyes, and she could see the hurt lingering there as she spoke of Alisa. "I would never hurt you," she promised. "For the last ten years, I have looked for someone to make me feel the way you make me feel, and now that I have found it, I do not intend to let it pass me by."

"I don't think I am ready for a serious relationship yet," Sully said.

"That doesn't matter. I am willing to wait as long as necessary for you to decide I am the woman for you," Bryn said, "but you can't compare me to Alisa."

"There really is no comparison," Sully said with a chuckle. "The two of you are night and day."

Bryn sat quietly, hoping Sully would expand upon that comment, but she didn't. The cool night air sent a chill through her body, and she shivered as goose flesh rose on her arms.

"Let's get you inside and out of this chill," Sully said as she stood and offered Bryn her hand.

Bryn allowed Sully to assist her from the chair and continued to hold her hand as they turned and started back toward the barn. They walked silently until they neared the barn, and Bryn asked, "Are you hungry?"

"I could eat," Sully answered.

"Camille sent us fried chicken, potato salad, and some leftover biscuits. I could warm it up if you would like."

"Or just eat it cold," Sully said. "Camille's fried chicken is just as good cold."

"That works for me. Let me check on the animals, and I will return."

"I will start laying out the food then," Sully said.

Bryn looked at her and started to say something. Then, she thought better of it and turned toward the stalls with a heart that felt much lighter than an hour ago. She could understand the hurt Sully felt and the hesitancy to allow herself to become vulnerable to that hurt again. Bryn would have to be patient with Sully and allow her the time to finish healing. She sighed to herself as she walked. Patience was never one of her strong points, but Sully was worth waiting for. When she turned to step into Sunspot's stall, she stopped in her tracks.

"Sully," she called out.

†

Sully heard Bryn's call in the office and dashed to the barn. She saw her standing at the entrance to the stall and rushed to join her. When she reached Bryn's side and turned to look inside the stable, she witnessed Bryn's excitement. Sunspot stood in the stall, nuzzling her mother through the railing. She had found the desire and strength to stand on her own without mechanical aid. Bryn smiled at Sully as they watched Sunspot take several wobbly steps toward them.

"I guess you are hungry too," Sully said as she stepped forward and hugged Sunspot's neck.

"I will bring Mom in," Bryn said, leaving the stall.

†

"You are such a fighter," Bryn heard Sully say to Sunspot.

It was terrific that the filly found the strength to stand independently after suffering such traumatic injuries. Bryn led the mare into the stall and knelt to examine Sunspot's wounds. The sutures were still intact and did not appear to hinder her movement at all. They watched as she began to nurse, and Sully turned toward Bryn.

"It is time for us to eat too."

They walked back toward the office together. “I think it would be safe to say Sunspot is well on her way to recovery. I will stay with her through tonight and start daily visits tomorrow if that suits you.”

“That will be fine,” Sully said as she toiled in the office to place the food on the table as Bryn washed her hands.

After the meal, they cleaned the table and returned to the barn. Sunspot had finished nursing and was quietly napping in the stall as her mother watched over her.

“She is in good hands if you want to get some sleep,” Sully said.

“I am not really sleepy yet, but I will lie down with you and talk for a while if you would like,” Bryn said.

†

Sully laid down on her back on the air mattress, and Bryn boldly snuggled in next to her and placed her head on Sully’s shoulder. They talked for hours about the women of their lives and how they feared they would never find the love that they sought. Bryn buried herself in Sully’s warmth and slowly began drifting. Sully asked Bryn a question, and when she realized Bryn had gone silent, she looked over at her to find her sleeping. Sully smiled a comfortable smile, glad that the evening had ended much better than it had begun. She closed her eyes and let her body float between sleep and dreams.

Sully awoke early and was preparing coffee in the office when Doc arrived to check on them.

“Good morning, Sully,” he said as he pushed through the door.

“Good morning, Doc. You are just in time for coffee.”

"Thanks, but I have already had a pot this morning. Is Bryn awake yet?" he asked.

"Not when I left, but you can wake her while I get coffee."

†

Doc nodded his head and left the office. He walked over to the air mattress and gently shook Bryn awake. "Rise and shine, sleepy head," he chided.

Bryn wiped her face and sat up on the mattress. "Good morning, Grandfather. What time is it?

"Almost seven," Doc said as Sully walked in carrying cups of coffee. "I can see you are getting spoiled already," he teased.

"We had a late night, but a good one," Sully said. "Go look in the stall."

Doc walked over to the stall and peeked in to look at Sunspot. "Good lord, she is up on her own already," he said.

"Yup, she is one tough little cookie," Sully said with pride.

Bryn took a sip of coffee. "I think we can return to daily visits now that the worst has passed."

"Great, I can finish making rounds with you now," Doc said.

"Have I been monopolizing her time?" Sully asked.

"Well, yes, but rightfully so," Doc said. "The most exciting thing she has for the rest of this week is worming steers and a couple of heifers to artificially inseminate. That is unless, of course, your mare goes into labor."

"She is getting close," Bryn said.

"Another day or two at most," Doc said.

Sully beamed, seemingly delighted at the prospect of her next generation of champions about to be born.

"Drink up so you can go shower and change. We have many miles to travel today," Doc said. He stood and walked from the barn.

†

"What plans do you have for the day?" Bryn asked.

"I thought I would leave Glen to watch over the animals and start cutting the hay," Sully said.

"Are you getting a bit restless?" Bryn teased.

"Maybe this life of leisure we've shared the last few days could spoil me," Sully joked.

"We certainly can't have you getting fat and lazy."

"Ha! That will never happen," Sully answered.

"I will drop by later today to check on Sunspot and the mare," Bryn said, "that is if it is okay with you."

"That would be delightful," Sully said as she stepped toward Bryn.

The space between them disappeared rapidly, and Bryn felt her heart lurch as Sully approached. Their eyes were locked on one another, and she could feel her cheeks flushing. Her breath caught in her throat as Sully stopped before her, caressed her cheek softly, and lifted her chin.

"I will see you this afternoon then," Sully said as she walked out of the barn, a devilish grin on her face.

"Damn," Bryn whispered. She walked out behind Sully and climbed into the truck beside her grandfather.

†

Sully climbed onto the tractor and watched as Doc and Bryn drove away. She would attach the bush hog, and if Glen hadn't arrived, she would leave him a note with instructions before driving out to the first field she would cut.

Just as she was finishing, Glen's truck pulled up in the yard, and he stepped out of the truck.

"Good morning, Boss," he said.

"Good morning, Glen."

"Are you going to start cutting the fields today?" he asked.

"Yes, I thought I would get a jump on cutting."

"You sure you wouldn't rather stay and work in the barn and let me cut?" he asked.

"No, I need some wide-open space today," she answered.

"Are you okay?"

Sully chuckled. "Yes, just feeling a little cramped up. Sunspot is doing well, so I can easily leave her to get started."

"Do you want me to go ahead and make the feed store run?"

"Yes, that would be great, Glen. Also, call the coach and ask him to round the boys up this weekend."

"Will do," he said.

"I will see you late this afternoon then," Sully said and climbed onto the tractor.

"See you later, Boss."

Sully reached down, picked up a pair of sunglasses, and covered her eyes as she started down the lane. When she reached the field, she would begin cutting. She climbed down from the tractor and swung the gate open wide. Ahead of her lay a hundred acres of land that, in a few days, would be dotted with thousands of bales of hay. The dry weather and warm days would help to cure the grass quickly. She drove the tractor through the gate, lowered the mower carriage, and engaged the blades.

# Chapter Ten

---

In her excitement to start mowing the fields, Sully neglected to bring food or water with her, and as the sun rose higher in the midmorning sky, she began to feel thirsty. The dust from the dry pasture coated her face and her parched throat as she turned the tractor toward home in search of food and drink. Sully hoped Glen had not found the leftover chicken in the office refrigerator as she chugged back toward the barn. Sully was relieved that Glen's truck was not parked in the yard as she rounded a bend, and the barn came into sight.

She parked the tractor and walked into the office. Sully opened the refrigerator and smiled when her eyes landed on the container of cold fried chicken. She placed the container on the table and walked into the bathroom.

"That's attractive," she said aloud as she looked at her image in the mirror. She lifted the sunglasses onto her head and leaned down to wash her face and hands. The water turned dark as it swirled down the drain.

Sully dried her hands and pulled a Mountain Dew from the refrigerator before sitting at the table. She reached into the container, pulled out a drumstick, and moaned when the flavor of the chicken accosted her taste buds. Sully hadn't realized how hungry she was until she remembered she had skipped breakfast. She picked the bones of two drumsticks clean like a vulture and was reaching for a third when she heard a vehicle approaching. She took her prize and walked to the door to see Glen pulling up with a full load of feed.

He parked and stepped out of the truck. When he saw Sully standing in the doorway with the drumstick, he grinned and said, "Is that from Camille?"

"Yes, leftovers from last night," Sully answered, wiping crumbs from her chin.

"I hope you didn't eat it all," he said.

"Nope, but if you had waited much longer to return, I could have. I did make a sizable dent in it."

"Well, at least you left me some," he teased.

"Help yourself. I will check on the animals and then get back to cutting," she said.

"Will you be ready for me to begin raking tomorrow?"

"Most definitely," Sully said. "I want to get at least halfway through the first field before dark falls tonight."

"Do you need me to stay late tonight?"

"No, why don't you make it an early day today, and we will work late tomorrow," she suggested.

"I will unload the feed and muck the stalls before I leave. Do you want me to check with you before I go?"

"No, I will be fine and will see you early tomorrow," she said as she walked back into the barn.

Sunspot heard her approaching and met her at the stall door. "Hey, little one," Sully said as she stroked the filly's head. "You are walking much better today."

Sully knelt to inspect Sunspot's wounds. She was pleased to find no weeping as the flesh began to mend, and there was no evidence of infection. "Looking good, baby girl," she said as she stood and hugged Sunspot's neck. She turned to walk further into the stalls to check on the pregnant mare and heard light hoof steps behind her. Sully stopped and turned to find Sunspot walking behind her.

"Do you want to visit?" she asked and continued walking, closely followed by the filly.

Sully opened the stall door, so Sunspot could follow as she stepped inside. She walked up to the mare, her belly sunken low as she prepared to give birth. Sully's hand ran down her side, and she could feel the colt moving. "Someone is getting restless."

The mare turned to look at Sunspot and nuzzled her sweetly. Sully watched the exchange with pride. It didn't matter that Sunspot wasn't her foal. The mare treated her just as warmly as she would her own. "She's a tough little cookie," Sully said as she stroked down the animal's sides. "It won't be long now," she promised the mare.

Sully spent several more minutes with the horses before she broke away to return to work. As she walked out of the stall, Sunspot followed. "Do you want to spend some time outside?" she asked.

Sunspot answered by walking past her stall, following Sully out of the barn.

"Do you know you have a shadow?" Glen asked as he looked up and saw Sully followed by the filly.

"Yes, I think she has a touch of cabin fever. Would you mind if she stayed out and watched you for a short while?"

"Not at all," Glen said as he walked over and stroked Sunspot's head. "I fixed you a small cooler with some water. You need to put it on the tractor so you will at least have something to drink."

"Thanks, Glen. Keep an eye on her, and if she appears to get tired, you may have to walk her back inside."

"I will watch her closely," he promised.

"See you tomorrow then," she said as she stepped inside the office to grab the cooler and take a ball cap off a peg on the wall. The cap was worn and would help keep the sun out of her eyes as the afternoon waned. She slipped the cap onto her head and pulled down her sunglasses as she walked from the office.

Sunspot tried to follow, but Sully watched as Glen placed a firm hand on her halter. "You have to stay with me, little girl," he said, holding her until she presumably pulled out of sight.

†

Bryn and Doc visited several clients and answered a call to assist with a calving. The calf had breached, turning his body in reverse of the correct birthing position, and was making no attempt to shift.

"You better take this one," Doc said.

"Why is that?"

"Because I have a suspicion that when Sully's mare gives birth, it won't be easy due to his size, and you can practice with this calf," Doc explained. He tossed Bryn a pair of shoulder-length gloves.

Bryn pulled the gloves onto her arms, held her hands out for lube, and covered her gloved hands and wrists with the smooth jelly.

"All set," he asked.

"Ready when you are."

Together, they walked over to the chute where the owner had placed the heifer to immobilize her. Doc gave her a brief examination and then lifted the heifer's tail. "The calf is going into distress, so you will have to work quickly," he said as Bryn gently inserted one hand into the animal's body.

"He is close," Bryn said as her hand contacted the unborn calf. "You are right, he wants to try butt first," she said.

"You will have to turn him," Doc instructed.

Bryn inserted her left hand and began the task of shifting the calf's body, moving him inch by slow inch. She was working up a sweat, and Doc took out a handkerchief and wiped her forehead. "Are you doing okay?"

"Yes, I think I just about have him turned," Bryn answered. "Her contractions are getting stronger, too."

"The heifer is trying to help you," Doc said. "When you have him turned, bring his front legs forward."

"Got him," Bryn said. "Okay, I have two hooves."

"Put them both in one hand and use your other hand to guide his head and start to pull."

Doc pulled on a pair of gloves and continued to talk Bryn through the process. "That's good," he said when a shiny black hoof emerged behind Bryn's right hand. "Keep pulling, slowly now."

Doc placed his hands on the calf's legs and helped Bryn pull the legs from its mother's body as Bryn gently guided the head through the birthing canal.

"Be ready to catch when the head is clear," he warned. "The calf will come quickly once the head is freed."

Bryn was relieved when the calf's head broke through, but her smile quickly turned to surprise when a strong contraction rapidly pushed the calf's body free. Bryn and Doc had to grab quickly to keep the calf from falling to the ground. They eased the calf to the ground, and Doc quickly severed the umbilical cord, and the sac of afterbirth fell to the ground.

The heifer was released from the chute, and instinctively moved to her calf and began cleaning it with her tongue.

"You have a brand-new bull, Mama," Doc said as the heifer attended to her calf. "Good job, Bryn."

"Thanks, Grandfather," she said.

"It's getting late. Let's wash up here and then get you home for a shower before you head over to Sully's," he said.

They dropped their gloves into a garbage can and used a small sink to wash up as best they could. Calving was rarely a clean job, and Bryn looked forward to a hot shower and clean clothes.

She couldn't help but glance toward Sully's as Doc's old truck bounced down their driveway. She was disappointed when she saw no signs of movement. Bryn would take a quick shower and then drive over to see how the animals and Sully were doing. It amazed her how much she missed Sully. *I sure hope you are not setting yourself up for heartbreak*, she thought as Doc's truck stopped.

"Will you be back in time for supper?" Doc asked.

"I am not sure, but don't wait on me," she answered.

"You know it would probably be good to get her away from the place for a little while," he said.

Bryn looked at him suspiciously. "Do you really think she would leave right now?"

"She might if you asked her to dinner, and I promised to come over to keep an eye on the animals," he answered with a wry grin.

Bryn returned his smile. "I guess it is worth a shot."

"Ask her then, and if she says yes, call me. We do have a rather good steak house in town, you know."

"A nice thick steak does sound good."

"You have earned it today. You did a great job with the calving."

"Thanks," Bryn said with a modest smile as they exited the truck and started for the house.

†

Sully stopped the tractor and took a long drink of water. She looked at her watch and found it was three in the afternoon. She promised herself two more hours, and *I will call it a day*. Sully was pleased with the day's work and thought she should reach her goal of half the field in two hours. The sun was still beating down as she lowered the sunglasses to cover her eyes and put the tractor in gear. She wondered how Bryn's day had gone and looked forward to seeing her later when she came to check the animals. Thinking of Bryn made her smile, realizing she had missed spending the day with her.

"You are getting soft," she said as she engaged the blades and continued the mowing.

†

Bryn showered and took great pains selecting an outfit to wear. Jeans were a given, and she pulled out a new pair, but she struggled to find the shirt she wanted to wear. After several minutes of searching, she settled for a brilliant blue oxford, a color that immediately reminded her of Sully's eyes. She buttoned the shirt and sprayed a light scent on her neck and wrists. Bryn inspected her image in a full-length mirror. *Not bad at all,* she thought. "I would date me," Bryn said and then chuckled. She felt like a teenager going out on her first date.

Camille and Doc were in the kitchen when Bryn walked downstairs.

"You look very nice," Camille said as Doc turned to look at Bryn.

"Well, don't you clean up nice," Doc teased.

She leaned down to kiss her grandfather on the cheek. "I will give you a call later," she promised.

"Good luck," he said.

"Thanks. I may have to call for reinforcements to get Sully to leave," she said.

"Just give me a call then," Camille said with a wink. "Sully knows she can't refuse me," Camille said with a chuckle.

"Enjoy your evening," Doc said.

"We will," Bryn said confidently as she walked toward the door.

†

Camille looked at Doc. "You wouldn't be playing matchmaker, would you, old man?"

"Who are you calling old?" he asked.

"That's what I thought."

"When is dinner going to be ready?" he asked.

"Soon," Camille answered, and with a smile, she turned back to the stove.

†

Bryn drove to Sully's and parked in front of the barn. She would check on the animals, and then if Sully had not made it in from the fields, she would go find her. The sun was making its way down the sky as she walked into the barn.

Sunspot had heard Bryn's approach and was waiting for her at the stall door when she arrived. Bryn opened the door and watched as Sunspot came dancing out into the aisle. "Well, aren't you feeling perky today?"

Sunspot lifted her muzzle to Bryn's face, and her soft lips brushed her cheek. "You are such a smoothie," Bryn said as she placed her hands on either side of the filly's head and kissed her forehead.

She knelt to inspect her wounds and was startled at how quickly she seemed to be healing. "You are doing so well," Bryn said as her hands caressed down each of Sunspot's front legs. "No muscle tremors at all. Amazing," she said, as she shook her head in disbelief.

Bryn walked down to the birthing stall and entered as Sunspot followed her closely. She examined the mare carefully and noted that she was continuing to dilate in preparation for birth. "It won't be much longer now," she told the mare as she ran her hand down her swollen belly. She checked the colt's heartbeat. "Beating strong," she said as the colt moved and the stethoscope bounced on the mare's stomach. She chuckled. "He is obviously ready to make his entrance," she said as she ran her hand up the mare's shoulder. "I know you are ready, too, Mom."

The mare nuzzled Sunspot, who stood patiently beside Bryn during the examination. "You will have a new playmate very soon," she told Sunspot. They walked from the stall toward the opening of the barn. There was still no sign of Sully, but in the stillness of the afternoon, Bryn could hear the tractor running in the distance.

Sunspot had walked to the entrance with her and stood next to Bryn. "Are you ready to go find your two-legged mom?" she asked.

Bryn started walking toward the path that would lead her to the fields, with Sunspot walking beside her. The exercise would do them both some good, and Sunspot was eager for a walk as she pranced a few steps ahead.

They walked toward the sound of the tractor, which grew louder with each step. When they reached the gate of the first pasture, Bryn could see the cloud of dust that the tractor stirred up trailing behind the mower. She and Sunspot walked through the gate, and the filly seemed excited to see Sully in the distance but remained close to Bryn.

†

Sully made a turn with the tractor, and movement at the front of the field caught her attention. She slowed the tractor and looked to find Bryn and Sunspot walking her way. Satisfied with what she had accomplished for the day, she reached down and turned the tractor's engine off. She pulled the keys from the ignition and climbed down from the tractor, slipping the keys into her pocket.

As she started walking toward them, she was surprised at how strong Sunspot's gait appeared. Even more pleasing was the beautiful smile Bryn was wearing as the distance between them began to shrink.

Sunspot trotted ahead of Bryn and reached Sully first. "Hello, my beautiful girl," she said as she stroked the filly's face.

†

Bryn watched the joy spread across Sully's face as she gave and received attention from Sunspot. At that moment, Bryn had serious doubts that anyone could create a love stronger than the love Sully shared with her animals. When she turned toward her, Bryn could see the sparkle in Sully's eyes.

"There was no way I was leaving the barn without her. I hope you don't mind me bringing her out here."

"Of course not. She was probably having some cabin fever."

"No, I really think she was missing you."

Sully leaned down and planted a soft kiss on Sunspot's muzzle. "Were you missing me, little girl?"

Bryn laughed as Sunspot nuzzled Sully. "See, I told you."

Sully turned to look at Bryn, her eyes taking in her entire body. Bryn's body quivered from the look she was receiving from her.

"You look very nice and smell good, too," she said.

"I got cleaned up so you could take me out for a steak dinner."

Sully smiled and draped her arm across Sunspot's withers as they turned and began to walk toward the barn. "A steak dinner, you say?"

"I worked up a huge appetite that I think a thick steak might satisfy."

"Let me have a shower and some clean clothes, and you have a deal."

"Grandfather said he would come over and animal sit while we are out."

"That is very nice of him."

"I will give him a call while you shower," Bryn said.

"So, you two have this all planned out?"

"All I needed to hear from you was a yes."

"Yes, then. I would be proud to take you out to dinner tonight, Ms. Barton."

"Why thank you, Ms. Sullivan," Bryn said, batting her eyelids at Sully.

As they walked to the barn, Bryn told Sully about her day and the adventure of the breached calving.

"You really did work up an appetite if you had to pull a breached calf."

"Of course, I did. Did you think I was joking?"

"Actually, I did. I thought you and Doc were mostly making introductory visits today."

"Well, it started off that way, but we got an emergency call to assist with the calving."

"That could be good practice for you if the colt decides to make his arrival difficult."

Bryn could not stifle her laughter.

"What is so funny?" Sully asked, a bit confused.

"That is exactly what Grandfather said earlier today."

"He is such a wise man," Sully said.

When they reached the barn, Sully stopped and turned to Sunspot. "Go back and have your supper, and I will see you later tonight," she said to the young filly. "I am going to take a shower. After you check the animals, come inside, and get comfortable. I shouldn't be long."

"I will call Doc and be inside in a few minutes," Bryn said, then watched as Sully walked toward the house. "Let's go, little one," she said to Sunspot and turned to enter the barn.

Bryn opened the gate to the mare's stall, and Sunspot walked over to her mother and began nursing. Bryn walked to the birthing stall. The pregnant mare was resting well. She checked to make sure she had feed and water before pulling out her cell phone.

"Hey, Grandfather."

"Hello, Bryn. Do you have a date tonight?"

"I do, in fact," Bryn answered. "Sully is showering now, and hopefully, we will head to town in no more than an hour," she said.

"I will drive over in an hour then," he said.

"Thanks, Grandfather."

†

"You are very welcome." Doc could hear the smile in Bryn's voice as she talked, and he was happy for his granddaughter. When he closed his cell phone, he found Camille watching him.

"I take it from the smile on your face that you have animal-sitting duty tonight?"

"Yes, the girls will be leaving in an hour for dinner."

"Would you like me to prepare a thermos of coffee for you?"

"That would be very nice. Thank you, Camille."

"You are welcome."

†

Bryn left the barn and walked to the house. She had been a young girl the last time she had entered the house now belonging to Sully. She walked through a large kitchen to a den area where she would wait for Sully. She could hear the shower as she walked to a wall covered with pictures of horses and of Sully with horses. She moved around the room, looking at the photographs that told the history of Sully's life. There were pictures of her with her parents as a young child, through her teenage years, and one of her adult life with her aging parents.

There was also a photograph of Sully with a beautiful woman on a beach surrounded by deep blue-green water. Sully looked so happy, and Bryn wondered if the woman in the picture was Alisa. She reached out to trace Sully's body in one of the photographs and quickly found herself lost in her thoughts.

†

Sully finished showering and dressed as quickly as she could. She was excited about their "date" and took extra measures to look nice for Bryn. She left her room and walked through the house to find Bryn looking at pictures in the den. Bryn had not heard her approach, so Sully leaned against the door frame and watched Bryn as she moved from picture to picture, picking one of them up for a closer look. She watched her study the images for several minutes until the large grandfather clock chimed and startled Bryn. She jumped at the sound and spun on her heels to find Sully watching her.

"I didn't hear you come in," she said, her face flushed with color as she placed the photograph back on a shelf.

Sully walked over to Bryn. "You were busy studying pictures."

"You certainly won a lot of awards when you were a child," Bryn said.

"Yes, I guess I did." Her eyes moved up a shelf until they rested on her favorite photograph. "This is my all-time favorite," she said as she reached up and pulled the frame down from the shelf.

The photograph was of Sully in her mid-twenties with a large palomino stallion. "This was the last picture I had with Sun Dancer. He was almost twenty-five in this image."

"I can tell how much you loved him," Bryn said. "I still see that look when you talk about your animals or especially when you are talking to Sunspot."

"He was such a special horse," Sully said as she drifted off in thought for a moment.

Doc's arrival in the driveway brought Sully back to the present. "It appears our animal sitter has arrived."

## CHAPTER ELEVEN

---

Bryn and Sully met Doc in the yard as he walked toward the barn.

"Thanks for giving us a break tonight," Sully said.

"My pleasure. I think you both deserve a break from all the hard work you have been performing," he said.

"I did work up an appetite with you today," Bryn told her grandfather.

"Do you think she can handle the porterhouse, Doc?" Sully asked.

Doc looked at Bryn. "I am not sure, but I think she would give it a heck of a try."

"Just how big is this steak?" Bryn asked.

"Twenty-four ounces of juicy T-bone," Sully said.

"I feel like I could eat a couple of them right now."

"I guess we had better get moving then," Sully teased. "See you later, Doc."

"You two have fun and take your time. Camille packed me coffee and a snack, and I have a new book to get started on, so there is no rush."

"Thanks, Grandfather," Bryn said as she walked around to the passenger side of Sully's truck.

Sully opened the door for her and, after seeing Bryn seated, walked around to climb in behind the wheel. "Here we go," she said as she started the motor and pulled out of the yard.

†

Bryn remained quiet, looking out the window as Sully drove the short distance into town. "I can't believe it still hasn't rained."

"This has been one of the worst droughts I can remember. Lakes are drying up, and farmers cannot water their crops." Sully shook her head. "Much longer, and they can scrub this year's harvest."

"We will get some relief soon."

"I hope you are right. I know a lot of farmers that are dependent on their crops to keep them from filing bankruptcy papers."

As they approached the small restaurant, the smell of grilling meat greeted them. "Oh, dear Lord, that smells great," Bryn said as she inhaled, filling her body with the aroma.

"It tastes just as good as it smells," Sully promised.

They parked and were seated immediately at a small table near a mesquite wood grill. A waitress came and took their drink orders. When she returned with the drinks, she asked Sully, "You cooking your own tonight?"

"Yes, I think I will, Greta," Sully said.

"Well, you know the routine. Have your salad, pick out your meat, and get to grilling," the older woman said with a grin.

"You cook your own here?" Bryn asked.

"You have the option of cooking your own steak or having one of the cooks do it for you," Sully explained. "It is a great opportunity to socialize around a grill and show off some cooking techniques, too."

"I have to admit, then, that I am not the greatest of cooks," Bryn said.

"Not to fear, ma'am, you are with the best in the county," Sully said with a grin. "Come on, and I will show you the salad bar, and later, we can pick out our steaks."

Bryn seemed impressed with the size and selection of the salad bar. "You might want to go easy on the salad. Don't forget you have a huge steak to eat, too," Sully reminded her.

"Bring it on," Bryn said with a chuckle.

"I will start cooking after we finish our salads."

Bryn ate half of her salad and then pushed the plate to the side. "I better save the rest of this for later," she said.

Sully looked at her and smiled, knowing full well that Bryn would never make it back to the salad once she started on her steak. She pushed back her own plate and said, "Grab your beer, and let's go find some meat."

Bryn stood and picked up her beer before following Sully to a refrigerated case filled with freshly cut meat.

"I am having a porterhouse, but feel free to pick out anything that strikes your fancy," Sully said as she opened the case and selected a large steak which she placed on a metal tray.

Seemingly not to be outdone, Bryn said, "I will have one of those, too."

Sully handed Bryn her beer and picked up the tray of meat. They walked back to the grill closest to their table, and Sully placed the steaks on the grill to begin her magic. Bryn took a seat on one of the bar stools surrounding the grill and sipped her beer as she watched Sully.

Sully picked up a paintbrush, dipped it into a container of drawn butter, coated both steaks and then picked up a shaker of seasoning. She covered the tops of both steaks before moving to sit with Bryn and sip on her beer.

"That part looked easy enough," Bryn said.

"Grilling is all about patience, timing, and good seasoning," Sully told her. "Too many people are impatient and cook the meat too fast, drying it out and losing the precious taste of the meat. It is so tempting to place the steak directly above the open flame, but that's the absolute worst thing you could do to a good piece of meat."

Greta came by with fresh beers for them. "Listen to her, honey," she told Bryn. "This woman can grill some meat," she said before sashaying off toward the kitchen.

"Your reputation precedes you," Bryn said. "So, you place the meat opposite the flame?"

"That's correct. It is called indirect heat, and it cooks the meat slowly to keep it juicy and tender."

"The butter, what is that for?"

"To help seal in the juices and to give the seasonings a base of support," Sully answered. "In a place like this, you really don't have the opportunity to marinate the meat, so the butter is used in its place with a variety of seasonings."

"That makes good sense."

Sully raised her hand to acknowledge a couple that had entered the pit on the opposite side of them, and she and Bryn watched them closely.

The man dropped the meat on the grill almost directly above the heat and dowsed the meat with salt and black pepper before turning to retrieve his beer from his wife.

Sully turned to look at Bryn. “They will be eating before we are halfway done cooking,” she said. “And you never salt beef before cooking,” she warned.

“Maybe you should offer him some lessons,” Bryn suggested.

Sully chuckled softly. “You never try to tell a man how to grill, my friend. Men think they were born to grill.”

“I guess you have a point there,” Bryn said.

They watched as the man used a large fork to turn the meat, poking large holes which allowed the juices to flow out in tiny rivers.

“Problem two, never use a fork on uncooked beef; always use a pair of tongs.”

“This is turning into quite a meal and cooking lesson all in one,” Bryn said.

“Sorry, but it is a pet peeve of mine to see someone ruin good meat like that,” she said.

“I love it. Who taught you all this?”

“My father taught me most of what I know about grilling, and the rest I picked up by trial and error.”

Sully stood and walked over to turn their steaks just as the young man across the grill was placing his meals on plates. She smiled at him, returned to sit beside Bryn, and took a long drink from her beer.

“Thank you for inviting me out tonight. I didn’t realize how much I needed a break.”

"I do believe the pleasure is all mine. I do, after all, have the best cook in the county cooking for me."

Sully smiled at Bryn. "That's correct." Sully noticed Bryn rubbing her arms. "Are they sore?"

"I had forgotten how strong a cow's contractions can be. She gave me quite a squeeze."

Sully chuckled at Bryn's comment. "I guess life in the country takes some getting used to."

"Possibly, but I am really enjoying the quiet, especially at night. There is nothing like walking outside and looking up to see stars."

"Not too much of that in the city?"

"Heavens no, with all the artificial light and smog, it is almost impossible to see any but the brightest stars."

"Some nights, I sit out by the lake for hours watching the stars while the fireflies dance," Sully said.

"That sounds romantic," Bryn teased.

"Well, I can be romantic at times," Sully said, feigning hurt feelings.

"I am sure you can," Bryn said with a wink.

Sully shook her head and walked to the grill. "These are getting close. Would you grab our plates and make us a baked potato at the bar," Sully said as she pointed in the direction of the potato bar.

Bryn walked over to retrieve their plates. "You want everything?"

"Everything but the kitchen sink. When you get done, the steaks will be ready."

Sully watched Bryn walk away. She definitely looked good in those jeans.

"Would you like fresh beers?" Greta asked.

Sully had not realized that Greta had returned. "What?"

"I asked if you wanted fresh beers, Romeo," Greta teased.

Sully blushed when she realized Greta had caught her eyeing Bryn. "No, I think we will switch to sweet tea."

"Tea it is, then."

"Thanks, Greta," Sully said, but the spirited waitress had already disappeared.

Bryn returned and set the plates on the carving board. "Those look and smell delicious."

"I hope you will be pleased," Sully said as she placed the steaks on the plates. "Let's eat."

Bryn followed Sully to the table where Greta had delivered their teas. They sat, and Sully watched Bryn as she cut into the steak and let out a delicious moan.

"Oh, my goodness, this is the best steak I have ever tasted," Bryn said between bites.

Sully's heart swelled with pride as she cut into her steak and watched Bryn eat heartily. "You still think you can eat the whole thing?"

"Probably not, but I am going to give it my best shot."

"They have excellent desserts, so save some room," Sully suggested.

"Forget dessert, I am going to eat my fill of this steak."

"Suit yourself," Sully said and began eating.

Sully ate quietly while she watched Bryn put a sizeable dent in the steak. When she finally put her fork down and pushed the plate away, Sully said, "Done already?"

"I am completely stuffed."

Sully stopped eating as well when she saw Greta approaching.

"Did you ladies save room for dessert," she asked.

"Of course I did," Sully said.

"Oh no, you have got to be kidding me. I have no room left."

"The usual?" Greta asked Sully.

"Yes, ma'am," she answered.

"I will be back in just a few then."

Sully saw Bryn watching Greta walk away, and then she asked, "What's the usual?"

"They serve the most amazing chocolate bread pudding."

"Dear Lord, you can eat that after the meal we just ate?"

"I told you to save room. I always eat dessert here," Sully answered with a smile.

Bryn shook her head and looked at the large portions of steak remaining on the plates.

"No worries, we will have leftovers for tomorrow."

"They were certainly too good to waste."

"They will taste even better tomorrow," Sully promised.

"Here you go," Greta said as she placed a bowl of tantalizing dessert in front of Sully. "I brought an extra spoon, just in case. Should I wrap these up to go?" she asked, and when Sully nodded, she took their plates away.

Bryn just shook her head. "I can't even begin to think of eating that."

"More for me then," Sully said as she picked up a spoon and took a bite. "This is really good," she said with a wicked grin.

†

Bryn could not resist leaning across the table and wiping a small trail of chocolate from Sully's chin with her finger and lifting it to her lips for a taste. "That is sinful."

"Yes, it is. Are you sure you wouldn't like a taste?"

"No thanks."

Sully continued to eat. Bryn watched bite after bite disappear, and when Bryn ran her tongue across her lips, Sully took a spoonful and offered it to Bryn. "Come on, you know you want it," she teased.

Bryn could no longer maintain her willpower. She closed her eyes and leaned forward as Sully placed the succulent dessert in her mouth. She let out a slow, sensual moan as her taste buds were seduced by the combination of the chocolate and creamy bread pudding.

†

The sound of Bryn's moan sent shivers through Sully's body. Images of her and Bryn in a lover's embrace flashed in her mind as she watched Bryn's tongue slowly trace her lips to capture every bit of the sweet taste.

†

Bryn opened her eyes to find Sully watching her intently.

"I told you it was good."

"Good is such an understatement, but I cannot find the words to describe how wonderfully it tastes," Bryn said. She was about to attempt to describe the luscious taste when her cell phone rang. She pulled the phone from her pocket and saw that it was her grandfather calling.

"Hello."

"I am so sorry to interrupt your evening out, but I need the two of you to come home as soon as possible," Doc said.

"What is it? Is the mare okay?" Bryn asked.

Sully sat straight up in her seat at the mention of the mare.

"No, the mare is fine, but there has been an accident, and I need you to bring Sully home," he said. "If I tell you anymore, she will hound you for answers that I can't give you right now, so just come home."

"We will be there as quickly as we can," Bryn said.

"Is the mare okay?" Sully asked.

"Yes, the mare is fine, but Doc needs us back at the barn. All the animals are fine," she repeated.

Greta returned to the table with their carry out boxes.

"Put this on my tab, please, Greta, and add a nice tip for yourself. There is an emergency at home, and we need to go now," Sully said.

"No problem, Sully. I hope everything turns out okay," Greta said as the two women rushed past her.

†

Sully drove quickly from the restaurant back to the farm. She quizzed Bryn but quickly realized she did not know what the emergency was. The news he had for Sully was not good, and he wanted her seated before he delivered it.

Sully's truck slid to a stop in front of the barn, and they raced inside to find Doc sitting in the office. Sully immediately noticed the worried look on his face.

†

Doc saw the lights of her truck bouncing down the driveway and decided to wait for them in the office.

"I need you two to sit down," he said.

Sully and Bryn both took seats across from Doc.

"What's the matter?" Sully asked.

"The animals are fine. I was sitting here playing cards when your phone rang, and I answered it." Doc reached across the table to cover Sully's hand with his own. "The call was from the Fulton County Sheriff's office. There has been an accident." Doc took a deep breath that felt like an eternity before he spoke again. "James and Caroline were killed in an automobile accident as they were going out to dinner tonight," he said.

James, Sully's only brother, was ten years older than her and was a successful lawyer in Atlanta. He and his wife, Caroline, had been married for eight years and had one daughter, Kendal, who was five.

"Oh my God, what about Kendal," Sully asked.

"She was at home with a babysitter," Doc said.

Sully remained speechless for several minutes as the shock of the news seemed to settle in. Bryn had placed an arm around her shoulder, and Doc was still holding her hand. She looked up at him and blinked.

"What else do you know about what happened?"

"Not much. The detective I spoke with said the driver of a large truck lost control of his vehicle and hit them head on, killing them both instantly."

"Dear God," Bryn said.

"I have the name and number of the detective. He wants you to call whenever you are up to it."

Sully turned to look at Bryn with a dazed look in her eyes. "Will you get me some water?"

"Of course," Bryn walked to the refrigerator and took out two bottles of water.

"Thanks." Sully looked up at Doc again. "Wake me and tell me I am dreaming this, Doc," she pleaded.

"I wish I could, Sully," Doc said.

"They are so young. This really cannot be happening," she said.

Bryn sat beside her and said, "I am so sorry."

Sully turned to her with tears blearing her eyesight. Bryn took her in her arms and held her tightly.

"I am going to step out for a few minutes to give you some privacy," Doc said. "I will check the animals."

†

Bryn nodded and watched her grandfather leave the room, a huge weight resting on his shoulders. She knew that Sully was like a daughter to him, and he longed for something to say to her to ease the pain.

She could feel Sully's sobs wracking her body as her tears began in earnest. Her hand smoothed down Sully's hair as she held her tight and felt her grief.

# CHAPTER TWELVE

---

Doc checked on the animals. The mare turned and looked him in the eyes. He knew that look all too well. Just as sure as he was standing there, he was certain the mare would give birth tonight. *Tonight, of all nights*, he thought as his hand ran across her withers. "I guess your time does not care about human tragedy," he whispered to the mare. "No worries, girl, I will be here to help you through."

He was sure Sully would leave for Atlanta tonight, although she was in no condition to drive. Bryn would be torn in her decision to go with Sully for support or to stay and help him with the mare. He would do his best to convince Bryn to go with her. Sully needed her most. He could still handle a birthing, and he would call Glen in for help if needed. His heart was breaking for Sully. She had looked up to James as her hero, even when, as a teen, he had little patience for a younger sister. Even though his heart was not into continuing the success of the farm, he called Sully often to check on her and see how things were going. Two summers ago, he even brought Kendal for a short visit. Sully was ecstatic to see her brother and the niece she doted on.

After twenty minutes, Doc decided it was time to return to the office and set the wheels in motion. Atlanta was only a five-hour drive, but the sooner they got on the road, the better, and he would not relax until Bryn called to say they had safely arrived.

†

Bryn held Sully until her body began to calm. She, too, was in shock from the news and was at a loss for words to say to Sully. She was relieved to see Doc enter the room.

Sully looked up at him as he returned to his seat beside her. "I don't want to rush you, but are you ready to make the call?"

"Yes, I guess so, Doc. There is no sense in putting it off any longer. Waiting won't change anything."

"That's true, and I would like you two to get on the road as soon as possible," he said.

Sully looked at Bryn. "Will you go with me?"

Bryn looked at Doc. "I can handle things here, so go."

"Are you sure?"

"I am positive."

"Yes, I will go with you then."

"Let's make the call, and you two can pack and hit the road," Doc suggested.

Sully took a deep breath and nodded her head. Doc stood and carried the phone to the middle of the table and pressed the speaker button. He looked at his scribbled notes and dialed the number the detective had given him.

When a female operator answered, Doc asked for Detective Gray.

"Gray here," a deep voice spoke into the phone.

"Detective Gray, this is Doc Barton, and I have Micah Sullivan here with me."

"Ms. Sullivan, let me first say I am very sorry for your loss. I knew your brother on a professional level, and he was a great man."

"Thank you, Detective. What do we need to do from here?" she asked.

"We were able to identify your brother and sister-in-law, but since there is a living next of kin, the morgue needs to obtain your signature to release the bodies to the funeral home," he explained.

"Can the forms be faxed?" Doc asked.

"Unfortunately, no. State law dictates they have to be made in person, so Ms. Sullivan will have to make a trip to the morgue."

"That's unfortunate," Doc said.

"Where is Kendal?" Sully asked.

"Your brother's partner, Josh Graves, has taken her home to his house. His daughter, Kayley, and Kendal are best of friends. He has already contacted the funeral home, and they will go into action as soon as you arrive."

"That's good. At least she is with a friend right now. Does she know?"

"No, Josh said he did not have the heart to tell her."

"I can understand that," Sully said.

"Can you come to Georgia as soon as possible?" he asked.

"I will leave tonight," Sully said.

"Is ten in the morning too soon to plan to meet you at the morgue?" the detective asked.

"No, that should be fine. We will arrive and try to catch some sleep and meet you then."

"Great, I will contact Josh and arrange for him to meet us as well. He stated earlier he would go into the office early and pull James's plan and will."

"Is there anything else I need to know?" Sully asked.

The silence at the other end of the phone line was deafening as Detective Gray contemplated his next words. "I am sorry to have to say this, but the services will have to be closed casket," he said.

Thankfully, he did not go into any further detail. His blunt statement was enough to tell them that the physical damage would be too disturbing to be viewed.

Sully got up and walked away from the table.

"Let me give you my cell phone in case you need anything," Detective Gray offered.

"Thank you," Doc said as he jotted the number down on a notepad.

"I will see you in the morning then, Ms. Sullivan," he said.

"She has stepped away, but I will pass on your message. Thank you for all your assistance, Detective Gray."

"You are very welcome. Good night," he said and disconnected the call.

†

Doc looked at Bryn. "Go pack for at least a week, and I will stay here and help Sully get her things together. Tell

Camille what has happened and have her pack some coffee and snacks for you," he instructed.

"I feel bad for abandoning you like this," Bryn said.

"Right now, Sully needs you more. If the mare goes into labor, I will call Glen in to help out."

"Okay, I will check on Sully and then get back here as quickly as I can," Bryn said.

She walked outside to find Sully sitting on a stump they had used as a mounting block when they were younger. Bryn sat down beside her and placed an arm around Sully. "I am going to go pack while Doc helps you get ready. I will be back as quickly as I can."

"Thanks," Sully said. Her tear-stained cheeks were flushed with emotion. "I can't believe this has happened."

"I know," Bryn said as she hugged her close. She planted a soft kiss on Sully's forehead and stood to leave. "I will be right back."

†

Sully watched Bryn jog to her truck and drive away.

Doc walked over to her and took her in his arms. "You will be okay," he promised. "I know your heart is breaking, but right now, you must be strong for Kendal. Her whole world has changed, and she will need you there to lead her through it," he said.

Sully knew he was right, but at the moment, she felt like she was totally lost and could never help Kendal cope with her loss.

†

Doc sensed her apprehension. "You are a strong woman, Micah Sullivan, and will come through this adversity even stronger."

"I am glad you are confident of this," Sully said. "I am terrified."

"Trust in your faith and upbringing," Doc said. "Like your horses, you come from good stock," he said with a wink. "Come with me, and we will get you packed and ready for when Bryn returns."

"Will you call me if the mare goes into labor?"

"Of course I will. I will call Glen in if she does and will call you when the birthing is complete," he promised.

Doc took her hand and lifted her to her feet. "I may be old, but I can still bring a colt into this world."

Sully smiled at him. "There is no one else I trust with that responsibility."

"I know, so I better not screw it up," Doc said as he led her into the house. "Let's go get you packed."

Doc followed her into the house. "Will you grab me a large suitcase from the front bedroom closet?"

"I sure will."

†

Sully walked into her room and began placing items on the bed. Her body moved mechanically as her mind rehearsed the clothing she would need. She had enough casual clothing laid out and walked into the closet. Back on the final rack was the dreaded black suit, the one worn only to funerals. She had hoped it would stay back in its place for a long time, but that was not to be. Never in her wildest dreams had she thought she would be wearing this outfit for James so soon. Her tears began to fall again as she reached for the suit and picked up black dress shoes to match.

Doc was placing her clothing in her suitcase when she walked from the closet. "Here, let me take that while you get a hygiene kit together," he said as he took the suit and hung it on top of the door frame.

Sully returned from the bathroom carrying a small kit and placed it on the bed. She stood there blankly.

"I will finish this up and bring the bag out to the porch. Why don't you go see Sunspot and the mare before you leave," he suggested.

†

Sully left the room and walked out to the barn. As soon as she reached Sunspot's stall, the filly came rushing to her. She could sense Sully's distress and nuzzled into her until Sully wrapped her arms around her neck. "You are such a good girl," she whispered into the filly's ear. "I will miss you, but I will be home as soon as I can. I will be bringing you a new friend who will need your love as much as I do."

Sully leaned down and planted a kiss on Sunspot's forehead. "Keep Doc good company while he is here," she instructed. She turned away to check the mare with Sunspot following closely behind her. Sully ran her hands over the mare. "You are going to be just fine. Doc will be here with you. I hate I will miss his grand entrance," she told the mare.

She heard Bryn's truck return and knew that Doc would be loading her suitcase into the truck. She left the stall and walked out to meet them. Sunspot refused to enter the stall, insisting on following Sully outside.

"She's going to miss you," Doc said as he stroked down Sunspot's neck.

Sully turned and hugged the filly's neck again. "I am going to miss her, too, but I will be home soon."

"Be careful," Doc said and hugged each of the women. "Call me as soon as you get checked into a hotel, and try to get some rest."

"Will do, Grandfather," Bryn said.

"Call if there is anything I can do," he said as he opened the passenger's door for Sully. "I will care for things here, so don't worry."

"Thanks, Doc." Sully looked at Sunspot, who was eyeing her sadly. "Stay with Doc," she said and climbed in quickly before her tears could start again. "Talk to you soon," she said as she pulled the door closed.

Bryn started the truck and carefully pulled away as Doc held onto Sunspot's halter. With darkness and silence surrounding them, they started the long journey to Atlanta.

## CHAPTER THIRTEEN

---

They rode for nearly an hour in silence; both women lost in thought. Sully stared out of the window as Bryn followed the broken lines down the center of the highway. She was at a tremendous loss for words to speak to Sully.

She finally broke the silence by asking Sully to pour her some coffee. "Camille packed a thermos of coffee. Would you pour me a cup?"

"Sure, where is it?"

"Right behind the driver's seat," Bryn answered.

Sully fumbled in the dark until she found the thermos and poured them both a cup of the presweetened drink. "Here you go," she said as she handed Bryn a cup.

Bryn took a sip. "Camille makes the best coffee."

"Yes, she does, she is an amazing woman."

"How are you feeling?"

"Still in a bit of shock, I would presume. My whole body feels numb."

"That is to be expected. I can find my way to Atlanta if you want to try to catch some sleep."

"I don't think I could right now, but thanks, and thank you for coming with me."

"Did you really think I would let you go alone?"

"Well, I was hoping you wouldn't," Sully said with a slight smile.

"There was no way you were leaving without me."

"I wish there was a way I could fast forward through the next few days. I know they are going to be awful."

"They will be stressful, yes, but it sounds like James had things planned out well."

"Of that I am sure. He was always a super-organized man and would prepare for every contingency," Sully said. Bryn could hear the pride in her voice as she spoke.

"I regret I never had the chance to meet him."

"You would have liked him," Sully said and then fell silent again.

They finished their coffee, and Sully put their cups away. The road was empty this time of night, and Bryn watched the miles slip away. Soon, they would be in Montgomery and would change interstates. Sully resumed staring out the window into the vast darkness.

Bryn pulled into a rest area just south of Montgomery. The coffee had run straight through her, and she needed to stretch her legs. "Do you need a bathroom break?"

"I probably should since we are stopped," Sully said as she opened her door. Her voice was so flat and emotionless that it worried Bryn.

After the quick break, they returned to the road. When they passed through the lights of Montgomery, Bryn noticed that Sully's head was beginning to nod. She reached into the back seat to grab a small travel pillow, which she placed on her thigh. She patted the pillow. "Why don't you curl up and try to get some sleep."

†

Sully was bone tired and emotionally drained. She did not want to sleep but curled up on the seat and placed her head on the pillow.

She enjoyed the way Bryn's fingers brushed through her hair. The closeness of her body and the light touch she gave were very comforting to Sully. She turned her head slightly, and Bryn's fingertips stroked across her cheek. A single tear slid down her face and encountered Bryn's fingertips.

†

Bryn felt the tear, and her heart continued to break. Her fingers continued to graze Sully's soft skin as she slowly succumbed to sleep. Bryn could hear the soft purring of Sully's breath as she slept, and she smiled. She placed a comforting hand on Sully's shoulder as she concentrated on the road ahead. Three more hours, and they could find a place to rest for the remainder of the night. Bryn was ready for that. The stress of the evening and the tension of driving were making her shoulder muscles ache, but she would not voice a complaint of her discomfort.

She could feel Sully's body twitching in the deep abyss of sleep and tried to remain very still to prevent disturbing her slumber. Sleep was probably the best thing for Sully at this time. The coming days would be horribly stressful for her, and any rest she could get would be a blessing.

Sully slept for two hours. Bryn looked at her fuel gauge and decided she needed to stop for fuel. When she saw the lights of Atlanta looming ahead of her, she located a station and pulled over. The deceleration of the vehicle woke Sully, and she bolted upright.

"What's wrong?" she asked, confused.

"Nothing, sweetie, I need to fuel the truck."

"Where are we?" she asked as she rubbed her eyes.

"Just outside of Atlanta," Bryn said.

"How long did I sleep?"

"Only about two hours, but I made good time."

"So, I see. I don't know about you, but I am ready for a room and a bed."

"I will not argue that with you."

"Let me get the fuel, and I can drive if you would like."

"You probably know the city better than me, so that would make sense."

"I know of a nice hotel that will hopefully have a vacancy and will be close to where we need to be," Sully said.

Sully stepped from the truck, slid a credit card in the pump, and filled the truck as Bryn got out and stretched her tired and stiff muscles.

†

Sully noticed how tired she looked and felt a pang of guilt for sleeping without sharing the drive. Bryn turned and smiled at her, and Sully's guilt melted away.

Sully slipped in behind the wheel as Bryn climbed into the passenger seat. "We should be there in a half hour," Sully said.

"Great," Bryn answered with another of those beautiful smiles.

†

Traffic into the city was unbelievably light, and Sully made a turn onto an exit ramp and pulled into the parking lot of a tall hotel. "Let me check to see if they have a room," Sully said as she parked the truck. "I will be right back."

Sully walked into the hotel lobby and approached the front desk. The woman behind the desk looked up at her and smiled. "May I help you?"

"Do you have any rooms available?"

"I have one king suite available."

"That's fine, we'll take it. Is it available for more than one night?"

"How long will you be staying?"

"At least three nights, maybe longer," Sully said.

"I will book it in for you then, Ms. Sullivan," the woman said after looking at Sully's credit card.

"Thank you."

"Here you go, you are all set," the woman said as she handed her the room key. "Is there anything else I can do for you?"

"Yes, please set it up for an eight am wake up."

"That's not much sleep," the woman said.

"I know, but I have business to attend to in the morning."

"I have it all arranged."

"Thanks," Sully said and returned to the truck. "I will grab the bags and wait for you if you will park the truck."

"Deal," Bryn said as she slid across to the driver's seat.

Sully pulled their bags from the back seat and pulled them inside the hotel lobby while Bryn parked the truck. When she joined her in the lobby, they located the elevator and rode it to the fifteenth floor. "I hope you don't mind, but they only had a king-sized bed available."

"I don't mind at all," Bryn said. "Right now, I just want to lie down."

"Thank you for bringing me to Atlanta," Sully said.

"No problem," Bryn said.

When the elevator stopped, they located their room, and Sully opened the door. The room was dark, and the curtains were open, showing a brilliant view of the downtown Atlanta skyline.

"What a view," Bryn said as she stepped into the room.

"Beautiful, isn't it?"

"Very much so."

Sully placed their bags on stands and turned on a light. She opened her bag to pull out a T-shirt and her hygiene kit. "Do you want to go first to the bathroom," she asked.

"No, go ahead while I take in this view for a minute."

†

Bryn could hear Sully in the bathroom brushing her teeth. She walked to her bag, pulled out a T-shirt to sleep in, and slipped out of her clothes. She was digging out her hygiene kit when the bathroom door opened, and Sully appeared, wearing a T-shirt and boxers. “The shower is all yours.”

“I will be right back,” Bryn said, then disappeared into the bathroom. She was excited to be in the same bed as Sully but was exhausted beyond belief. She wanted nothing more than to roll over and wrap her body around Sully to sleep the night away but was careful not to rush Sully.

†

Sully pulled back the crisp, cool sheets and climbed into the bed. It felt good to stretch out, and she was so relaxed. She jumped when the bathroom door opened, and Bryn entered the room. She turned out the light and climbed into the bed beside Sully.

Sully knew she was vulnerable to Bryn, and the closeness of their bodies was unbearable for her. “Would you hold me until I fall asleep?” she asked Bryn in a hushed whisper.

†

“Yes, I will,” Bryn said, her heart racing wildly as Sully appeared to read her thoughts. “Roll onto your side.”

“Thank you for everything. I had a great time with you tonight,” Sully said.

“I did, too,” Bryn said as she turned her body to face Sully and wrapped an arm around her waist. She snuggled her hips into Sully and was enveloped in her warmth immediately. “This feels good,” she whispered.

“Yes, it does,” Sully said as she covered Bryn’s hand with her own.

Bryn rested her head near Sully's shoulder, taking in the fresh smell of Sully's hair. "Get some sleep."

"I will. Good night, Bryn."

"Good night, Micah."

Bryn was perfectly content and quickly found her mind slipping into unconsciousness, her arm and body wrapped in Sully's warmth.

†

Sully smiled at the sound of Bryn speaking her name. She closed her eyes and allowed her body to drift off to sleep.

Sully woke hours later as the sun began to shine through the window. They had left the drapes open when they arrived last night. She crept quietly from the bed, pulled the drapes closed, and looked at the clock. In twenty minutes, they would receive a wakeup call, but she couldn't resist climbing back into the warm bed beside Bryn. Bryn had rolled onto her back and slept soundly as Sully propped up on her elbow and watched her sleep. Her face was so beautiful and relaxed, making her appear angelic as she slept. Sully was tempted to reach out and stroke her face but decided instead to enjoy the last few moments of sanity before their hectic day began.

Sully observed Bryn until a loud clamoring from the hallway caused her to stir. She watched as Bryn's eyes began to flutter, and then she opened to find Sully watching her.

"Good morning. How long have you been awake?"

"Not long," Sully answered.

"Did you sleep well?"

"I barely remember putting my head on the pillow. Did you rest?"

"I think I was asleep five seconds after you," Bryn said as she stretched her arms above her head.

Bryn's stomach chose to break a moment of silence with a loud growl. Sully smiled. "Are you hungry?"

"I don't know how I could be after last night's dinner, but I guess I am."

The phone rang, and Sully reached over to pick up the receiver. The automated recording was playing as she replaced it in the cradle. "Would you like some breakfast then?"

"Something light, maybe."

"You can go first in the shower," Sully said.

"It will save time if we shower together," Bryn said.

"Yes, that is true," Sully admitted.

"But?"

"But what, let's go."

They climbed from the bed and walked to the bathroom. Bryn started the shower while Sully placed towels close at hand. After taking a deep breath, Bryn pulled the T-shirt over her head and slipped out of her panties.

Bryn had the advantage of already seeing Sully naked when she had given her the massage. On the other hand, Sully found her heart racing as Bryn stripped before her eyes. Her body was firm with well-placed curves, and her eyes enjoyed taking her body in slowly as Bryn flushed with modesty. When their eyes met, Sully smiled. "You are beautiful," she said.

"Thank you," Bryn said as she stepped into the glass shower.

Sully quickly removed her clothing and joined Bryn in the shower. Bryn had moved under the water and was wetting her hair. Sully reached for the bottle of shampoo and filled her palm with the silky liquid. When Bryn stepped from beneath the water, Sully said, "Turn around."

Bryn turned to face Sully, who lifted her hands to Bryn's hair and began to work the shampoo into a soft lather.

†

Bryn closed her eyes and enjoyed the voluptuous feeling of Sully's hands working on her scalp. She worked the lather throughout Bryn's hair, then placed her under the flow to rinse the shampoo from her head before reaching for a washcloth and some fragrant soap.

Bryn slicked her hair back on her head and watched with delight as Sully lathered a washcloth. Sully stared at her neck, softly swirling the cloth across Bryn's skin. She caressed Bryn's full breasts slowly before moving upward to wash her shoulders and then down each arm. Sully then knelt in front of Bryn and bathed her stomach, across each hip, and then down her shapely, long legs. Bryn's knees grew weak under Sully's caresses, and she reached for the wall to support herself.

†

Bryn felt Sully making slow, teasing strokes up the inside of Bryn's thighs, and she felt a shiver run through her body. Sully looked up to find Bryn's desire-filled eyes tracking her every movement. She smiled and handed Bryn the washcloth. "You want to finish while I wash my hair?"

Bryn was speechless as she took the cloth and washed between her thighs as Sully lathered her hair. The soapy cloth moved smoothly across her swollen lips as Bryn's body quivered with excitement. *Damn, Sully, for getting me so worked up,* Bryn thought as she planned her revenge. She dropped the cloth in the back of the shower and joined Sully under the flow of the water. Sully had finished rinsing her hair and had turned toward Bryn. Bryn circled Sully's waist with her hands and pulled her body close. Bryn used her lathered front to coat Sully's body and pressed into her, moving her body slowly from side to side. Bryn locked eyes with Sully and smiled as she covered Sully's lips with her own.

Sully barely had time to close her eyes as their lips met. The softness of the tip of Bryn's tongue teased her lips open as their kiss grew more sensual. Bryn's hands stroked Sully's back as her tongue danced an alluring dance inside her mouth. Bryn moaned softly when her hardened nipples brushed across Sully's, sending vibrations through Sully's mouth into her body.

Sully's hands reached down to cup Bryn's ass in her hands to pull her body closer as their bodies moved together in a sensual rhythm. The kiss lasted for several minutes. When Bryn realized it had gone further than she intended, she broke the kiss.

"If we don't stop now, we are going to be late," she said.

"I know, but that felt really nice. We will continue this later, right?" she asked.

Bryn's heart skipped. "Yes, we will," she promised. "But for now, I need to rinse, and you need to bathe," she said with a devilish grin and pushed past Sully to rinse her body.

Sully was grinning widely as Bryn rinsed and stepped from the shower to begin drying her body. Bryn's heart was still pounding in her chest as she wrapped the towel around her and walked into the bedroom. She sat on the bed to steady her quivering body. She was overwhelmed by how excited Sully could make her feel.

†

Sully bathed her body and shut off the water. The brief physical encounter in the shower with Bryn had temporarily distracted Sully from the depressing events scheduled for her today, but as she dried her body, the reality of why they had come to Atlanta struck home.

## Chapter Fourteen

Bryn and Sully shared many shy smiles while they dressed for the day. When they were finished, Sully reached for Bryn and embraced her.

"Thanks again for being here with me. I can't begin to tell you how much this means to me."

"You are very welcome, and I feel honored to be your friend," Bryn answered.

"You are so much more than that," Sully said.

She leaned forward and kissed Bryn, who felt the breath leave her body. In a split second, the arousal she felt earlier in the shower returned, raging through her veins. Sully had the power in her kiss to instantly turn Bryn's world upside down, and she adored the way Sully could make her feel. The tender kiss left her wanting so much more, but that would have to wait for a different point in time.

"Let's go find some breakfast," Sully said as she led Bryn toward the door.

Downstairs, they found a small dining room where they shared a light breakfast of bagels, juice, and coffee. After they had finished a second cup, Sully asked for coffee to go and looked at her watch.

"We are fairly close, but you never know about the traffic here."

Bryn nodded her head. She could feel how much Sully dreaded the events of today but knew that nothing they could do would make them go away. When the coffee arrived, Sully signed the check to charge the breakfast to the room, and they left the dining area.

Bryn handed her the keys. "Since you know where we are headed."

†

Sully took the keys. She unlocked the door, walked to open Bryn's door, and closed it behind her once she was comfortably seated in the truck. Sully walked around the truck and climbed in behind the wheel.

The county morgue was only ten minutes away, and the dread had already begun to weigh on her. After they finished the morning's business, she would go to Kendal and find a way to gently break the news to her. More than anything else, Sully prayed that Kendal would be able to forgive her for giving her the news that would change her world forever.

As she slipped the key into the ignition, she placed her head on the steering wheel as a memory came flooding back to her. Her thoughts went back to the day James had called, so excited to share the news with her that Caroline was pregnant. His second comment completely astounded her when James asked her to be Godparent to their child, stating that he wanted their child to be raised by her if anything were to ever happen to him and Caroline. She had excitedly agreed, thinking that James was covering all his bases and that he and Caroline would live to see their future grandchildren, never once giving thought to being asked to raise a child. That reality came rushing home, terrifying Sully, and she felt her heart begin to race. After all, what did she know about raising a child?

Bryn watched her curiously. When Sully laid her head on the steering wheel, she asked, "Are you okay?"

"I was just remembering back to when James called with news of the pregnancy, and he asked me to be Godparent to his child." She looked over at Bryn. "When Kendal was born, James had me sign guardianship papers, just in case anything like this happened in the future. Now, I realize I have no idea how to raise a child."

Bryn chuckled softly. "From what I have seen from the way you care for your animals, raising a child will come naturally for you. I have a feeling you will make an excellent mother."

Sully smiled at Bryn. "I am glad you are so confident. I am terrified."

"You will be just fine, and you will have plenty of support from your friends and family."

Sully turned the key in the ignition. "That is comforting."

†

Sully pulled the truck out of the parking place and turned onto the street. They remained silent during the short drive to the morgue. Sully was lost in her own world of thoughts. She was concentrating so intensely that she almost drove past the looming hulk of a building that served as the county morgue. She turned into the parking lot and searched for a parking spot.

After two circuits of the lot, Bryn spotted a man walking toward a vehicle on the front row. "There," she said as she pointed at the man.

Sully pulled the truck around and waited as the man slowly settled into his car and pulled out of the spot. Sully maneuvered the truck and put it into park, killing the engine. She sat there with her hands on the steering wheel and took a deep breath.

"Here we go," she said and opened her door.

†

Bryn was unsure of what to say to Sully and followed her out of the truck. She noticed Sully looked a little pale. "Are you okay?"

"Yes, I am fine. I just dread where we are going. Can we please go back to the hotel and start over?"

"Unfortunately, it won't change anything, my love," Bryn said.

Sully perked up at her words. "I know, so let's get this over with."

Bryn walked beside her and glanced over at Sully to watch her closely. Her color had returned to normal by the time they reached the front entrance to the building. As they approached, a man stood up and walked toward them.

†

He looked vaguely familiar to Sully.

"Ms. Sullivan," he said.

"Yes, I am Micah Sullivan," she said.

The man smiled and held out his hand. "I am Josh Graves, your brother's partner. We have met before, but that was several years ago."

"Yes, I remember now. Thank you for meeting us today." Sully turned to Bryn. "This is my friend, Dr. Bryn Barton."

Josh smiled at Bryn and shook her hand. "It is nice to meet you. I wish it were under different circumstances."

"Nice to meet you," Bryn said as she firmly shook his hand.

"Detective Gray told us Kendal is staying with you. How is she doing?" Sully asked.

"She is a little confused about why she can't go home, but she and Kayley have been playing, and they are at the zoo with my wife this morning. They will meet us at home after lunch," he explained.

"Thank you so much for all you have done for her."

"She is a wonderful child, and I know Kayley will miss her friendship," Josh said.

"We will have to make the effort to keep them in touch," Sully said.

"Yes, I believe they would both love that. They have grown up so close."

Another large man walked up dressed in a suit, and when he opened his mouth, Sully knew the deep-voiced man was Detective Gray.

"Ms. Sullivan," he said as he held out his hand.

"Detective," Sully answered as their hands clasped.

Detective Gray shook hands with Josh. "Good to see you again." Then he turned toward Bryn with a brilliant smile.

"This is Dr. Bryn Barton," Josh said to introduce them.

"Bryn will do," she said, taking his offered hand.

"My pleasure, ma'am," he said, his southern accent resonating in his deep voice.

Selfishly, Sully felt a twinge of jealousy over the attention the Detective gave to Bryn. *She is all mine, big boy*, she thought with a smirk.

"Are we ready to go inside?" he asked.

"Yes," Sully answered.

"Follow me then," he said as Josh opened the door for them.

They followed Detective Gray onto an elevator and rode up to the third floor. "You will need to sign some forms for the Medical Examiner's office, and he will be able to answer any questions you may have."

"I don't think we have any. Your phone call last night pretty well answered any questions we had," Sully said.

"Your brother was a fantastic lawyer, and he will be missed a great deal," Detective Gray said.

"Thank you. I am glad you had an opportunity to know him."

He smiled at Sully. "There is no doubt you two are related. You look so much like him."

Sully chuckled. "There was never any doubt. We could have passed for twins if it had not been for the ten-year age difference. Many people told us that when we were growing up."

"Uncanny," the Detective said as he shook his head.

Sully smiled at Bryn, who was still watching her closely.

The elevator doors opened, and the small group followed the detective to a small waiting area. “I will let Dr. Jack know we are here and be right back.”

Sully, Bryn, and Josh took a seat and waited for his return.

Moments later, the door opened, and the detective returned with a man who looked young enough to still be in college. “Dr. Jack, this is Micah Sullivan, Dr. Bryn Barton, and Josh Graves,” he announced to the group.

“Ms. Sullivan, I am so sorry for your loss,” the young man said. “It is a tragedy when a young life is taken so swiftly, and your brother and his family had such a brilliant future.”

“Thank you, Dr. Jack,” Sully said. “This whole ordeal is still such a shock. I am not sure everything has sunken in yet.”

“I understand. I apologize for making you come here for a signature, but I must follow state law. I need two signatures from you, and you can be on your way to attend to other matters,” he said warmly. He handed her two release forms with post it notes pointing to the area where her signature was required.

Sully quickly added her signature to the forms and handed them back.

“Thank you. I will contact the funeral home and arrange for the release. Again, I am so sorry for your loss.”

“Thank you, Dr. Jack,” Sully said.

He nodded his head and turned away.

“Is there anything else?” Sully asked.

Detective Gray shuffled his feet. “There is one other matter I need to discuss with you.”

“What is it?” Sully asked.

"The driver of the truck that killed James and his wife was driving impaired," Gray said.

Sully looked up at him and blinked.

"He was a long-haul trucker who had high levels of antihistamines in his system. He was taking large doses to stay awake to make it home to his daughter's birthday party." He took a deep breath. "They aren't illegal drugs, but it is up to the victim's family to determine if they want to press charges for vehicular homicide since deaths occurred."

"There is no need to ruin another family, and I am certain the mental havoc he has caused himself will be punishment enough for the man. There is no need to add to the tragedy," Sully said.

"I understand and agree," Detective Gray said. "Thank you. If you are done here, I will walk you out."

Sully stood, followed by Bryn and Josh, and they were led back out to the morning sunshine by the Detective.

"I hope everything goes well for you this week, and if there is anything I can do, please do not hesitate to ask," Detective Gray said, and with a final handshake with Sully, he was gone.

Sully released a deep breath. "What do we need to do next, Josh?"

"We need to drop by the funeral home and make the final arrangements. Sometime in the next day or so, we need to go to James's home to pick out a suit for James and clothing for Caroline."

Sully looked at him blankly.

"I know it seems odd, especially since it will be a closed casket service, but it is protocol for the funeral home. I can handle that if you would like."

"Yes, please, if you would," Sully answered.

"Once we finish at the funeral home, I suggest we pick up some lunch, and then we will go to my home so you can visit and talk with Kendal."

Sully swallowed hard at the reminder of the difficult talk she would have to have with Kendal. Once more, her skin turned pale.

"I think I will drive. Since we are following Josh, I can't get too lost," Bryn teased to lighten the moment.

"I promise I won't lose you," Josh said.

They walked into the parking lot. Sully remained silent as they climbed into the truck and followed Josh across town.

As they wove through the traffic, Bryn glanced over at Sully. "Are you okay?"

"Yeah, I am just trying to think of a way to break the news to Kendal," Sully said.

"I haven't much experience, but I think we adults take children for granted too often. They seem to know and handle things much better than we do on many levels." Bryn reached over and took Sully's hand in hers. "I know when the time comes, you will say the right things to her."

"I love your confidence in me," Sully said. "Would you rub my head and send some of it to me?" she asked teasingly.

"I think you need to give yourself more credit, too," Bryn said. "You have a sense of calmness about you that allows you to handle things without panic taking over. Remember how you calmly picked Sunspot up when she was hurt?" Bryn looked over at Sully. "Even with my medical training, my first instinct was to rush back to the barn to find some method to transport her, and you just calmly reached down and picked her up."

"I had to take care of my baby," Sully said.

"Aha, my point exactly. You took care of what was yours and will do the same with Kendal."

†

Much to Bryn's relief, Sully smiled brightly. "When did you get so smart?" she asked.

"It must have happened while we slept," Bryn said with a wink.

Josh turned into a parking lot and pulled up to a beautiful brick building. Bryn followed him and found a parking spot close to him.

They were greeted at the door by the funeral director and, after a brief meeting, made the final arrangements for a graveside service for James and Caroline. When that part was done, Josh suggested they stop off for a bite to eat before they went back to his home to meet up with Kendal.

†

They followed him to a small diner and ordered burgers and fries. While they waited, Josh made small talk, trying to keep Sully's mind off the troublesome task of informing Kendal about her parents. He could not do it and felt guilty for passing the task off to Sully, but he felt sure she would do a good job.

When the food arrived, Sully picked through her fries and ate half the burger. Obviously, her mind was distracted, and neither Josh nor Bryn pressed her to join in the conversation. When they had finished eating, Josh paid the bill and walked them out to the truck.

"When we get to the house, and you are ready to talk to Kendal, I would recommend the backyard. We have a large garden that would give you ample privacy to have your chat without distraction."

†

"Thank you, Josh," Sully said.

Josh surprised Sully by stepping forward and giving her a hug. "I am sorry I couldn't do this for you."

"You have done so much already, Josh, so don't you regret anything," Sully whispered to him.

When Josh stepped back, Sully saw that he had tears in his eyes. He, too, was suffering from his loss. He and James had been partners for many years, so he must also be feeling a significant loss from his death.

He opened the door for Sully. "We don't live too far, maybe another fifteen minutes. Just follow me," he said, and closed the door behind Sully.

Bryn pulled into traffic behind him, and Sully reached over for her hand. Bryn smiled as she slipped her smaller hand into the warmth of Sully's grasp. "The worst part will be over soon," she said.

"I know," Sully said as she fought back the tears that so desperately wanted to flow.

## CHAPTER FIFTEEN

---

Sully took a deep breath as Bryn parked behind Josh in the driveway. "I better do this soon before I lose my nerve," she said.

"Relax, baby, you will be just fine."

They exited the truck, and Sully was relieved to learn that Kendal had not made it back from the zoo yet. Josh's wife had called to say they were running late and would be home in ten minutes. Josh gave them a quick tour of the house, and then he and Sully walked out into the garden.

He was right, he did have a beautiful garden, Sully thought as they walked toward a small gazebo. "This is magnificent," Sully said to him.

"We spend a lot of time on the weekends out here, so we wanted to create something special," he said.

"You have certainly done that."

"If you don't mind a suggestion, why don't you stay out here? When the girls come home, I will send Kendal out to you. I know you are anxious to talk to her."

"Yes, I think that would be wise," Sully agreed. "This place is perfect for a troubling conversation," she said as she sat beside a bubbling brook.

"Good luck then. I will be here if you need me," Josh said.

"Thanks," she said, then watched him return to the house.

She closed her eyes and concentrated on the sound of the gentle movement of water and, for a few moments, allowed the real-world worries to slip away.

†

Josh returned to join Bryn in the living room. "I think the best plan is to send Kendal out to Micah and let them have some privacy for their talk."

"That is an excellent idea, Josh."

"They should be home very shortly, and after a brief introduction, I will send her out to the garden to find her aunt. We can observe from here without intruding on their privacy, and she can signal us if she needs our assistance."

"Thank you for being so supportive to both Kendal and Micah," Bryn said.

"James was like a brother to me, and I know how much he loved his sister and his daughter. I will do anything within my power to ensure they are safe and get the best care they can."

"I wish I could have met James and his wife," Bryn said.

"They were both great people and will be dearly missed by the community as a whole."

Their conversation was brought to a halt by the front door being flung open as Kayley and Kendal rushed in, followed closely by Josh's wife, Laura.

Both girls put on their brakes when they realized there was company in the house. Josh hugged them both and then turned to Bryn.

"Ladies, I would like you to meet Dr. Bryn Barton," he said. "Bryn, if I may introduce my wife, Laura, our daughter, Kayley, and Micah's niece, Kendal. Kendal, Dr. Barton is a friend of your Aunt Micah."

Bryn saw a frown of confusion pass over Kendal's face. "A doctor," Kendal said, "Is Aunt Micah sick?"

"No, Kendal, Micah is just fine. I am an animal doctor," Bryn said.

"A veterinarian," Kendal said. "You keep her horses from being sick?" she asked.

"Yes, a vet for short, and I help her keep her horses healthy," Bryn said with a smile.

"That's cool. I love to visit and ride the horses."

"They are so much fun," Bryn said.

Kendal looked puzzled again. "Where is Aunt Micah?"

"She is out in the garden, Kendal. Why don't you go visit with her and bring her back inside," Josh suggested.

"Okay. It is nice to meet you, Dr. Barton," she said so sweetly.

"Nice to meet you, too, Kendal," Bryn answered.

She watched her bounce out the door to the garden. "She looks just like Micah," she said as she turned to look at Josh.

"Kayley, honey, why don't you go up to your room with your mom while I visit with Dr. Barton," he said.

"Yes, Daddy," she said, taking her mom's hand as they climbed the stairs.

"Laura will update Kayley on what happened with James and Caroline. I think she knows something is wrong but is not sure just what."

"They can be very perceptive at that young age," Bryn said as she turned to watch out the window. Kendal had just spied Micah and was racing toward her beloved Aunt.

†

Sully cringed when she heard the house's back door open, and she knew when she opened her eyes and turned around, Kendal would be in sight. Her mouth was suddenly filled with cotton, and she bit her lip to hold back the tears that were on the brink of falling. When Kendal saw her, she began running toward her, a broad smile gracing her beautiful face. Sully's heart broke a little more when Kendal ran into her arms and hugged her tightly. She could feel the child's heart racing as she picked her up and held her close.

"I am so glad to see you, Aunt Micah," Kendal said. "I met your doctor friend inside," Kendal said in an excited voice. "She takes care of your horses, doesn't she?"

"Yes, she does, Kendal; she is my best friend."

"She is also very pretty."

"I will certainly tell her you think so," Sully said with a chuckle. "It will make her day. So, how are you doing," she asked Kendal.

"I am good. I came over to spend the night with Kayley. This morning, we went out to breakfast and then to the zoo," she said excitedly.

"Oh, I just love the zoo here and all the animals," Sully said.

Kendal, who was now proudly poised upon Sully's left knee, cocked her head to the side with another of her puzzled looks. Her tiny hand came up to stroke her aunt's face. "Have you been crying, Aunt Micah," she asked.

Sully's body stiffened at the child's question. "Yes, Kendal, I have. I am very sad right now."

"Is it about Daddy and Mommy?" she asked.

"What about them?" Sully asked, totally shocked by Kendal's question.

"I know something is not right, and all the adults are acting strangely. Even Kayley noticed it this morning. Besides, Daddy always calls me when he and Mommy are on their way home, and last night he didn't call."

Sully felt a huge lump in her throat. She tried to swallow, but her mouth refused to cooperate.

"I don't know exactly how to tell you this, Kendal, but I have some news that will make you very sad," Sully said.

"Like you?" Kendal asked.

"Yes, like me, I am afraid." She took a deep breath and closed her eyes for a moment. When Sully opened her eyes, she found the same crystal blue eyes that she and James shared staring up at her. She felt her tears begin to flow down her cheeks as she began to speak and silently cursed herself for not being strong enough to keep them in check.

"Last night, your mommy and daddy were in a bad accident," Sully said. She nearly choked on those words as recognition began to show on Kendal's face.

"Are they gone to heaven?" Kendal surprised her by asking.

"Yes, Kendal, as bad as they wanted to be here with you, they could not be. God decided he needed them in heaven," Sully said to follow the little girl's lead.

"So, they will be with angels?" she asked. "Daddy always said he would be with the angels when he had to leave me," she stated calmly.

James had done a superb job preparing Kendal for such an event, and Sully was shocked at the maturity Kendal displayed. "Yes, they are with the angels."

Sully choked back her tears and lifted Kendal's chin with her fingertips. She smiled at the niece she adored so deeply. "When your father first told me about you, he asked if I would care for you if he had to leave," Sully said. "He was so excited about you coming to him and your mother but wanted to know that you would be safe and happy if anything ever happened, and I promised him then that I would love you and care for you the best that I could." Sully waited for her words to register with Kendal. "I told him that you would come to live with me on the farm, and I would help you become anything you wanted to be." Kendal wiggled in her lap when she talked about the horses, making Sully smile, knowing how much she loved them.

"I would love that, but what about my friend Kayley?" she asked.

"Josh and I have agreed that the two of you should continue to visit as often as possible, and we will make that happen," she promised. "I know how hard it can be leaving a best friend behind."

"But I will have you and Dr. Barton, and I am sure I will make more friends," Kendal said.

"Yes, you will have plenty of friends and all the animals to spend your time with. As a matter of fact, I know of a little filly that needs a best friend right now," she said.

"Really, Aunt Micah?" she asked.

"Yes. Her name is Sunspot, and she has been hurt and needs someone to help her get better," Sully explained as Kendal's eyes lit up.

"I can do that," Kendal said.

"I think you would be perfect," Sully said with a big hug.

They sat in silence for a few minutes, just holding on to one another. Sully could not believe that Kendal had yet to shed a tear. Concerned, she took another approach to speaking with her.

"Kendal, you do realize that Mommy and Daddy won't be coming back, right?"

"Yes, Aunt Micah, just a few weeks ago, they took me to a funeral, and I saw how all the friends and family said their goodbyes. Some people cried, but most were happy that their friend had gone to be with the angels."

"There will be a funeral for your mommy and daddy in a few days where you can tell them goodbye and their friends, and I can do the same," Sully explained.

"I will be there to hold your hand as you say goodbye to Daddy," Kendal said. "I know how much you love him, too."

"Yes, and I will miss him dearly, but I am glad I will have you to share a life with."

Kendal reached up and stroked Sully's cheek softly. "We will be just fine."

†

Bryn and Josh watched the interaction between aunt and niece with curiosity. When Bryn saw Kendal reach up and stroke Sully's face, she whispered, "I wonder who is consoling who?"

"It seems to be going pretty well," Josh observed. "Kendal is very mature for such a young age, and James did not believe in sheltering her from the realities of life."

"That is probably the best thing he could have done for her." Bryn stared out the window. "I swear if I didn't know better, I would think they were mother and daughter. I can't believe how similar their appearances are."

"Must have been quite a family trait to have those blue eyes and the dark, wavy hair," Josh said. "Caroline's blonde hair and brown eyes were such a contrast to James and Kendal."

"Have you known them for long?"

"James and I became partners shortly after we both passed the bar. We met in law school, and from the start, there was no doubt we would become partners," Josh said.

"Caroline and Laura became good friends, and we spent a lot of time together on the weekends, and on occasion, we vacationed together." Josh turned his head to look out the window to hide the tears pooling in his eyes.

†

Bryn could hear the admiration in his voice as Josh spoke of James. She turned to see Sully and Kendal walking back toward the house and watched as Kendal's hand instinctively reached for Sully's as they walked together. Bryn smiled when she saw Kendal's small, warm hand slip inside of Sully's and she turned to smile warmly at Kendal. Bryn's heart was touched by the tenderness between them at that moment, and she prayed that the rest of the week would pass quickly and painlessly.

Caroline and Kayley must have also been watching from upstairs. Kayley rushed down the stairs and met Kendal at the door with a huge hug. “I am sorry about your mommy and daddy,” Bryn heard her say to Kendal.

“Everything will be fine,” Kendal said. “I will be going to live with Aunt Micah, and she has promised you can come for a visit as often as you would like,” Kendal said with another of her charming smiles.

“Can we ride horses?” Kayley asked excitedly.

“Yes, we can,” Kendal said.

Kayley looked up to Sully, who nodded her head. “I have so many horses and not enough time to ride them all, so you two would be doing me a favor,” she told Kayley with a wink. “Maybe later this summer, you can come for a long visit before you two start school in the fall,” Sully said.

“Can I, Daddy?” she pleaded.

“Yes, you can,” Josh said with a smile to his daughter. “Maybe Kendal can join us for our annual camping trip to the Smoky Mountains, too,” he added.

“I would like that very much,” Kendal said.

“How about some grilled chicken for dinner tonight?” Josh asked the girls.

“Yummy,” they said in unison. “Can we have some of those grilled sausages, too, please, Daddy?”

“Yes, I will be sure to cook those too. Do you two want to go play for a while?” he asked.

The girls answered by rushing to the stairs and disappearing in a roar of giggles.

†

The sound of their laughter was music to Sully's ears. She watched them fly up the stairs and turned back to Josh.

"That went much better than I expected."

"It was hard to tell who was comforting who," Bryn said.

"She is an amazingly mature child for her age, but it worries me that she hasn't cried," Sully admitted.

"When the time comes for her to mourn, she will," Laura said. "James and Caroline taught her about death well and that it was a time for celebration, but even so, there will be sadness and loneliness that she will have to face." Laura reached over and took Sully's hand. "She is lucky to have an aunt she loves so much."

"I am the lucky one," Sully said.

"We won't eat until about seven," Josh said. "I know you two couldn't have gotten much sleep last night, and today has been so hectic, so if you want to take a nap, I can give you directions back to the hotel."

"A nap would be nice," Bryn said.

"You must be tired. You did all of the driving last night," Sully reminded her. "Is there anything we can bring for dinner?"

"Just good appetites," Josh said. "Laura and I have dinner all planned, and the girls will play well into the afternoon before we put them down for a nap."

"I have a GPS in the truck, so if you will write down your address, we should be able to find our way back," Bryn said.

Josh walked over to a small desk and wrote down the address and phone number. "I included the house phone number, too, just in case," he said with a grin.

Sully took the slip of paper from him. "We will see you before seven then," she said.

"Get some rest," Josh said as he walked them to the door. "I will let Kendal know you will be back for dinner."

Laura stepped forward and placed a hand on Sully's arm. "Would you mind if she stayed here with us at the house until you are ready to go home?" Laura asked.

"I don't think that would be a problem, and I know she wants to spend as much time with Kayley as she can."

"Thank you. I think it will be good for both of them," Laura said.

"Thank you for everything," Sully said. "James and Caroline could not have had better friends."

Josh and Laura stood in the doorway and waved as Bryn pulled the truck out of the drive. Sully lifted her hand to wave back.

†

"So, how are you?" Bryn asked.

Sully let out a deep breath. "Relieved, I am very relieved to have that over," she said. "Tired too. I was glad when Josh mentioned a nap."

"Me too," Bryn said. "A nap and a shower to freshen up, and we will be good to go."

"Yes, we will," Sully said as she reached for Bryn's hand.

## CHAPTER SIXTEEN

---

The drive back to the hotel passed quickly. Sully placed the Do Not Disturb sign on the door and closed it behind them. Then she sat down in one of the high-backed chairs next to the bed and started taking her shoes off.

"I am so ready to lie down," she said as she pulled the shirt over her head.

"Do you want me to set an alarm?" Bryn asked.

"I will set my watch alarm," Sully said, adjusting her watch.

Bryn had also removed her shoes and stripped down to a sports bra and panties. She pulled back the covers and climbed into the bed.

Sully smiled and walked over to close the heavy drapes. "We won't make that mistake again," she said. She walked back around the bed, stepped out of her pants, and dropped them onto the chair.

Bryn had turned onto her side and was watching Sully as she climbed into the bed and lay down facing her. She reached out her hand to caress Sully's cheek. "I am glad your talk with Kendal went well."

"She is an incredible child," Sully said. "She seems to be handling the whole situation much better than me."

"You had many more years with James and are completely aware of your loss. Kendal is still young enough to adapt to changes easily, and even though she will miss them, she will bounce back quickly."

Sully reached up and took Bryn's hand in hers, bringing it to her lips. She kissed the palm of her hand and then pulled Bryn closer until their bodies touched. She could feel Bryn's warm breath on her neck as their eyes locked. Sully smiled and leaned forward to kiss Bryn, softly at first, as her hand stroked down Bryn's side.

†

Bryn closed her eyes and allowed the moan to escape her body as the touch of Sully's hand made her skin burn with desire. Bryn reached across Sully's waist and slowly rolled onto her back, pulling Sully on top of her as their kiss deepened. Sully's hips molded perfectly between Bryn's open thighs, their body heat merging as skin pressed into skin.

Sully broke the kiss and propped herself on an elbow as her fingers brushed the hair from Bryn's face. "You are so beautiful," she whispered as her fingertips traced the lines of Bryn's facial bones.

†

Bryn's hands moved down Sully's sides and came to rest on her hips. Her body ached with need, and Sully could feel Bryn's body quivering beneath her. She planted soft kisses down Bryn's face until she reached her lips, her tongue slowly savoring the taste of her soft lips before entering her mouth.

Bryn's hips began to undulate slowly, grinding her body into Sully's hips while her hands encouraged reciprocal movement from Sully's body. Sully felt the heat and wetness spread between them as her hips slowly pushed deeper into Bryn, their pubic bones grinding together in a slow, seductive dance. She felt Bryn's fingers grabbing her ass, pulling her hips as her body begged for release. Sully slowly increased the speed and power of her movements, responding to the urgent messages Bryn's body was sending hers.

Bryn broke off the deep kiss to gasp for breath. She buried her face in Sully's neck and breathlessly begged, "Please, Micah, make me come."

"Does this feel good?"

"Yes, baby, that feels so good," she growled and nipped the soft skin of Sully's neck.

The feel of Bryn's teeth on her skin and the husky sound of desire in her voice made Sully's body move more urgently as she reached the brink of control.

"Come with me, Bryn," Sully said as her body began to convulse. She heard a loud groan from Bryn and felt the intense rippling of pleasure flow through Bryn's body as they moved together.

"Oh yes, Micah," Bryn cried out, then covered Sully's mouth with a crushing kiss.

The kiss maintained the sexual bliss that had passed between them for several minutes. When Sully opened her eyes and broke the kiss, she saw the look of complete contentment on Bryn's face. When Bryn opened her eyes, Sully smiled and said, "That was intense."

"That was fantastic," Bryn said.

"Very fantastic," Sully said as she rolled onto her back. She guided Bryn to rest her head on her shoulder.

†

Bryn's hand glided across Sully's stomach as they lay together in silence. No words were needed to explain the feelings of complete satisfaction they both felt. After several minutes of continued silence, Bryn felt Sully's muscles begin to twitch, and she realized Sully had fallen asleep. She laid her head back on Sully's shoulder and closed her eyes, reveling in the warmth of her body as sleep claimed her, and she drifted into unconsciousness.

†

Hours later, the alarm sounded, and they showered and dressed for dinner. Sully could not wipe the grin off her face each time she looked at Bryn, and Bryn's cheeks would flush. Before they left the room, Sully took Bryn in her arms and held her close.

"This afternoon was beautiful," she whispered to Bryn.

Bryn lifted her face to look up at Sully. When she started to speak, Sully lifted her fingers and placed them across

Bryn's lips to silence her. Then she replaced her fingers with her lips to place a soft kiss on Bryn's lips.

†

Kendal met them at the front door when they returned for dinner. Kendal climbed into Sully's arms and hugged her closely.

"I am so glad you are back," she said.

"We needed to take a nap, too," Sully answered.

"Do you feel better now?" she asked.

"I feel much better, thank you," Sully said as she kissed Kendal's cheek and lowered her back to the floor.

Kendal's hand found Sully's as she led them through the house and out to the patio where Josh and his family were sitting around a grill.

"Welcome back," he said.

"Thanks," Sully answered.

"May I offer you two an adult beverage?" Josh asked, holding up a beer bottle.

"That would be wonderful," Bryn said.

Josh walked over to a small refrigerator and turned back to them. "You can have beer or beer," he said with a grin.

"Beer will do just fine," Sully replied.

Josh carried two beers to where they were sitting. "You look refreshed."

"It is amazing what a nap and a shower can do for a body," Sully said.

Kayley and Kendal were playing in the garden. "Did the girls take a nap?" Sully asked.

"A short one after all the giggles subsided," Laura answered.

"They are very close, aren't they?" Sully asked.

"Yes, best friends," Josh said. "I do believe we will be doing a great deal of traveling in the future, you and me," he said with a grin to Sully.

"You are so right, but I think they will both enjoy their time together."

"They always do," Laura added. "I hope you and Bryn will consider going on the camping trip with us, too."

Sully looked at Bryn, who was shocked by the invitation. "I will have to see how the practice is running, but it sure sounds like fun," Bryn said.

"We would be very happy if you could make it," Josh said. He turned toward the grill and opened the lid.

The air was filled with fragrant smoke, immediately making Sully's mouth water.

"Something smells delicious," she said.

"The girls love sausage on the grill for appetizers," he said as he turned the meat. "We can munch on these while the chicken finishes cooking," he said as he began taking the links of sausage off the grill. The girls came running at the sound of sausage. "Let them cool for a few minutes, and then you can dig in."

Kendal crawled up in Sully's lap as they waited for the meat to cool. Bryn was still amazed at the resemblance between the two as Sully and Kendal chatted away. If Sully ever had a child, Bryn was certain it would look just like Kendal.

Kayley and Kendal assisted Josh in serving the sausage once it had cooled.

†

Sully enjoyed the spices as she ate several pieces.

"I can see why you two like this so much," she said to Kendal. "It tastes really good."

"Yes, it does, Aunt Micah. Do you like to grill?" she asked her aunt.

"As a matter of fact, I do. I have a big Fourth of July cookout every year," Sully said.

"With fireworks?" Kendal asked.

"Yes, whenever possible. I am not sure about this year. It has been so dry, but if we get rain between now and then, I think we will be good."

"That sounds like fun," Kayley said.

"If you don't already have plans, you are more than welcome," Sully said to Josh.

"Can we go, please, Daddy?"

"We will see. I don't think we have anything planned for the holiday," Josh said as he looked at Laura.

"Great, I have plenty of room at the house, so you can stay with me, and the girls can have some time together."

"Can we ride horses?" Kayley asked.

"Yes, you can," Sully answered.

"How much longer until the Fourth of July, Daddy?"

"Just a few more weeks," he answered.

"This summer is moving so quickly," Laura said.

"That it is," Sully said as she stole a glance at Bryn.

After they finished the sausages, the girls helped Laura set the table on the patio. It was such a lovely night that they all agreed to eat outside. When dinner was over, they returned to their comfortable seats and shared a few more drinks. Kayley was curled up in Josh's lap, and Kendal was in Sully's, and both had fallen asleep. Sully enjoyed the closeness with Kendal and was slightly disappointed when Josh spoke.

"Should we take them upstairs?" he asked Sully.

"I guess they would be more comfortable."

Josh led Sully into the house and up the stairs to Kayley's room. The bed covers were still drawn from their naps, so both she and Josh placed the girls on their backs and gently removed their shoes before covering them up. They stood over them for a few minutes to ensure they were sound asleep.

"They look like angels," Sully said.

"They usually are unless they get too much sugar in them," Josh teased.

"I will make a note of that," Sully said.

"Don't worry about notes. You will learn quickly enough, and Kendal will be a great teacher." Josh placed a comforting hand on her shoulder. "You will do just fine."

"I hope you are right," Sully said.

They walked downstairs to join Laura and Bryn on the patio.

"If you would like, we can go to James's tomorrow, and you can instruct me on what to do with the household items," Josh said to Sully.

"I hadn't even thought of that, but I guess we should get started and pack some stuff up for Kendal."

"I can probably rent the house fairly easily if you don't want to sell it outright," Josh said. "I know of several people in the firm who would jump on renting or buying the property."

"Rent it at first, and we will see how things go," Sully said. "Will you also set up a trust for Kendal?"

"Of course I will. I promise she will have the best investments money can buy," he said.

"Thank you, Josh. I know James would be proud," Sully said.

"I know he would do the same for me if the tables were turned, and I will do everything in my power to ensure Kendal has the funds necessary to ensure a bright future."

"Should we meet at the house around nine, then?" Sully asked.

"Nine would be fine," Josh said.

"I think we will head back to the hotel then and see you in the morning," Sully said.

"Thank you for a terrific meal," Bryn said.

"You are more than welcome," Laura said. "If you don't want to go with Josh and Micah in the morning, you can come spend the day with us girls," she added.

"Thank you. I may do that," Bryn said.

Josh walked them out to the truck, and they started back to the hotel. "Would you prefer to come back here tomorrow?" Sully asked.

"That depends on whether or not I can be of assistance to you tomorrow."

"You are always a great help, but tomorrow may be a bit painful. Why don't you spend the day getting to know Kendal a little better and let Josh and I take care of business."

"If that is what you wish, I certainly don't mind spending time with the girls."

Sully reached over and took Bryn's hand. "Thank you for being here with me."

"There is no need for you to thank me. I am where I want to be," Bryn answered.

# Chapter Seventeen

---

When they returned to the hotel, Bryn and Sully stripped off their clothes and climbed between the fresh sheets. Bryn turned toward Sully, who took her in her arms and pulled her close. The warmth of her skin gave Sully great comfort as she snuggled into Bryn's softness.

"You feel so good next to me," Sully whispered. "Such a sweet relief."

"I was just thinking the same thing," Bryn said, then shivered as Sully's hand glided across the curve of her hip.

"Are you cold?"

Bryn softly chuckled. "No, not at all, Micah. Your touch sends shivers racing through me."

"Like this?" Sully asked as her fingers trailed up Bryn's side.

"Umm, yes, just like that," Bryn answered, her voice growing husky.

For the next two hours, Sully took delight in torturing Bryn's body with light kisses and soft touches. With a final shudder, their bodies melted together as their desires were satisfied for the moment.

Bryn's body was tucked into Sully when she whispered, "It is incredible how you move me."

"It feels so natural with you," Sully said.

"Yes, it does," Bryn agreed.

"Do you want to spend the day with the girls tomorrow?"

"Yes, I think I need to spend some time with Kendal since she is going to be a huge part of our lives."

Sully lifted Bryn's face with her fingertips. "Yes, she will be, for many years to come, I hope."

"I don't plan on going anywhere," Bryn said as she snuggled into Sully.

"Fine, Josh and I will take care of business and join you as soon as we can."

"When do you think we will be going home? I really should call tomorrow and check on Grandfather," Bryn said.

"Holy cow, I can't believe I haven't called him to check on the animals," Sully said.

"You have had your hands full here. He would call if he needed to talk about one of them with you."

"True. The services are scheduled for the day after tomorrow, so we will start home Thursday morning."

"Let's give him a call in the morning before we leave for the day."

"Sounds good," Sully said as she buried her face in Bryn's hair.

†

The room grew quiet as Bryn listened to the strong beating of Sully's heart. Her hand rested on Sully's hip, her fingers aching to stroke her lover, but Bryn knew that Sully had an emotionally draining day ahead of her and needed her rest.

"Good night, Micah," she whispered.

"Good night, Bryn."

†

The next morning, when the alarm woke them, Sully rolled onto her stomach and stretched her arms above her head while Bryn reached for her cell phone. As she turned back toward Sully, her eyes took in the curves and swells of Sully's body.

"I could get used to this," she said.

"What's that?" Sully asked as she rolled onto her side.

"Waking up next to your beautiful naked body," Bryn said as her hand trailed up Sully's thigh across her hip.

Sully saw the cell phone in Bryn's hand. "Be sure to ask Doc how the animals are doing, please."

"I will," Bryn said as she dialed her grandfather's number.

Sully reached over and began to tease Bryn's left nipple as she waited for Doc to answer the phone. She gave Bryn a mischievous grin as she moved closer, and her tongue flicked across a swollen nipple.

Bryn gasped with surprise when Doc answered the phone. "Hello, Grandfather," she said.

"Good morning. How are things going?" he asked.

"Pretty well so far," Bryn answered as Sully's mouth covered her left breast. "How are the animals?"

"You can let Sully know her new colt arrived safely last night, and he and his mother are doing well," he said.

Sully moaned, sending vibrations across Bryn's sensitive flesh. "I will be sure and tell her. Are you doing well?" she asked.

Sully's hand slipped between Bryn's thighs and found her lover's lips damp with excitement. She slipped a finger between them and slowly stroked her wetness as Bryn bit her lip.

"Yes, I am doing fine, and Glen is taking good care of all the animals. When do you think you will be home?" he asked.

"We should be there sometime late Thursday," she said.

Sully's teeth grazed Bryn's nipple as a second finger entered her wetness.

"How is she holding up?" he asked.

"Sully is doing very well," Bryn said. "Kendal took the news better than anticipated and is looking forward to living with Micah."

"That is wonderful news," Doc said. "Tell her she is in my thoughts and prayers."

"I will, Grandfather, and I will call again after the services, but call before if you need anything," she said.

"I think I have everything under control," he said. "Love you and will talk with you tomorrow," he said.

"Love you, too," Bryn said and ended the call as she spread her legs open to allow Sully better access to her body. "You are so naughty," she growled as her hand pressed on the back of Sully's head.

"Would you have me stop?" Sully asked.

"Oh Lord no, please don't stop," she answered.

Sully curled her fingers deep inside Bryn, causing her to moan loudly as her fingertips lightly stroked her G spot. Sully positioned her body to straddle Bryn's left thigh, her wetness soaking Bryn's skin as her fingers plunged in and out of Bryn's body. Bryn's breathing was quickly becoming ragged as she slipped her hand between Sully's legs and entered her, smoothly sliding deep into her wetness.

Sully groaned as Bryn matched her movements, her muscles wrapping around her fingers with each stroke into Bryn's body. The thrusting of her hips drove Bryn's fingers deep inside her, and Sully felt her climax rapidly approaching. Her thumb located Bryn's swollen button and rubbed across it as her teeth stretched Bryn's nipple, causing her to erupt, sending Sully tumbling over the edge with her as their bodies shook violently together.

Sully removed her fingers and moved up to kiss Bryn passionately.

†

Bryn's fingers were still buried inside Sully, and she could feel her muscles pulsing as she slowly curled them back and forth, extending Sully's pleasure.

When Bryn felt Sully's body relax, she slowly removed her fingers. The kiss lingered as a soft swirling of tongues as their bodies recovered.

"That was fantastic," Bryn said when the kiss ended.

"Uh-hmm," was all Sully could manage.

She rolled onto her back. "I will miss you today."

"Would you rather I go with you?" Bryn asked.

"No, I am just letting you know I am going to miss being with you," Sully said.

"That is so sweet. I will be a call away if you need me."

Bryn rolled onto her side, facing Sully. "We still have two nights together," she said.

"Yes, we do, and I hope to take full advantage of them," Sully said with a grin.

Neither woman wanted to discuss how things would have to change once they returned home. Bryn was content with what Sully had to offer in the present and figured the future would take care of itself. She knew they had a future. "Are you ready for a shower and some breakfast?" she asked.

"Yes, I am starved."

"You worked up an appetite," Bryn said.

"That I did, and it's not for breakfast," Sully said.

Bryn felt her heart drop into her stomach. "We will just have to see if we can satisfy your hunger tonight, then," she boldly said, stepping from the bed and offering Sully her hand.

After a shower and a hearty breakfast, they left the hotel and drove to Josh and Laura's. Sully spent a few minutes with Kendal explaining what she and Josh were doing before they left the house.

†

"I have a teddy bear on my bed. Would you bring that for me, please, Aunt Micah?" she asked.

"Of course I will. Is there anything else you want right now?"

"Just some clothes and my dress for tomorrow," she said.

Sully hugged Kendal tightly. "Bryn has my number if you think of anything else, okay?"

"Yes, Aunt Micah," Kendal said and kissed her cheek.

"I will be back as quickly as I can."

"That's good. I can spend the morning with Dr. Barton, and I will see you later," Kendal said.

"You know what Kendal? Bryn would prefer you call her by name rather than Dr. Barton."

"I can do that," Kendal smiled.

"Ready?" Josh asked.

"As ready as I am going to get," Sully said.

"I will drive," he said as they left the house.

Sully's heart grew heavier with each moment that passed. She had never dreamed she would be entering James's house under these circumstances, and the dread weighed heavily on her shoulders.

# Chapter Eighteen

James's home was just as impressive as Sully remembered it to be. The lawn and garden were superbly maintained, and the interior was spotless. As Josh turned the key to open the front door, she took a deep breath and held it until she stepped inside the foyer. It felt strange to be entering her brother's home, knowing he would never be there again. Sully felt like she was walking through a dream.

Every room was filled with photographs of the loving family, and their home was a shrine to the love and dedication each felt for the other. As they walked through the house, Sully realized the immensity of the task ahead of them. The house was much larger than she thought and filled with so much life. As she and Josh made their way through a tour of the house, Sully was overwhelmed at how devoted James was to his family. Every picture portrayed a perfect family with broad smiles that were genuine and loving.

When they entered the master bedroom, she noticed the closet door was ajar and stepped forward to close it when she realized James was probably the last person to enter the room. She took a step inside and marveled at the almost obsessive organization of the closet. Suits were meticulously organized by color and style, while white business shirts were starched and crisply pressed, eagerly awaiting James to choose them for the day's attire. Even his shoes were organized and polished to perfection. Sully leaned down to lift the arm of a robe to her face, and just as she expected, it smelled like James. Her heart ached for the brother she would no longer be able to pick the phone up to talk to or share holidays with. She knew she was being selfish, but just for the moment, Sully believed she deserved to show a little of the grief she felt.

Sully emerged from the closet to find Josh sitting beside the large king-sized bed, staring out a window onto beautiful green gardens. She felt his pain and understood this was not an easy task for him either. She walked over and sat down on the bed near him.

"What would James have wanted with all of this?" she asked.

"I think he would want the personal keepsakes and possessions saved for Kendal when she grows older and can truly value their worth." Josh turned back toward Sully. "The clothing, furniture, and household odds and ends can be sold in an auction or estate sale, or if you prefer, the house could be rented or sold furnished."

"Which do you think would be best?"

"I think it would significantly raise the value of the home to leave it furnished. However, I think there are several items you will want shipped to your home," he said.

"I would like to keep Kendal's room intact as much as possible to provide her some comfort during this time," Sully said.

"Also, in the family room is a large leather chair. James and Kendal spent hours watching television or reading together in it. I think that would hold very special meaning for her."

"That is a wonderful idea. Now that I think about it, I know exactly which chair you are speaking of," Sully said with a smile of remembrance.

Josh stood and walked to the door, seemingly eager to escape the room his friend had spent so much intimate time in. He and Sully made their way down to Kendal's room. It was a fairy tale dream of a room, one any young girl would be proud to claim.

†

Sully was again struck by the large number of photographs on the walls and covering the dresser. Kendal was definitely her Daddy's girl and was pictured with him in every photograph. She walked over to the bed. Sitting on the nightstand was a recent picture of Kendal with her parents at the beach, in their swimsuits, sporting sunburned noses and sunglasses. She couldn't resist a smile as she picked up the photograph.

"I will go into the basement to get a few suitcases if you want to start picking out some clothes to pack for Kendal," Josh said.

"That would be wonderful. Thank you, Josh," Sully answered as she replaced the photograph and turned to look at him.

"I will be right back then," he said, leaving the room.

Sully entered a much smaller but no less organized version of Kendal's father's closet. She was initially shocked at the lack of dresses hanging in the closet. It was obvious Kendal's taste in clothing was much more tomboyish, probably much to her mother's chagrin and James's delight. Blue jeans were pressed and hung in row after row, and a pile of shorts was stacked three feet tall. Sully grinned when she saw a pair of well-worn ropers that would do well for life on the farm amongst a pile of tennis shoes and sandals.

Her heart plummeted when her eyes found the dress Kendal had requested for the funeral. Sully's hand trembled as she reached out to pick up a small, plain black dress still in the plastic from the dry cleaners. Sully remembered Kendal telling her she had recently attended a funeral, and this must have been the dress she wore. She could no longer hold back her tears as she clutched the dress tightly to her body.

†

Josh had returned from the basement carrying the suitcases and heard Sully sobbing in the closet. He quietly laid the luggage on the bed and left the room to allow her time to collect herself. He walked into the study and began making phone calls to arrange to move items to Sully's place and pack up others for storage.

†

Inside the closet, Sully heard the soft click of the bedroom door and emerged to find that Josh had placed the luggage on the bed and left the room. She still held the black dress and walked over to lay it out on the bed. Seeing the suitcases enabled her to break free from the emotional distress she was experiencing and begin the task at hand. She opened each of the suitcases and then walked over to a dresser and began opening the drawers, pulling out panties, socks, pajamas, and tucking them into a suitcase with loving care. Her tears began to subside as she quickly gathered clothing, filled the suitcases, and added the photograph from the nightstand, wrapping the frame in a pair of soft pajamas before tucking it securely between the layers of clothing.

She wanted Kendal to have the photograph with her when she arrived at her new home to remind her of the happy times she had shared with her parents. When they returned, Sully and Kendal would pick out her bedroom and then would paint it to Kendal's taste. She would not have a room as grand as this one, but she would have a room that she had complete control over decorating.

When Sully had finished packing the suitcases, she walked from the room and located Josh in the family room, with a telephone book in front of him. He saw Sully and smiled at her as he ended the call.

"I have contacted movers, and they will be here Thursday morning to pack the items you want to be shipped, and prepare to transport them to your home," he said.

"I hope to leave for home before lunch," she said.

"That won't be a problem. I feel I have a good idea of the items you wish Kendal to have now, and I will see these are delivered and the rest stored properly for her future."

"You are an angel, Josh," she said.

"Hardly an angel, but I know you don't need to have to deal with making these arrangements and decisions right now, so just relax and let me do it."

"I have absolutely no problem with that," she said.

"Were you able to finish packing some clothes for Kendal," he asked.

"Yes, I have quite a few things for her."

"Do you think we should take them today, or do you think Kendal needs to come pick them up Thursday to get some closure on this part of her life?"

"I know she will have a painful goodbye tomorrow, but I think if it were me, I would want to see my home one last time," Sully said.

"I agree with you but will respect your decision if you change your mind at any time," he said.

"Thank you, Josh."

He smiled sweetly at her. "You are most welcome."

"Is there anything else we need to do here?" Sully asked.

"No, I think I can handle things from now on out. Did you pick out her outfit for the services?" he asked.

"Yes, I left her dress and shoes on the bed."

"Wait here then, and I will go get them," Josh said.

Sully nodded her head and sat down in a deep leather chair, feeling emotionally exhausted. Her eyes burned from the tears she had shed in Kendal's bedroom, and she hoped they weren't as bloodshot as they felt. One glance in a mirror confirmed her fears. She stood and walked to the bathroom. She smiled when she opened the medicine cabinet to find a bottle of eye drops on the bottom shelf. She took them out and dosed each eye with the cool, liquid relief of the drops.

Josh returned carrying the black dress, white stockings, and black patent leather shoes Kendal would wear tomorrow as she said her final goodbye to her parents. Tears threatened to fall again, so she quickly turned her focus away from the dress.

"Are you ready?" he asked.

"Yes, I am."

Josh led them outside into the afternoon sun. Sully was amazed by how much time had passed while they were in the house. It seemed like they had spent just a short time inside, but Sully exited to find four hours had passed. As they walked to the car, Josh said, "I need to call the funeral director this afternoon about transportation arrangements. Do you want to come to the house where we can all be picked up together, or do you want to be picked up at the hotel?"

"I would like to be here to help Kendal prepare," Sully said.

†

Josh smiled at her, happy with the choice she had made. "I think that is a wise decision. You will need each other tomorrow," he added.

"Probably me, more so than Kendal," Sully said. "I can't believe how strong she has been through all of this."

"She is a tough little girl, but there will be a time soon when she breaks down," Josh said. "She won't be able to hold her grief back forever."

Sully nodded her agreement. "I just hope I am ready."

"Have faith you will be," Josh said as he bent down to open the door for her.

# Chapter Nineteen

---

When they returned to Josh's home, they found the house empty. Josh carried Kendal's funeral clothing upstairs and then joined Sully in search of the girls. As they approached the back of the house, their ears picked up the sounds of laughter, and when they looked out the window into the backyard, they found two adults and two children engaged in a heated game of badminton.

Kendal and Bryn had teamed up against Kayley and Laura. Sully and Josh watched from the family room as several points were played.

"Should we go out and challenge the winning team?" he asked with a grin.

"I am not sure. They look like they are taking their game pretty seriously," Sully answered.

"You do have a point there," Josh said as Kendal screamed out a cheer when Laura's shot fell short of the net.

Sully opened the door, and they were able to approach undetected until Kayley saw her dad.

"Daddy," she shouted as the shuttlecock dropped onto her head. Kayley laughed as the game piece fell to the earth, and she ran for her daddy's arms.

"Time out," Laura said once she could stop laughing.

"Who is winning?" Sully asked Kendal.

"I think we are, but just barely," Kendal said.

"Let's take a lemonade break," Laura suggested.

"That is a wonderful idea," Bryn said, her cheeks flushed a rosy red.

"How long have you girls been playing?" Josh asked.

"I guess about an hour or so," Laura said. "We had sandwiches for lunch and then started playing."

Josh poured glasses of lemonade. "Lunch, that's what we forgot, Micah. Are you hungry?"

"I think I could eat a sandwich," she answered.

"Me too. You sit tight, and I will go fix us one," Josh said.

Kendal scrambled up in her lap and reached for a glass of lemonade. She took a long drink. "Boy, was I thirsty."

"You look like you were playing pretty hard," Sully said.

"Badminton is my favorite game," she answered.

"We will have to buy a set once we get home then," Sully said.

"That would be great, Aunt Micah," she said as she wiggled around to hug Sully's neck.

When Josh returned with sandwiches, he said, "When you finish this game, Micah and I want to challenge the winners."

"That should be us then," Kendal said as she hopped down from Sully's lap. "Let's finish them off, Bryn," she said with a grin as she took Bryn's hand.

Josh and Sully ate their meal as they watched the game continue. Once Bryn and Kendal scored the final point, Kendal ran over to Sully and grabbed her hand. She allowed Kendal to pull her onto their court and handed her a racket.

They played several games until both the child and adult were exhausted from laughing and playing. Partners were exchanged several times, and the most potent team was Kendal and Sully, who won every game they played.

Josh cooked burgers while the women of the house relaxed on the patio. The afternoon of exercise was taking a toll on the two girls, who quickly started nodding off after the meal.

"I think it is time you two go get ready for bed," Josh said.

"Will you come tuck us in?" Kendal asked Sully.

"Yes, when you come back to say your good nights, I will go up with you," she promised.

Kayley and Kendal made a dash for the house and disappeared.

"I have no idea where they get their energy," Sully said, turning back to the adults.

"I don't either, but I think they are both about tapped out and will sleep well tonight," Laura said.

"Especially since they didn't get a nap this afternoon," Bryn said.

"That's right, they didn't," Josh agreed.

"I don't think they will only sleep well tonight. I haven't played like that for years," Sully said.

"You will get used to it," Laura promised.

The girls returned, and after saying good night to the other adults, they each took one of Sully's hands and led her into the house.

†

Bryn smiled as she watched the girls leading Sully.

"She is going to make a terrific mother," Laura said.

"Yes, I think she will, too," Bryn said.

"Tomorrow is going to be a long day for both of them and you, too," Josh said. "I called earlier today, and the limo will be here at ten to pick us up. Micah said she wanted to be here to help Kendal be ready," he added.

"Did you bring her clothes?" Bryn asked.

"Yes, we put them upstairs when we got home."

"I will have Micah here by nine if you think that is early enough."

"That should be fine."

"I will have coffee, juice, and Danish if anyone feels like breakfast," Laura said.

"Coffee will be great, but I doubt she will eat," Bryn said.

†

Sully watched the girls climb into the bed and then sat down with them. "I had so much fun playing with you two today," she said.

"We did, too," Kendal said, with Kayley nodding in agreement.

"We will have to hold a tournament when you come to visit," Sully said to Kayley.

"I would like that a lot," Kayley answered.

"I will introduce you to the foxes, too," she said.

"Foxes?" Kendal asked.

"Yes, I have a mother fox and two pups I have been feeding for a while," Sully said. "I love to sit and watch them play."

"I can't wait to see them," Kendal said.

"I will need to go feed them very soon after we return," Sully said.

"Do they have names?" Kendal asked.

"Well, no, as a matter of fact, they don't. I think that would be a good job for you, to name them," Sully said.

"Can I really, Aunt Micah?"

"Yes, you can." She smiled at the excited girls. "But for now, you two need to get some sleep. I will see you in the morning," she said, kissing each one on their foreheads.

"Good night, Aunt Micah," they both said.

"Sweet dreams, girls," Micah said and stood to leave the room. She stopped at the door and turned back to the bed. "Good night," she said and flipped off the light.

She could hear the soft giggles coming from the bed as she started down the stairs, and the sound brought a smile to her face. When she walked out to the patio, Laura and Bryn had finished picking up the dishes.

"I timed that just right, didn't I?" she asked.

"We didn't have much to do anyhow," Laura said sweetly.

Sully sat beside Bryn and could feel the warmth of her body seeping through her thigh as they touched. She looked at Josh. "Is there anything else we need to do for tomorrow?"

"No, everything is set. The limo will be here at ten, and Bryn promises to have you here at nine to help Kendal prepare. We will have a light breakfast for anyone who is hungry."

"Thanks, but I am not sure I will be able to eat," she said.

"You need to set a good example for Kendal and try at least some juice and Danish if you can. It will be a long morning," Laura chided.

"I will try," Sully said.

"Why don't you call it a night and try to get some rest, too? I know today was hard on you," Josh said.

"I think we will," Bryn said. "Thank you for a great day," she said to Laura.

"It was fun," Laura said. "I hope we will have a chance to be together again soon," she said as she hugged Bryn.

"Me too," Bryn said with a smile.

"We will see you in the morning then," Sully said.

Josh stood to walk them out. "Sit tight. We can find our way out," she said.

"Good night then," he said.

"Good night," Sully said, and she and Bryn walked through the house to the truck.

†

Josh locked the door, settled back in beside Laura, and placed his arm around her shoulders. "I hope we all survive tomorrow," he said with a sigh.

"We will, my love," Laura answered as she rested her head on his shoulder.

†

Sully handed Bryn the keys. "Would you mind?"

"No, not at all."

They climbed into the truck, and Sully stared out the window in silence as Bryn drove back to the hotel. Bryn understood she was deep in thought and remained quiet to allow Sully to sort through her thoughts.

When they reached the room, Bryn closed the door behind them. "I think we need a quick shower and a good night's sleep."

†

Sully felt completely exhausted. "That sounds great," she said and managed a weak smile. "Right now, I just want to curl up in your arms."

"Good, so let's go shower and hit the sack," Bryn said.

†

After showering, Bryn stretched out on the bed and reached for Sully. She could see the tears in her eyes, which crested when her head rested on Bryn's shoulder. Bryn softly stroked Sully's hair and held her close until she cried herself to sleep.

†

The following morning, they woke up early and refreshed. Bryn had brought a skirt for the service, so she would need to shave her legs in the shower. "Why don't you go first, and I will shave when you are finished," she suggested.

"Okay, I won't take long," Sully said as she walked to the bathroom and started the shower.

Bryn dozed until she heard the shower turn off. Moments later, Sully emerged wearing a towel. "The bathroom is all yours," she said.

Bryn climbed from the bed and walked toward the bathroom. As she walked past Sully, she reached out and took Bryn in her arms for a light kiss. "Mmm, that was nice," Bryn said.

"Enjoy your shower."

†

Sully busied herself dressing in a tailored black suit and low heels. She disliked funerals but enjoyed wearing the suit. It gave her a weird sense of confidence; one she especially welcomed this morning. As she finished dressing, she heard the shower turn off and waited for Bryn to emerge.

†

Bryn toweled off and wrapped a towel around her. When she stepped from the bathroom, Sully stood and walked forward. "Oh, dear Lord," she said.

"What?" Sully asked.

"You look beautiful, baby," Bryn said as she motioned for Sully to turn in a circle so she could get the full effect.

Sully turned slowly. "I am glad you approve."

"Seriously, you look amazing," Bryn said.

"Thank you," Sully said.

Bryn tore her eyes away from Sully long enough to get dressed, but a smile was plastered to her face. "I really can't get over how great you look," she said as she turned toward her lover.

"Thanks," Sully said as she took Bryn in her arms. "You look terrific, too, and I am proud to be with you."

Bryn smiled and leaned into Sully for a kiss. "You make me a very happy woman, Micah Sullivan."

"Likewise, Dr. Barton," Sully replied.

"Thank you for suggesting Kendal call me by my name. I smile to know she's comfortable enough to do that."

"You're welcome. Dr. Barton is just too formal. We better get on the road or be late."

"I know, I just had to have another kiss," Sully said.

"Would you like me to drive?"

"That would be great," Sully said as she opened the door and handed the keys to Bryn. She followed her from the room and smiled at the way her hips swayed so seductively.

†

The morning sun was burning brightly as they stepped outside. "It looks like we will have a beautiful day," Bryn said.

"I hope so," Sully said as she opened the door for Bryn and walked around to the passenger's seat. She would need all her help to lift the black mood that threatened to suffocate her this morning.

# CHAPTER TWENTY

---

When they arrived, Kendal met them at the door. "You look very pretty, Aunt Micah," she said as she reached up for a hug.

"Why thank you, Kendal," Sully said as she leaned down to hug and kiss the small girl.

"You look very pretty, too, Bryn," Kendal said when Sully released her from the hug.

"Thank you, Kendal," Bryn said.

"Kayley's dad said to bring you in for coffee and Danish," she said as she took Sully's hand.

"Have you eaten yet?" Sully asked Kendal.

Kendal smiled up at her aunt. "I was waiting for you."

"Let's go eat then," Sully said.

†

Bryn smiled, knowing that Sully would have to eat at least a little something since Kendal and Josh had trapped her so well. She followed them into the breakfast area and took a seat next to Kayley.

"Good morning, everyone," she said.

"Good morning, ladies. I hope you rested well," Josh said.

"Yes, we did, thank you," Sully said.

"Can I get you coffee or juice?" Laura asked from the kitchen.

"Juice for me, please," Sully said.

"I will take some coffee," Bryn said.

"Apple or cheese Danish?" Josh asked.

"That's a tough one," Sully said. "What are you having, Kendal?"

"Cheese," Kendal said with a grin.

"Cheese it is then," Sully said to Josh.

"What would you like, Bryn?" he asked.

"I think I will try the apple," she said.

"The girls have already had their showers, so after we eat, we can get them dressed," Laura said.

"I thought I smelled apple blossom shampoo," Sully said.

"What's with all this apple stuff and your family?" Josh asked.

"Apples are good for you, Uncle Josh," Kendal said.

"I know they are good to eat, and the juice is good, but apple shampoo?" he teased her.

"It makes your hair smell fresh and clean," Kendal informed him.

"Maybe I should try it then," he said.

"Uncle Josh," Kendal said with a smug smile, "it's only for girls."

"Does it say that on the bottle?" he asked.

Kendal tilted her head with a puzzled look on her face. "I don't know," she said. "I will have to check," she added.

"I guess I will have to stick with my boy stuff," Josh said.

"I don't think you would smell good with apple hair, Daddy," Kayley said, sending her and Kendal into a fit of laughter.

"That is just not right," Josh said and pouted out his lower lip.

"That's okay, baby. I love the smell of your hair," Laura said.

"Well, I am glad I can charm some of the women in this house," he said.

"You are so outnumbered here," Sully reminded him.

"I know, and I'm enjoying every minute of it," he said, keeping the mood light.

"Speaking of minutes," Laura said, "Ours are slipping away. Finish up, girls, and go brush your teeth."

Kayley and Kendal finished their breakfast before brushing their teeth upstairs. "I will be there in a minute to help you get dressed," Sully said.

"Okay, Aunt Micah," Kendal said.

"She seems in good spirits," Bryn pointed out.

"They have had a good morning with each other," Laura said.

"That's good," Sully said.

†

She gave them a few moments, and then she and Laura went upstairs to help the girls get dressed. When they stepped into the room, both girls were sitting on the bed, waiting patiently.

Sully felt a huge lump in her throat when she saw the black dress hanging on the door frame and had to swallow hard before she spoke to Kendal. “Are you ready, Kendal?”

“Yes, Aunt Micah,” she answered.

“Off with those clothes then, and let’s get these hose on you.”

Kendal pulled the shirt over her head, slipped out of the shorts she was wearing, and sat back on the bed. Sully kneeled before her and slipped the left stocking over her toes. Personally, she hated these things but realized it was proper attire for funeral wear for a young girl. Still, she struggled to raise the hose up Kendal’s legs without putting a run in them.

“Okay, up you go, and we will finish these hose,” she said.

Kendal stood up as Sully pulled the hose the rest of the way up her legs. “There, how does that feel?”

“Like I am stuffed like a sausage,” Kendal said, surprising Sully.

She couldn’t help but laugh. “That’s exactly how I feel when I have to wear them,” she told Kendal. “When we get back, you can come straight up and change,” she said.

“Good, I much prefer my shorts,” Kendal said.

“Me, too,” Kayley said from across the room.

“Yes, honey, you can change, too,” Laura said.

Sully picked up the patent leather shoes and helped Kendal buckle them. She was delaying touching the dress until the last moment. With the hose and shoes finished, she walked to the door, took the dress from the plastic, and removed it from the hanger.

"This is a pretty dress," she said.

"I guess so," Kendal said.

Sully slipped it over Kendal's head and then reached behind her to zip the dress closed. "Go get your brush, and let's brush your hair again," she said.

Kendal walked into the bathroom and returned with a small brush. She looked very pretty in the dress, Sully thought as she walked across the room. "Sit up here with me, please," she said as she patted the bed.

Sully ran the brush through Kendal's thick hair. It was soft and curly, so much like her own, she thought as she brushed it.

"Okay, I think that has you ready," Sully said. "Stand up and let's have a look at you."

Kendal stood and turned in a slow circle for Sully. "You look marvelous," Sully said.

"Thank you, Aunt Micah," Kendal said.

Kayley was also finished and was dressed very much like Kendal. "What a pair of beauties," Sully said when they stood side by side.

"The car is here," Josh called from downstairs.

Kendal took Sully's hand and asked, "Shall we go?"

Sully nodded her head, unable to speak for a second as the young girl so bravely faced burying both of her parents. They joined Josh and Bryn downstairs, and together, they all walked out to the long black limousine.

Sully took a deep breath as the driver stepped out to open the door for them. "Good morning, ladies," he said sweetly.

"Good morning," Kendal and Kayley said as they stepped into the car, followed by the group of adults.

## CHAPTER TWENTY-ONE

---

Kendal sat between Sully and Bryn during the ride to the church for the services and held her aunt's hand the entire time. There was little conversation between adults, but Kendal and Kayley continued their chatter during the ride. Maybe it was Kendal's way of keeping her mind off the task at hand, but regardless, Sully was impressed by her young niece's strength of character.

To say the church was huge would have been an understatement. It could easily be larger than every church combined at home, and the parking lot was already crowded with cars for the service. The driver pulled the limousine directly in front of the large oak doors that opened to the church. He got out, walked around to open the door for them, and stood back to allow them to emerge from the spacious vehicle.

Two flights of marble steps led to the entrance of the church, and taking Kendal's hand, Sully started the climb. A man whom Josh introduced as a deacon of the church met them at the doors, and when the party had all arrived, he swung the doors open and ushered them down the aisle.

The church was just as beautiful on the inside as out, and every pew was filled with friends and associates of James and Caroline. At the end of the center aisle, two matching caskets rested before the altar, with a small table between them holding a picture of Sully's brother and his wife.

Sully swallowed hard as she took a seat at the end of the first pew, and Kendal settled in next to her. Bryn sat next to Kendal and gave Sully a warm smile as Josh and his family took their seats. A moment of silence hung in the air before the organist began playing a song, and the minister entered the church from a side door and walked behind a podium to begin the service.

"Dear Brothers and Sisters of God," he began, and then Sully's world went silent as the service was nothing more than a blur to her. She appeared attentive, but her mind blocked out the words she so dreaded to hear: the final goodbyes to James and Caroline.

She glanced over to Kendal, who listened intently to the words of the minister she had listened to for several years, and she smiled when he addressed her individually. Sully moved through the service like a robot, standing with the crowd and bowing her head in prayer or moving her lips through hymns she knew by heart from her childhood.

When the service had concluded, the congregation stood as the minister moved to comfort the family as the caskets were carried from the church and loaded into the back of matching hearses.

"Thank you for a beautiful service," Sully remembered saying.

"You are most welcome. James and Caroline were very popular members of our church, and though they are with the Father now, they will be missed greatly," he said as he placed a fatherly hand on Sully's shoulder. "I know that brings you little comfort at this time," he said with a warm smile. "I will perform the brief graveside service, but if there is anything I can do for you or Kendal, please let me know."

"Thank you again," Sully said.

The deacon who had seated them returned to usher them from the church to the limousine as the congregation followed and disbursed them to their vehicles. The two hearses were parked in front of the limousine and would lead the procession to the cemetery. The driver waited for them with the door open as they carefully maneuvered down the steps. He welcomed them inside and closed the door behind them as the motorcycle police arrived to escort the procession.

The funeral director allowed the congregation to return to their vehicles, and the ushers began forming a line of vehicles behind the limousine. Sully glanced out the back window to see a long line forming behind them. James would have been proud to see how well loved he was she thought as she turned back to Kendal.

"How are you doing?" she whispered.

"I am good, how about you?" Kendal whispered back.

"I am good, too," Sully said as she leaned over and planted a kiss on Kendal's forehead just as the limousine began to pull away from the curb.

Sully watched as a county sheriff's department cruiser rushed ahead to clear traffic at the next intersection, and she knew this routine would be repeated for each intersection until they reached the cemetery. She peered out the front windshield at the line of oncoming traffic that had pulled onto the shoulder of the road and turned their headlights on out of respect for the deceased. Sully smiled as she remembered attending a funeral up north many years ago and curiously asked why people did not pull over as the procession passed by. She was quickly informed that it was a Southern tradition that was not practiced above the Mason-Dixon Line. She thought it a shame that it was not practiced as it symbolized respect for those who had passed on.

†

The ride to the cemetery would normally take fifteen minutes but seemed to last an eternity. When they finally turned between the heavy cast iron gates, the driver slowed down to give the hearses a small lead to the grave site. He crawled along slowly to allow the pallbearers time to unload the caskets and place them on the electric lifts beneath a green tent. They rolled slowly past two fresh mounds of earth that had been piled and covered with artificial turf to conceal their presence. The limousine pulled up behind a second green tent and pulled to a stop.

As Sully stepped from the vehicle, she looked at the train of cars that were parked throughout the cemetery. It looked as though over half of the vehicles from the church had followed. She and Kendal sat under the tent and waited as others crowded around the tent, umbrellas in hand, as dark clouds were forming in the sky.

As soon as the crowd settled in, the minister started the graveside service, and as the winds picked up, so did his rate of speech. He had barely completed the final prayer as the first tears from heaven began to fall, and the crowd began to rush for their cars. It seemed perfect, though, as it gave them some privacy. After several minutes, Bryn, Josh, and his family entered the limousine.

The funeral director took two red roses from the family blankets, one draped over each casket, and handed them to Sully and Kendal. He also took the picture of her parents and presented it to Kendal. "Take all the time you need," he said as he left the two of them alone at the gravesite.

Kendal looked up at Sully. "Can we come back later, Aunt Micah, when everything is finished?" she asked.

"I think that would be a great idea," Sully agreed.

"Let's go then," she said as tears filled her eyes.

†

Sully stood and took Kendal's hand as they walked toward the limousine. The driver stood awaiting them with a large umbrella and sheltered them from the falling rain as they rushed to the car. As they settled into their seat, Sully heard Kayley ask her dad, "Why does it always seem to rain at funerals?"

Josh smiled at his daughter. "It is because everyone in heaven is happy to welcome their friends and family home," he explained. "That's why they are called tears from heaven."

"That makes sense now, Daddy," Kayley said. "Thank you."

"You are most welcome," Josh said as he placed an arm around Kayley.

The driver returned them to Josh's and carefully escorted them into the house. "Thank you for your services today," Sully said with a warm smile at the door.

"It was my pleasure, ma'am," he said with a nod and turned to rush back to the car.

Kayley was waiting for her inside the foyer. "May I change now?" she asked.

"Yes, you may. Do you want some help?"

"No, Kayley can unzip me, and I can take it from there," Kendal said.

"Very well, I will see you in a few minutes."

Kendal threw her arms around Sully's neck and hugged her tightly. "I love you, Aunt Micah," she said.

"I love you, too," Sully told her.

Kendal and Kayley scampered up the stairs to change clothes while the adults settled into the family room. "Can I get you a drink?" Josh asked.

"Yes, I would appreciate that," Sully said.

"Something light would be nice," Bryn said.

"I make a mean frozen drink with bananas and strawberries that the girls like," Josh said. "Of course, I will leave the rum out of theirs," he said with a chuckle.

Sully smiled at him. "I promised Kendal I would take her back to the cemetery, so better make mine light, too," she said.

"Okay, make yourselves at home while I change clothes, and I will fix us some light drinks," he said with a chuckle.

Bryn sat next to Sully. "How are you doing?"

"I am okay," Sully answered. "I think Kendal was on the verge of crying before we left but didn't want everyone to see."

"I was thinking that, too. Taking her back for some private time may help, and she may be comfortable enough with you to let her emotions go," Bryn added.

"You could tell she was really trying to hold back at the gravesite," Laura added.

"Yeah, I can't get over how strong-willed she is."

"She is just like her father and probably her aunt," Laura said.

Sully grinned at Laura. "I am not strong-willed. I am just flat-out stubborn," she admitted.

Bryn chuckled at Sully's remark. "I can attest to that."

Josh returned dressed in jeans and a pullover.

"You look comfortable, darling," Laura said. "I think I will go change too and check on the girls."

"You don't need to. I checked on them and told them we were having frozen drinks, so they should be flying down the stairs at any moment."

Laura had barely left the room when she passed Kendal and Kayley. When they entered the room, Josh looked up and said, "Ah, here are my assistants now. Would you ladies like to go to the kitchen with me to get the ice and fruit?"

"Sure, Daddy," Kayley said.

Josh and the two girls left the room to get the ingredients for the drinks, leaving Bryn and Sully alone for a moment. Bryn looked into Sully's eyes and asked, "Are you really okay?"

"Yes, darling, I am. I am ready to be done with this and back home."

"I understand, and that time is growing near," Bryn said.

"One more sleep, and we will be headed home. We need to call Doc tonight to let him know we will be on our way and to check on the animals."

"I know he will be glad to see us," Bryn said with a grin.

Josh returned with the girls and supplies. "Would you two peel these bananas for me?"

"Yes, Daddy," Kayley said, and they began peeling the bananas as Josh began filling the blender with ice and fresh strawberries.

"Is there anything we can help with?" Bryn asked.

"No, ma'am, the girls and I have this covered," Josh replied.

"Is anyone hungry?" Laura asked as she entered the room.

"I have the munchies, Mom, but I'm not really hungry," Kayley said.

"So, how about I pull out some chips and salsa to go with our drinks?"

"That would be great," Kayley said.

"Would anyone else like anything more substantial?" she asked.

"Nope, chips and dip for me too, please," Josh said.

"How about you ladies? I have some crackers and cheese I can bring out?"

"That would be fine. May I help you?" Bryn asked.

"Sure, you can lay out some crackers while I slice the cheese."

The rain began to diminish as they ate their snacks and drank the frozen drinks. Kendal climbed up on the couch next to Sully, who placed a comforting arm around her shoulder.

"It looks like the rain is letting up," Josh said, glancing out the window. "I feel like cooking some spaghetti tonight," he announced. "I hope you two will stay and join us for dinner."

"Of course, we will. Your home cooking is fantastic," Sully said.

"His spaghetti is really good, Miss Micah," Kayley said.

"Are you hungry?" Sully asked.

"No, not yet," she answered.

"Let me know when you are ready to take our ride," Sully said.

"I am ready if you are," she answered.

"Let's finish our drinks, and we will go."

"I think I am getting a sweet tooth craving," Josh said. "What should we have for dessert?"

"I do believe I have a yellow cake mix and some chocolate frosting," Laura said. "Would you like to help me bake it while Kendal and her aunt are gone?" she asked Kayley.

"Yes, ma'am, especially if I get to lick the bowl," Kayley said.

"You can if you beat your father to it," Laura answered with a chuckle.

"I will distract him for you, Kayley," Bryn offered.

Kendal finished her drink and placed her glass back on the table before looking up at Sully. Sully took the subtle hint from her niece and stood. "We will be back later," she told them, walking Kendal to the door.

†

The rain had stopped, and they were blessed with a fairly comfortable late afternoon. The humidity that would normally accompany rain showers was mysteriously absent to Sully's delight. She walked Kendal to the truck and helped her into the seat belt before walking around to the driver's side door. Taking a deep breath, she opened the door and climbed behind the wheel. She looked over at Kendal. "Did you want to drive?"

"Aunt Micah, you know my legs aren't long enough yet," Kendal said.

"Don't worry, they will be before long," Sully promised.

She easily found her way back to the cemetery and parked where, just hours earlier, the hearse had been. The large green tent was still in place, and the grave sites had been filled in and fresh sod put in place. Flowers and potted plants surrounded the headstones as Sully and Kendal made their way to the chairs placed at the end of each grave. Kendal selected the seat at her father's feet, and Sully sat beside her.

They sat in silence for several minutes, each lost in their own private thoughts. A bird called in a distant tree, breaking the silence, and Sully looked at Kendal. Her heart broke when she saw the sadness in the young girl's eyes and watched her lower lip trembling with emotion. Sully waited for Kendal to make the move, and when Kendal reached her arms out to Sully, she quickly pulled her into her lap and hugged her close just as the dam of tears broke.

Sully stroked Kendal's hair and softly whispered, "It's okay to cry."

Her small body was wracked with sobs as her tears fell uncontrollably, soaking the front of Sully's blouse. Sully was also unable to hold back her tears and felt comforted by the child seated in her lap. She suddenly realized they were the only family left. Sully held Kendal until her sobbing subsided, and she looked up into her aunt's face, seeming to read her mind. "It is just you and me now," she solemnly stated.

"We will be enough," Sully promised as she lifted Kendal's chin with her fingertips. "I cannot replace your parents, but I will do my best to make your life happy."

"I know you will, Aunt Micah," she said as she turned back to look at the headstone. "I miss them so much," she said, her tears threatening to fall again.

"I do, too," Sully said. "We will have to work very hard to support each other and remind ourselves to remember the good times when we get sad," she said. "Do you think we can do that?"

Unable to speak, Kendal nodded her head.

"We can share stories of growing up with your mom and dad, and you can tell me what you did with them," Sully said. "Knowing my brother, you had many exciting adventures you can share with me."

Kendal smiled for the first time since returning to the cemetery. "We had lots of fun," she said.

They sat holding onto one another for nearly an hour before Kendal climbed down from Sully's lap to walk over to the headstone, where she pulled two yellow roses from an arrangement. "Goodbye, Mother and Father," she softly said, causing Sully's heart to drop to her knees. Kendal turned and walked back to the chairs to offer one of the roses to Sully.

"These are so beautiful," she said.

Sully lifted the rose to her face and breathed deeply of its sweet scent. "They smell really good, too."

"Will my heart ever stop hurting?" she asked.

"Eventually," Sully said. "I wish I could make it heal faster, but it will take time."

"I am glad that I have you to be with me," Kendal said.

"I understand. I couldn't go through this without you either," Sully said sincerely. "I lost a brother, but you lost your parents, and with a lot of love, we will make it through," she promised.

"Thank you, Aunt Micah."

"No, thank you for making me strong," Sully said.

Kendal smiled up at her aunt, and though tears still made them shine, Sully could feel the love in them. "Are you ready to go?" she asked.

"I am just waiting on you," Sully teased.

Kendal reached for Sully's hand, and they walked back to the truck. Sully opened the door and looked down at Kendal. "Are you sure you don't want to drive?" she asked with a grin.

"You are so silly, Aunt Micah," she said.

"Yep, but you love me," Sully answered.

"Yes, I do," Kendal said as she reached for Sully.

"Up you go then," Sully said as she placed her on the seat.

Sully walked around the rear of the truck and stopped, looking back at the graves. "Goodbye, dear Brother," she said and resumed walking.

# Chapter Twenty-two

After a delightful meal, Sully and Bryn decided to return to the hotel. They had an early departure planned for the morning and needed a good night's sleep.

"We will see you bright and early in the morning," Sully told Kendal as she walked them to the door.

"I will be ready, Aunt Micah," Kendal said as she released her aunt's hand.

"I really do wish you could drive," Sully teased as she knelt to hug her niece tightly.

"One day soon," Kendal said, hugging Sully. "Goodnight."

"Sleep well tonight. We have a long drive tomorrow."

"I will. I love you."

"Love you too," Sully said.

When she stood, Josh and Laura had joined them at the door. "Thanks again for everything," she said.

"It was our pleasure to help out with what we could," Josh said. "See you in the morning."

"Good night," Sully replied and walked Bryn to the truck. "Would you mind driving?"

"Not at all," Bryn said as she took the keys from her lover.

†

Sully was startled when Bryn turned off the engine. She had been lost in her thoughts and did not realize they had arrived at the hotel. "That was fast," she said with a grin.

"I am getting good with the route," Bryn teased as they left the truck.

Bryn took her hand as they entered the elevator. "You must be exhausted."

"I am totally drained," Sully admitted.

"I called Doc while you were at the grave site, so if you wish, we can call it an early night and get some sleep."

"That would be great. I could sleep for days."

Bryn slipped the key into the door to enter the room and turned to face Sully. She smiled warmly and reached out to caress Sully's face. "I have to tell you just one more time how beautiful you look."

"Thank you, Bryn," Sully said, forcing a smile.

"Now, let's get you out of these clothes and into bed," Bryn said as she began to undress Sully. "Do you want a nightshirt?"

"No, I want to feel your skin next to mine," Sully said with a light blush.

Bryn smiled and took Sully's face between her hands. "I was hoping you would say that, now into the bed with you."

She pulled the covers back, and Sully crept between the fresh sheets.

Dark eyes watched as Bryn slipped out of her clothes and placed them carefully in the suitcase.

"I will be right back," Bryn said, disappearing into the bathroom.

†

When she returned moments later, Sully's eyes were closed in sleep. Bryn climbed softly into the bed and pressed her body into Sully's back, wrapping an arm around her body. Bryn felt a tear drop softly onto her hand and realized Sully was crying in her sleep. She snuggled in closer, held her lover tightly, and planted a light kiss on her shoulder.

"Rest well, My Love," she whispered. The warmth of Sully's skin was comforting to Bryn, and it did not take long before the sound of Sully's breathing drew her into sleep.

Bryn awoke early and called down to cancel the wake-up call to allow Sully to sleep just a little longer. Sully's sleep had been restless most of the night, but she had finally fallen into a deep, restful sleep, so Bryn carefully left the bed. She quietly laid out clothes for them and packed the rest of their belongings back in the suitcases. Sully slept soundly as Bryn entered the shower.

†

Sully awoke to the sound of running water and reached for Bryn to find the bed empty. She climbed from the bed and walked to the bathroom, wiping sleep from her eyes.

Bryn's head was covered with shampoo lather as Sully peeled open the shower curtain and slipped into the steamy shower. She circled Bryn's waist with her arms to hold her close.

"Are you starting without me?"

"I was letting you sleep a little longer," Bryn answered.

"Thanks, but I would rather be here with you," Sully said as she turned Bryn under the flow of the water and rinsed her hair.

When her hair was rinsed, Bryn opened her eyes and met Sully's dark gaze with a smile. "Good morning, lover," she said as she leaned into Sully for a kiss.

Sully's hands pulled Bryn close, and they kissed deeply as the water caressed their skin. When they breathlessly ended the kiss, Bryn's sparkling eyes were filled with longing. "I wish we had time," Sully started to say but was interrupted by Bryn.

"It's okay. We will have time soon," Bryn promised and softly kissed Sully. Her fingers stroked down the scar on Sully's back, making her shudder. "Are you feeling okay?" Bryn asked.

Sully grinned mischievously. "Oh yeah, just looking forward to some time with you."

"Things will be back to normal soon."

Sully wondered what that normal would be but kept her thoughts to herself for the moment. They had not considered how their lives would change with Kendal now a part of their immediate family, and if it would change their relationship. *Only time will tell,* Sully thought as she took a towel to dry off before following Bryn to the bedroom to dress.

Dressed in Levis, boots, and a pullover shirt, Sully felt more comfortable and found herself excited to return home. “This feels so much better.”

“Now that’s the beautiful lady I fell in love with,” Bryn said, taking in Sully’s appearance.

They kissed and then gathered their bags for the trip home. Sully stopped at the front desk to check out while Bryn pulled the truck to the front of the building. After a short exchange with the manager, Bryn and Sully were on their way to pick up Kendal for the trip south.

†

Kendal had her bag packed and was sitting in the backyard talking with Kayley when they arrived. Josh and Laura were seated at the breakfast nook, sharing coffee, and watching the two young friends.

“May I get you two some coffee or juice?” Laura asked.

“No thanks, we plan to stop for an early lunch,” Sully said.

“I think the girls are about ready then,” Josh said as he tapped on the window to get their attention and motioned them to come inside.

They raced to the door and hugged Sully and Bryn when they entered the house. “Good morning,” Kendal said, barely containing her excitement.

“Good morning to you, ladies,” Sully said.

“We have been talking about the visit next month,” Kendal said.

“That is great,” Sully said with genuine excitement. “We will all have a great time.”

“I can’t wait to ride a horse,” Kayley said.

"There will definitely be plenty of time for riding," Sully promised.

"Are you ready to go home?" Kendal asked.

"Ready when you are," Sully answered. She could see tears welling up in Kendal's eyes. She knew it must be tough on Kendal, leaving her best friend behind.

Kendal hugged Josh and James before turning back to Kayley. "I already miss you," she said and then hugged her friend.

Sully choked back tears and looked to Bryn for a comforting smile.

"I will be there soon," Kayley promised. "Now come on, let's get your bags, and I will help you carry them out to the truck."

The two girls disappeared, and Sully, Bryn, Josh, and Laura exchanged embraces.

"Keep in touch and let us know how she is doing," Josh said.

"Please be sure to let us know if there is anything we can do for either of you," Laura added.

"We certainly will," Sully said as they walked outside to the truck.

"Bye, Kayley," Kendal said with a final hug before turning to Sully for a lift into the truck.

"Up you go," Sully said as she lifted Kendal onto the seat. She then turned to Kayley. "We will see you soon and will call tonight to let you know we made it home."

Kayley's face lit up with a smile. "Thank you," she said politely.

†

Sully drove to James's home and opened the door for Kendal. They entered the house together while Bryn waited for them in the truck. Kendal remained quiet as they walked up to her room to collect the bags Sully had packed for her.

"I've just packed a few things to get you started," she told her. "The rest of your clothing and the furniture from your room have already been shipped, but if there is anything else you want to take, I'm sure we can find room."

Kendal left the room and returned a few moments later carrying several picture frames holding pictures of her and her parents. "Can we take these?"

"Yes, we can, and the rest will come soon, I promise," Sully said as she kissed her forehead. "The movers will be bringing more of your things down later," she added.

Kendal took the smaller of the bags in her hand and looked up at Sully. "I'm ready to go home," she said with tears welling in her eyes.

"Let's go then," Sully said, picking up the remaining bags.

Bryn met them and took the bag from Kendal as she clutched the picture frames. She and Sully loaded the truck, and then she lifted Kendal into her seat.

Sully climbed in behind the wheel, and Bryn climbed into the truck. With a final look at the house she had called home, Kendal turned and nodded at Sully, who pulled out of the drive. They drove to the Interstate to begin their journey home.

## CHAPTER TWENTY-THREE

---

They stopped for an early lunch just outside Montgomery, and when Sully glanced over a half hour later, Bryn and Kendal huddled sound asleep. A smile crept to her face as she looked upon the two most important people in her life. She was filled with thoughts of the future as the afternoon and the miles slipped away. Two hours later, she slowed the truck and pulled onto the exit ramp to locate a gas station. The change of speed caused Bryn to stir, and she carefully sat up, trying not to wake Kendal.

"Hey, sleepyhead," Sully whispered.

"I guess we drifted off."

"Yes, I think you did," Sully added with a grin. "I don't know who snores the loudest."

"It was Bryn," Kendal said as she sat up and rubbed her eyes.

Bryn playfully punched her shoulder. "I am not so sure about that, young lady."

"Well, all I know is you were both rattling the windows," Sully teased.

Kendal looked up to her aunt with a smile. "Are we home yet?"

"Not quite, but we have to get some gas," Sully answered.

She pulled the truck into a station. "Would you like a drink?"

"I could use a bottle of water."

"Me, too," Kendal said.

"I will be right back then. You want to go in with me?" Bryn asked Kendal.

"Sure. Be right back, Aunt Micah," she said as she slipped off the seat and out the door.

Sully filled the truck and waited for Bryn and Kendal to return. Moments later they emerged from the store, Bryn carrying a bag of drinks and Kendal carrying an ice cream cone and wearing a smile as she reached for Bryn's hand.

Bryn opened the door and placed the bag on the floorboard, and then turned to lift Kendal into the truck.

"Look what I got, Aunt Micah," Kendal said holding her chocolate cone toward her.

"Yummy, my favorite, too," Sully said.

"Really?"

"Yes, really."

"Would you like some?"

"No thanks, but you will have to remind me to get some from the grocery store."

"I will," Kendal said as she resumed licking her ice cream.

"Here you go," Bryn said as she handed her a bottle of cold water.

"Thanks," Sully said and took a long drink of the cold liquid. "Ah, that's good."

"Will we be home in another hour or so?" Bryn asked.

"That should be just about right," Sully said as she merged back onto the interstate.

"I didn't even ask, but would you like me to drive?"

"No, I am good, thanks. I will be glad to make it home, though, and have a chance to stretch out my legs," Sully answered.

"I know you can't wait to see the animals," Bryn said.

"I bet Sunspot has grown a foot since we have been gone."

Kendal perked up at the mention of the young filly. "I can't wait to meet her," she said.

"You two will make quite the pair," Sully said.

"I bet she will be nearly healed," Bryn said. "Another day or so, and I can take out her stitches."

"We will be getting back just in time for the last week of hay season," Sully said.

"No rest for you then," Bryn said.

"I am pretty sure you will have to hit the ground running, too," Sully answered.

"Probably so. I am sure there will be plenty for me to catch up on."

"What can I do?" Kendal asked.

"I plan to teach you how to drive a tractor so I can put you to work," Sully said with a wink to Bryn.

"Aunt Micah, you know my legs aren't long enough to reach the pedals yet," Kendal said.

"You are right, maybe we can find something else for you to do."

"If not, I can always use an assistant a couple of days a week," Bryn said.

"I would like that," Kendal said.

"My ranch hand, Glen, has a daughter your age who will be starting school this year, too," Sully said.

"What is her name?" Kendal asked.

"Cathy," Sully said. "Glen has brought her to the ranch a few times to ride. I think you will like her."

"I am sure I will," Kendal said as she took a bite of her cone with a loud crunch.

They fell into a comfortable silence for a while, each lost in her thoughts as the final miles passed. When Sully turned on her blinker to exit the interstate, Kendal sat up in attention.

"Are we there?"

"Another ten minutes, and we will be," Sully answered.

Kendal watched out the window as they passed through the small town and the school she would be attending in the fall. It was small, nothing like the schools in Atlanta that seemed to stretch on forever. Sully slowed the truck and turned into a long driveway.

"Still no rain," Sully said to Bryn. "Everything is dry as a bone."

"At least the lake still has some water," Bryn said.

"Can we swim in it?" Kendal asked.

"Yes, we can," Sully said.

†

Glen was leaving the barn when he turned to see Sully driving into the yard. He smiled and waved as he waited for her to park the truck.

"I am so glad to see you home," he said as he opened her door.

"Is everything okay?" Sully asked.

"Oh yes, everything is fine, but Sunspot has been pacing all day as if she knew you were coming home today," he answered.

Sully chuckled, and when the filly heard her voice, she came rushing out of the barn.

"See what I mean," Glen said as Sunspot trotted up to Sully and nuzzled her hand.

†

Sully knelt and hugged Sunspot's neck. "My, you have grown, little one," she said as she patted her neck. "You have all but healed up, too."

Bryn lifted Kendal down from the truck, and she rushed around the front. Sunspot looked at her closely, then moved her head to sniff her.

"Kendal, this is Sunspot and Glen," Sully said.

"Nice to meet you, Kendal," Glen said.

"You, too," Kendal said, but her eyes were fixed on Sunspot. "I have never seen anything so beautiful," she said and then giggled as the soft hairs of the filly's muzzle tickled her chin.

"Hiya, Doc, welcome home," Glen said to Bryn.

"Is everyone healthy?" she asked.

"All is good," he said. "You just missed Coach and the boys. They just finished stacking the last of the hay in the barn."

"What? I thought we had at least another week to go," Sully said.

"The boys have been working overtime to surprise you. They knew Kendal was coming home with you and wanted to be finished so you wouldn't have to worry about getting the hay in when you got home," he said.

"That is fantastic," Sully said, relieved not to have to jump right back into the heavy work of making hay in the heat. "I will have to do a special cookout for them," she added.

"I know they would love that, but you know those boys can put some food away," Glen said.

"Well worth it to have the hay taken care of already. I can't believe they have gotten it done so fast."

"They worked way past dark to get it done, but they were eager to do it for you, Sully."

Bryn must have noticed Sully's eyes getting misty and broke in to say, "I am going into the barn to check the animals."

†

Sully welcomed the distraction. "I will take the bags into the house and join you in a minute."

"No, I will get the bags. You need to go see the new colt," Glen said.

For a moment, Sully had forgotten all about the colt that could be the new legacy of the Trace. "You have a deal," she told Glen, taking off after Bryn with Sunspot and Kendal in tow. "Just leave them in the parlor," she shot back at Glen.

"Will do," Glen hollered back as she disappeared into the barn.

Sully joined Bryn at the door to a stall where she stood staring.

"He is a beauty," Bryn said as Sully walked up.

Sully slid the handle to the door and pushed it open. They walked inside the stall to greet the new arrival. The mare turned her head to look at them as the young colt began to suckle. As Doc had predicted, he was large, and his conformation was the best Sully had seen in years. She felt confident that he would follow in his sire's footsteps and improve the breeding stock for years to come.

She turned to find Kendal and Sunspot standing in the doorway. Kendal had an arm draped over the filly's shoulder. "You two can come in and meet your new baby brother," Sully said.

They approached quietly, and Sully was amazed to see the two foals so close together. The new colt was almost as tall as Sunspot already, even though she was weeks older. She nuzzled the colt as Kendal softly stroked down his side. He stopped nursing long enough to look at them with dark brown eyes and then returned to the task of nursing.

"He is beautiful, too," Kendal said. "Does he have a name yet?"

"No, I haven't given him one. It will need to be a very special one to pay tribute to his father," Sully explained.

†

Sully looked into the next stall and found it empty. Sunspot's mother had been there before they left, which confused her for a few moments when she found it empty. There was sweet feed in the small feed trough.

Glen had walked into the barn.

Sully frowned with confusion.

"Where's the mare?"

"Sunspot decided to wean herself early, and the mare has returned to the herd."

"A little eager, aren't we?" Sully said to the filly as she stroked her back.

"I thought so, too, but she is eating the sweet feed well," Glen said.

"Funny she didn't return to the herd with her mother," Sully said.

"I tried taking her out to the back pasture for two days, but she kept returning to the barn, so I stopped."

Sully chuckled. "Looks like we are going to have a permanent resident at the barn then."

"I do believe so. She follows me around all day as I am completing chores."

"That is good she is not having any problems with her gait," Bryn said.

"Heavens no, she is fast as the wind when she runs," Glen said. "I have been stopping every morning to get the mail from the box, and when she hears my truck, she comes barreling out of the barn and reaches me before I can make it halfway down the drive."

"That is fast," Sully said as Sunspot nudged her hip. "I missed you too, little one," Sully said as she hugged the filly close.

Glen leaned on the wall of the stall. "The moving truck arrived yesterday, and I put the boxes in the bedroom as you asked. I took down the other bed, placed it into storage, and assembled Kendal's bed for you."

"Thank you, Mr. Glen," Kendal said.

"Yes, thank you."

"You are both very welcome," he said. "My daughter, Cathy, is so excited to meet you."

"Why don't you bring her tomorrow, and the girls can get acquainted," Sully said.

"I would like that," Kendal said.

"That sounds good to me, too," Glen said. "She asks me every day if you have arrived yet," he said with a grin. "Oh, I almost forgot. Camille called earlier and said she expected the two of you for dinner at five."

"I guess you get a taste of her cooking right off the bat then," Sully told Kendal. "Just don't expect my cooking to be near as good, though," she teased.

"I am sure I won't starve, Aunt Micah," Kendal said with a smile. "Besides, I can make pop-tarts and cereal," she teased back.

All three of the adults broke out in laughter at Kendal's witty remark.

"If you don't need anything else, I think I will head to the house," Glen said.

"I think we will just get settled in a bit before we head off to dinner. See you in the morning, Glen, and thanks for everything you did while we were gone."

"My pleasure, ma'am," he said and then tipped his hat. "I will see you all tomorrow."

"Goodnight, Glen," Bryn said.

†

"I think I will start out, too," Bryn said. "I have some catching up to do with Doc. I will see you both in a couple of hours."

"See you soon," Sully said.

Kendal walked over to hug Bryn.

"I hope you two will be hungry. Camille is probably preparing a feast," Bryn told her.

"I will be starving by then," Kendal said.

Bryn shook her head. "Just like your aunt," she said with a smile.

Bryn hugged Sully, and with a quick wink, she left the barn.

†

Sully checked her watch. It was barely three. "We have two hours before we are due next door. Do you want to get settled in the house first or go with me to check on the fox?"

"Silly question," Kendal said.

"Okay, but you have to drive," Sully told her.

They walked over to the golf cart, and Sully saw that Glen had already placed a bag of dog food in the back. Sully climbed in behind the steering wheel and reached for Kendal.

"If you stand here, you should be able to reach the pedals and steer as well," she instructed.

"You are serious," Kendal said.

"Of course I am. We all have jobs to do around here."

"Okay, I will give it a try."

"The long pedal to the right is the gas, and the wide one on the left is the brake. You can reach down and turn the key now to start us up," she told Kendal. "Go easy at the start until you get the hang of things."

Sully had no sooner said the words when Kendal pushed down on the gas pedal, and the cart lurched forward, startling Kendal, who immediately removed her foot from the gas.

"See, the gas is very sensitive. Let's try again, a little softer this time."

Kendal placed her foot on the pedal and gently pushed down until the cart began slowly moving forward. She was so excited she forgot all about steering until Sully said, "You might want to turn to the right just a bit to keep from hitting that gate post."

Kendal's head whipped around, and she successfully guided the cart through the gate with a smile growing on her face.

"That was very good."

Sully caught a flash of movement out of the corner of her eye and turned to see Sunspot trotting beside the cart. "Look, we have an escort."

Kendal carefully turned her head and saw the filly trotting beside them, letting out a round of giggles.

Halfway across the open field, Kendal was beginning to get the hang of driving, and Sully told her to come to a stop. Having learned a lesson from the gas pedal, Kendal gently depressed the brake until the cart came to a stop.

"Very nice," Sully complimented her. "Do you see that path over to the left?"

"Yes, ma'am."

"That is the one we need to take to see the fox, so you head that way, and, if needed, I will assist."

Kendal carefully guided the cart down the path until they came into a large clearing, and Sully instructed her to stop near the edge of the woods. Sunspot stopped as well and waited to see what the two humans would do next. She watched with excitement as Sully and Kendal left the cart and Sully carried a bag of food over to a small trough beside a large oak.

Sully carefully opened the bag and poured its contents the length of the trough, rolling the spent bag into a tight ball.

"What do we do next?" Kendal asked.

"You drive us over to the mouth of the path, and we wait," Sully answered. "Hopefully the mother fox heard the approach of the cart and will bring her kits for a meal."

With Sunspot in tow, Kendal drove the cart back to the path and turned it to face the woods.

"Okay, you can turn the key off, and we will wait."

Sully scooted back on the seat to make room for Kendal, who climbed up between her legs. Sunspot moved closer and stuck her head into the cart for some attention as they waited for any signs of the fox.

They waited patiently for a half hour, and there was no sign of the beautiful red creatures. "Do you think they forgot you?" Kendal whispered.

"Maybe so or maybe they are just bashful. I usually don't bring anyone else along and the scent of Sunspot may have old mama fox a bit spooked."

Kendal looked genuinely disappointed. "No worries, we will come back out in the morning and see if the food is gone. If so, we will wait a day or two and bring more food. The kits must be getting big by now and eating much more."

Kendal slid down off the seat and turned the key back on, and slowly drove back onto the path. If they had looked deeper into the woods on their right, they might have caught a glimpse of the foxes as they were hidden behind a berry bush.

When they returned safely to the barn and parked the cart, Sully said, "We had better head inside to get ready for dinner. Ms. Camille does not take kindly to guests arriving late." She also took her cell phone out. "We also need to call and let Josh, Caroline, and Kayley know we have arrived."

Sully and Kendal started for the house, leaving Sunspot in the barn. Kendal surprised Sully by taking her hand as they walked the short distance to the house.

## Chapter Twenty-four

---

"This is your room," Sully said as she gave Kendal a tour of the house. "Glen has placed your bed in this room, but if you don't like it, you can have your choice of rooms."

Kendal's breath was caught in her throat when Sully opened the door to the large bedroom. She had always thought her bed was big, but it was dwarfed by the size of the room. She dropped her aunt's hand and walked around the room. "This will be just fine," she said with a grin.

"We will have to get you some more furniture to go with your bed. I thought a nice desk and a computer station would look good over there," she said, pointing toward a large bay window.

"I can really have a computer?" she asked.

"Yes, Kayley's parents and I agreed that a computer for you both would be a good way for you to stay in touch."

"Awesome," Kendal said. "Mom and Dad promised me one when I started school," she added with a sad note to her voice.

"I figured we could go shopping tomorrow and see what best suits your needs. Heck, I might have to break down and get one, too. Do you think you can teach me how to use it?"

"You don't have one already?" Kendal asked somewhat puzzled.

"No, I have been a little on the stubborn side when it comes to technology."

Kendal giggled at the expression on Sully's face. "Don't worry, Aunt Micah, Dad taught me a lot about the internet and how to use several programs."

"That's a big relief," Sully said. She looked at her watch. "We have just enough time to put away your clothes and take a quick shower before we are due for supper."

"May I wear shorts tonight?"

"I don't see why not," Sully answered.

Together they carried Kendall's bags in from the foyer and started putting items in the small dresser.

"I like these," Kendal said.

"I think those will do just fine. What top would you like to wear?"

Kendal picked out a red pullover shirt to go with the jean shorts while Sully found her tennis shoes and socks.

"You know we will have to do some shopping for school soon, too."

"Maybe Bryn can go with us," Kendal said.

"I think she would like that very much. Why don't you ask her tonight?"

"Okay, I will."

†

Sully walked into the bathroom to ensure there were plenty of shower supplies and towels for Kendal. "Do you need any help?"

"No, Aunt Micah, I can shower on my own," she said.

"Let's call before we forget," Sully said and dialed Josh's number.

After quickly letting him know they had arrived, they put the girls on the phone. Kendal spoke excitedly about the horses and her new room as Sully put away the remainder of her clothing. When she ended the call, she handed Sully the phone.

"Very well. I am going to get cleaned up and will see you in just a bit." Sully pulled the door behind her and walked back to the foyer to get her bags. She tossed the dirty clothes in the hamper and headed off for a shower of her own.

†

"How is the little one doing?" Camille asked Bryn as she fussed around the table.

"If you are talking about Kendal, she is doing remarkably well. She is mature much beyond her years."

"If she is anything like her aunt, she will weather this storm very well."

"To look at her, you would think she was Sully's daughter," Bryn remarked. "They look so much alike, it is amazing."

"That's not at all surprising, really. Even despite the age difference, there was no denying James and Micah were siblings," Camille said.

"They were what, ten years apart, is that right?"

"Yes, James was older than the baby sister he doted on from the day she was born. It wasn't until he went off to college that they weren't always together," Camille remembered. "Micah always loved the animals, but James's heart was filled with a love of learning, and when he decided to enter law school, the family was so proud. There was never any hope he would return to run the family business."

"I would say that Micah has done a remarkable job of that," Bryn said.

"Her father and grandfather would be very proud to see how much she has accomplished since taking over."

"She is an amazing woman," Bryn said with a dreamy quality to her voice that did not go unnoticed by Camille, who smiled softly to herself.

"That she is indeed," Camille agreed with a chuckle.

"I hope they hurry, that chicken smells wonderful," Bryn said.

"Why don't you go join your grandfather on the porch while we wait? I am almost finished here," Camille suggested.

"I think I will. Should I take him some tea?"

"I bet he would love that."

†

Bryn poured two glasses of tea and walked to the front porch where Doc had just finished with the paper. He placed the paper on a small table and looked up at Bryn.

"You must have been reading my mind," he teased and accepted the glass of tea Bryn offered. "Thanks."

"You are very welcome. Have I missed much the last few days?"

"No, not really, things have been rather quiet."

Bryn sat down beside Doc in a well-worn rocking chair and looked out across the yard at the dark clouds that were forming above the horizon.

Doc saw her glance and said, "I hope those bring us some rain tonight. For three days they have formed, and then disappeared as night fell. I don't know how much more the animals and crops can take."

"Maybe we will get lucky tonight," Bryn said.

"A nice gentle rain all night long would do us good."

The sound of a door closing took Bryn's attention to the Trace. "Looks like the girls are finally on their way," she commented.

"About time, too, I am starving," Doc chided.

"Smelling Camille's fried chicken is torture, isn't it?"

"You would think after all these years I would be used to it, but I think it only gets worse."

"I can see that happening. To make things worse, she has hot biscuits and chicken gravy, too," Bryn warned.

†

Sully helped Kendal fasten her seatbelt and then climbed into the truck. She was hungry and looked forward to Camille's good cooking. "Are you ready to feast?"

"I feel like I haven't eaten all day," Kendal answered.

Sully chuckled. "Camille is going to love your appetite."

Kendal grinned back at Sully.

When they pulled up in Doc's front yard, Sully saw Doc and Bryn sitting on the front porch. She parked and quickly helped Kendal from the truck.

"Good evening," Doc said. "You must be Kendal," he added as the young girl bundled up the steps to crawl in Bryn's lap.

"Yes, sir, and you must be Doc Barton," Kendal replied.

"That I am, missy," he teased with a wink. "I am glad you have arrived. Bryn was about to start chewing on my leg," he said.

"Grandfather, you know that was your stomach growling, not mine," Bryn teased back.

"Naw, that was the thunder in the distance you were hearing."

"Well, I hope it brings us some rain," Sully said as she climbed the steps. "Is that fried chicken I smell?"

"You should have guessed Camille would cook your favorite," Bryn said. "She has baked biscuits and gravy, too."

"Good Lord, who is going to drive us home?" she asked.

Doc chuckled at Sully's comment. "You haven't taught Kendal to drive yet?"

"I drove the golf cart by myself," Kendal proudly said. "My legs aren't long enough for the truck yet, though," she said dead seriously.

"Soon enough they will be," Doc said. "Let's go in and not keep Camille waiting any longer," he suggested.

Kendal climbed out of Bryn's lap and followed Doc inside the house. Sully gave Bryn a soft hug. "I miss you already," she whispered.

"I miss you, too," she whispered back.

They followed Doc and Kendal into the kitchen and listened as Kendal introduced herself to Camille.

"It is so nice to meet you, Miss Camille," she said so politely. "Dinner smells good, too," she added.

"I hope you are hungry," Camille said.

"Yes, ma'am, I could eat a horse," she said with a grin.

"No horses here, but I do have a platter of fried chicken," Camille said.

†

Kendal climbed up into a chair and Doc saw that she was still well short of reaching the table. "Hang on one second," he said, disappearing into the pantry, returning with a small step stool. "Let's try this." He placed the stool on the chair, and when Kendal sat down, it was the perfect height.

"That should do; now, who is saying grace?"

Camille volunteered and said a short blessing for the meal and good friends. A chorus of "amens" was followed by a flurry of passing bowls of food.

"What piece of chicken do you like?" Camille asked Kendal.

"Thighs and drumsticks," Kendal said.

Camille shot a look at Sully, who was grinning widely. "She is definitely your niece," she said while serving a thigh and drumstick to Kendal.

Kendal smiled as she watched Sully take the platter of chicken and pick out the same pieces of chicken she had.

"She is at that, but I bet she has never eaten anything as good as your biscuits and chicken gravy," Sully said.

"That does look good," Kendal said as she watched Doc split a biscuit and cover it in rich brown gravy.

Camille watched with a growing smile as Kendal matched Sully bite for bite, amazed at the child's healthy appetite. "Did you not feed this child today?"

"You would think not from watching her attack your chicken," Bryn said.

Kendal smiled at Camille. "This is the best chicken I have ever eaten," she said between bites.

"Thank you, Kendal," Camille said. "I am so glad you are enjoying it."

"I may just have to send her over here for meals," Sully said.

"She is welcome anytime," Doc said, as he bit into a slice of biscuit.

"I should warn you two that we also have dessert," Bryn said with a sheepish grin.

"Hot apple pie," Doc added.

Sully placed her fork on the plate, leaving half a biscuit untouched. "Time to stop then," she said with a wink to Kendal. "Take a hint here."

Kendal placed her fork on the plate and pushed it forward on the table. "I love apple pie."

Camille stood and began clearing the plates from the table. "Here, let me help," Sully offered.

"Nonsense, you sit still and get ready for some pie." She took a handful of plates into the kitchen. "We have ice cream or cheese, whichever you would like."

"Cheese on apple pie?" Kendal said.

"Oh yes, it is wonderful," Bryn said. "You should try it."

"I think I will," Kendal answered.

"Ice cream for me, please, Camille," Doc said.

"What about you and Micah?"

"Cheese and cheese," Sully said.

Camille served the pie and brought coffee for the adults and a glass of milk for Kendal. "So, what do you think of cheese and pie?"

"It is delicious," Kendal said.

†

Sully noticed Kendal was halfway through the slice but beginning to struggle to finish. Sully, however, had left plenty of room and devoured her slice and was sipping the hot coffee while the others finished. With a final bite remaining, Kendal looked up at her aunt, and Sully saw that her niece's eyes were beginning to get heavy. There was no doubt she would sleep well tonight.

Kendal sat quietly while Doc brought Bryn and Sully current on affairs during their absence.

†

Camille also noticed how drowsy the young child had become.

"Would you help me clear the table, Kendal?"

"Yes ma'am," Kendal answered and picked up pie plates and carried them into the kitchen.

Camille took the dishes and placed them on the counter. "Thank you for helping. I have some chicken leftovers. If you would like, I can make a doggie bag for you and Sully," she offered.

"That would be great for lunch tomorrow," Kendal said.

"Would you like biscuits and gravy, too?"

Kendal grinned and nodded her head.

"I will put it together for you then if you want to go back with the others."

"Thank you for a great meal," Kendal said.

"You are most welcome," Camille said, then watched Kendal leave the kitchen.

Kendal returned to the dining room and crawled up into Sully's lap.

"Did you get enough to eat?"

"I am stuffed," Kendal said, rubbing her full stomach for emphasis.

"Good, I can't be accused of letting you starve."

"I don't think there is much to worry about that," Kendal said. "Besides, Miss Camille is making us a doggie bag in case we get hungry."

"She is, is she?" Sully asked.

"I am," Camille answered from the kitchen. "You have a growing child on your hands, so you are going to have to start eating three meals a day," she added.

"I am going to blow up like a house," Sully teased.

"Not as hard as you work," Camille said. "Besides, you could stand an extra pound or two."

Camille returned to the table and set a plastic bag beside Sully. "For later or lunch," she said with a wink.

Kendal had rested her head on Sully's shoulder and was soon asleep.

"I think someone is ready for bed," Bryn said.

"I see that too. Thanks for such a great meal," she said to Camille.

"It is always a pleasure to cook for people with a healthy appetite," Camille said.

"I think you have won over a new customer tonight," Sully whispered.

"She is welcome at any time."

"I will carry out your bag while you take Kendal," Bryn said.

"I am sure we will see you all again, soon," Sully said as she stood and started for the door.

†

Bryn held the door for her and then followed her out to the truck. The night had fallen, and they could see flashes of heat lightning in the distance. "If we could only get some rain," she said as she opened the passenger door.

Sully carefully laid Kendal across the seat and closed the door. "Maybe we will soon," she said as she reached for Bryn, holding her close. "I will miss you tonight," she whispered softly.

"I will miss you, too," Bryn said as she kissed Sully's lips. "I will see you tomorrow."

"Goodnight then," Sully said as she walked around the truck.

†

Sully watched Bryn disappear into the house and then carefully drove home. She carried Kendal into the house and got her into bed without waking her fully. Then she stepped back onto the porch and sat in a rocking chair to watch the night sky. The false lightning was still lighting up the sky, and Sully quietly prayed for rain.

Feeling the effects of the large meal, Sully found her head starting to nod, so she headed off to her bedroom and, after changing, collapsed into her bed, exhausted.

# CHAPTER TWENTY-FIVE

---

Sully was beyond tired, and she lay on the bed staring up at the ceiling, willing her body to rest. Her mind would not shut down as her thoughts volleyed back and forth between Kendal and Bryn. Her relationship with Bryn had begun to blossom so sweetly, but Sully had to change her mindset from single woman to single mother. She was all that was left of family for the young child sleeping in the next room over, and she would have to rearrange her priorities for the future.

As her thoughts continued to wander, Sully began hearing light tapping noises, which grew steadily as the minutes passed until she realized the sound was raindrops falling on the tin roof. To startle her back to her senses, a flash of lightning lit up her room, directly followed by a loud clash of thunder. *That was really close,* she thought. She doubted that even as tired as she was that Kendal could sleep through that sound, but she decided to wait a few minutes before she would check on Kendal. She closed her eyes and listened to the steady drum of raindrops on the roof. The sound was heavenly to her ears, and she welcomed the cleansing rain that had begun to fall in earnest.

Another bright flash illuminated the room. Not as close this time, but the sound of thunder still shook the windows as it vibrated through the house. She was about to climb out of bed to check on Kendal when she heard rapid footsteps on the wooden floor of the hallway, and Kendal darted into the room.

Sully instinctively scooted over on the bed, and Kendal dove under the covers. "That was really close," she said as Sully pulled the covers over her body.

"Yes, it was," Sully answered.

"Are we safe here, Aunt Micah?"

"Yes, we are very safe, Kendal," she answered.

"Can I stay with you?"

"Of course, you can as long as you don't snore," Sully teased. Sully lay down beside Kendal. "It is just a storm and nothing to be scared of," she said.

"I just don't like lightning," Kendal said. "It is too noisy."

"Do you want me to get you some earplugs?"

"No, I will be okay here with you."

A flash lit up the room, and Sully could see Kendal shudder with fright as she waited for the boom of thunder to follow. She curled her body around Kendal's and placed a protective arm across her waist. "I am right here," she whispered.

"Thanks, Aunt Micah," Kendal whispered back, apparently feeling more secure with her aunt.

"Do you think you can sleep now?"

"I think so," Kendal answered.

"If you get scared, wake me up, okay?"

"I will. Goodnight, Aunt Micah."

"Goodnight, Kendal."

Sully stayed close until she felt Kendal's body relax and her breathing deepen as she slipped off to sleep. She waited several more minutes to make sure Kendal was deeply asleep before carefully moving over on the bed. Kendal, sensing her absence, moaned softly and turned on her side to face Sully.

Sully reached out and brushed a stray lock of hair from Kendal's face. She laid her head on a pillow and watched Kendal sleep until the drone of the raindrops lulled her to sleep.

†

Bryn, too, lay awake listening to the rain and watching the flashes of lightning out her large balcony doors. She wondered how Kendal and Sully were faring in the storm. She had grown accustomed to sleeping beside Sully over the past few days, and Bryn felt utterly alone in her bed. Her thoughts kept returning to the feel of Sully's warm body next to hers, causing a dampness to form between her thighs. She closed her eyes and remembered the taste of Sully's kisses, and with a smile playing on her face, she finally slept.

†

Sully woke at six the next morning to find Kendal had kicked off all the covers and was sprawled across the bed.

The rain was still steadily falling outside, and the sun was hidden behind dark clouds. She crept from the bed and walked to the kitchen, stopping to turn a television on to the weather channel to check the day's forecast. She was surprised to hear the reporter discussing a rapidly forming tropical storm named Alex that was sitting off the coast only fifty miles away. Sully prepared a cup of coffee and walked into the room to watch the weather news. A graphic showed a display of the storm across the screen. Alex wasn't large but was projected to be slow moving and would provide two days of much needed rain. Sully was even more thankful that Coach and his boys had finished bringing in the hay. This type of rain would definitely have delayed the harvest and jeopardized the whole cutting for fear of molding from the extended wetness.

Sully sipped her coffee as the television showed video of waves crashing against a county pier, drenching the fishermen that had fearlessly ventured out to test the waters.

Sully had finished her first cup and was halfway through her second when she looked up to find Kendal coming down the hall, rubbing the sleep from her eyes.

"Good morning, Kendal."

"Good morning, Aunt Micah. Is it still raining?"

"Yes, it looks like we will have rain for a couple of days," Sully said. "I guess we will be shopping after all."

"I forgot to ask Bryn if she would go with us last night," Kendal said with a frown.

"Let's give her another hour or so and give her a call. I doubt she will be able to do much in this weather either," Sully said. "Are you hungry?"

"A little bit," Kendal answered.

"How do pancakes sound?"

"Great," Kendal answered.

"Let's see what we can round up then," Sully said.

Together they went into the kitchen and found the necessary ingredients for pancakes. Sully removed butter from the refrigerator and poured Kendal a glass of juice.

"I guess we should do some grocery shopping, too," she said, looking at the bare shelves.

Sully pulled a barstool close to the stove and lifted Kendal onto it. "There, you can watch and tell me when you think they are done."

"Deal," Kendal said with a broad smile on her face.

†

Bryn had also gotten up early, dressed, and was drinking coffee when she saw the lights come on in Sully's kitchen. She had already decided she would stop by and see how the girls were doing before making a few rounds, and then placed her coffee cup in the sink.

"No breakfast this morning?" Camille asked.

"Are you kidding? I am still stuffed from dinner last night."

"Good Lord, you didn't eat that much," Camille tossed back at her.

"I thought I would check in on the girls before making some rounds this morning," Bryn said. "Tell Doc I will call to check in with him later."

"I do believe he just got your message," Camille said as she pointed toward Doc, who was coming through the dining room door.

"Looks like we have a tropical storm churning off the coast, and the forecasters say we will get two days of this rain."

"Good morning, Grandfather," Bryn said.

"Morning," he said as he stopped and stretched. "Did you leave me any coffee?"

"I think there might be a drop or two left," Bryn answered. "I am going to drop by the Trace and then make some rounds. Is there anyone in particular I need to check in on?"

"Tom Jackson has a few new calves you can check on, but everyone else should be in good shape. Be careful driving around out there. They didn't mention winds, but you can never be too careful."

"Yes, sir, I will," Bryn said as she reached for the slicker hanging by the back door. "I will see you two later," she said and scurried for her truck.

†

Sully poured batter onto the griddle into two large circles. "That should be enough to at least get you started," she teased. "Hmm, wait a second, I have an idea," she said as she walked back to the pantry, Kendal watching her every move. "How about some chocolate chips in the pancakes?" she asked.

"Sounds yummy," Kendal said as she watched Sully scatter the chips into the batter.

Sully opened a cabinet and pulled down two plates, handing them to Kendal. "You better get another," Kendal said as she motioned her head toward the kitchen window.

Sully turned to look out the window and saw Bryn step out of her truck and make a dash for the door. "One more it is," she said and reached for a third plate. "Why don't you go let her in the door?"

Kendal climbed down from the stool, ran for the front door, and reached it just as Bryn rang the doorbell. She opened the door wide and rushed forward to hug Bryn.

"Good morning, Bryn," Kendal said.

"Good morning, you are up early," Bryn answered.

"We are making chocolate chip pancakes for breakfast," Kendal said as she took Bryn's hand and all but dragged her into the kitchen.

"That sounds good," Bryn said.

"Good morning," Sully said as they entered the kitchen. She took the first two pancakes off the griddle and handed Bryn the filled plate. "Will you help Kendall while I cook some for you?"

†

"I most certainly will," Bryn answered, taking the plate from Sully. Their hands touched briefly, and she could feel Sully's warmth on her skin. "Looks like we are in for some wet weather the next few days," she said as she carried the plate to the table.

"A tropical storm is exactly what we needed," Sully said. "I am ever more thankful Coach and the team got the hay in now," she said as she poured more batter onto the griddle.

"We are going shopping today. Will you go with us?" Kendal asked.

"When are you planning to go?"

"Later this morning if you can join us," Sully said.

"I have one stop to make, and then I will be free for the rest of the day," Bryn replied. "What kind of shopping are we doing?"

"A little bit of everything from computers to school clothes to some groceries," Sully answered.

"Computers," Bryn said surprised. "Are you finally going to make it into the twenty-first century?"

"Aunt Micah said we could both get laptops," Kendal said excitedly as she stabbed a bite of pancakes.

"That is great news," Bryn said.

"Here you go, my friend," Sully said as she placed a plate in front of Bryn. "Would you care for some juice or coffee?"

"I think I will join Kendal in some juice. I have already had my fill of coffee."

"Juice it is then," Sully said as she moved to the refrigerator.

She poured a glass and handed a cold glass of juice to Bryn. "I will join you two in just a minute," she said and poured the last of the batter onto the griddle.

"These are really good," Bryn said after swallowing a bite.

"Did you have any doubts?"

"No, not really. As quiet as Kendal got when she started eating. I knew they were good then."

"Is Doc's house wired for internet?" Sully asked.

"No, I will have to call the cable company to get it set up," Bryn said.

"I need to call today. Do you want me to place an order for you, too?"

"That would be great," Bryn answered.

"Consider it done," Sully said as she flipped the pancakes onto her plate and turned off the burner.

"Anybody need anything while I am up?"

"Nope, I think we are good here."

"Do you think you will need more pancakes?" Sully asked Kendal.

"I don't think so. I am already getting full," she answered.

"These are good," Sully said, after taking a bite.

"You are a good cook, Aunt Micah," Kendal said.

"Yes, you are," Bryn agreed.

"I can already see that I will have to expand my skills with the two of you around," Sully said.

"No more TV dinners for you," Bryn teased.

"I am not that bad," Sully said. "I just rarely cooked for just me, but now I have plenty of company to cook for," she said.

"I think that is plenty of family," Kendal quickly corrected her.

"I stand corrected. I have plenty of family to cook for," she said with a wink to Bryn.

Bryn's heart raced in her chest. Even a gesture as innocent as a wink from Sully made her heart flutter, and she felt a slight blush rise in her cheeks.

Kendal pushed her plate away. "I can't eat anymore," she said.

"You did very well," Sully said. "Do you want to go take a shower so you will be ready to go to town?" she asked.

"Yes, ma'am. I will see you later, Bryn," she said as she left the table.

"I will try to hurry," Bryn promised.

Sully looked across the table. "You look well rested. Did you sleep okay in this storm?"

"Once I realized it was raining, I relaxed and let the sound lull me to sleep. How did Kendal do?"

"Pretty well until the lightning got close. Then I had a bed partner for the rest of the night."

"I am so jealous," Bryn said with a grin.

Sully reached across the table and covered Bryn's hand with hers. "No need to be jealous; besides, she kicks like a mule."

Bryn laughed at Sully's comment. She stood to clear the table as Sully finished her breakfast.

"Just put them in the sink, and I will load the dishwasher later," Sully said.

"Believe it or not, I can do it," Bryn said.

"Knock yourself out then," Sully answered.

†

Sully heard the water turn on in Kendal's bathroom and took her plate to the sink where Bryn was busy rinsing dishes. She reached around her from behind and placed her plate in the sink and then slowly turned Bryn around to face her.

"Good morning," she said as her fingers trailed down the side of Bryn's face across her lips.

"Good morning," Bryn answered as she pulled Sully closer.

Sully leaned down and softly kissed her lips. Bryn's lips parted, welcoming Sully's tongue into her mouth for a slow, sensual kiss.

Despite all her efforts to control her body, Sully could feel Bryn's body trembling as they kissed.

"Damn, that felt good," Bryn breathed as Sully broke the kiss with a smile on her face. "I could do with a few hundred more of those," she said.

"Me, too," Sully said. "Why don't you plan on staying over tonight?"

"You think Kendal is ready for that?"

"We are all family, remember," Sully answered.

"I would like that."

"Get going then and stop by for a change of clothes before you come back, and we will have a day of shopping and a movie night tonight."

"Sounds great," Bryn said, and after another soft kiss, she was out the door, racing for her truck.

Sully looked at the clock and decided it was late enough to place a call to the cable company. After ordering their service calls, she walked back to her room to shower.

## CHAPTER TWENTY-SIX

---

Kendal and Sully finished dressing and sat in the kitchen making out a shopping list for groceries. "You will have to tell me what you like and don't like to eat," Sully said.

"I will eat just about anything but mushrooms," Kendal said. "They taste funny," she added.

"That is good. I don't particularly care for them either."

"Captain Crunch is my favorite cereal, and I like brown sugar cinnamon pop tarts."

"Frosted or unfrosted?" Sully asked.

"Unfrosted, the frosted ones are way too sweet."

"Perfect answer," Sully said.

Together they created a menu for the coming week and made a list of items they would need for the meals. "I have asked Bryn to stay over tonight. Is that okay with you?"

Kendal looked up at Sully and cocked her head to the side. "Bryn loves you like Mommy loves Daddy, doesn't she?"

Sully was completely taken back by Kendal's question. She did not hesitate with her answer, though, looking directly at Kendal, she replied. "Yes, Bryn and I love each other very closely to how your parents love each other," she said and waited for a reaction from her niece.

Kendal wasted no time posing the next logical question. "Then why doesn't she live here with you?"

"We hope to be living together soon but wanted you to have plenty of time to get settled in and comfortable with both of us," Sully answered honestly.

"I am home now, and you two are my family," Kendal said in such a grown-up way.

Sully felt the tears pooling in her eyes and got up quickly from the table, walking to the pantry to feign checking for something to give herself a moment to collect her emotions. Kendal's response had floored her. She had not expected such a comment from someone so young. She pushed a near empty jar of peanut butter to the side and took a deep breath before turning back to face Kendal.

"Yes, you are home, and we are family. I just want you to feel comfortable before Bryn moves in," Sully repeated.

"Can we move her in when it stops raining then?" Kendal asked.

Sully broke out in laughter. "I think we will have to ask Bryn that question. I think she will be very pleased with your request."

"Good," Kendal said. Moving on, she asked, "Smooth or crunchy peanut butter?"

"Smooth for me," Sully answered.

"Good, me too," Kendal said with a smile.

They spent the rest of the morning making lists of school supplies and clothing she would need to start school. The rain was relentless, but at least it had calmed to a gentle rain and the lightning had moved off in the distance.

"I need to go check on the animals in the barn since I gave Glenn the day off," she said. "Would you like to go?"

Kendal bounced to her feet. "Yes, ma'am, I would like that."

Sully walked to the front porch with Kendal by her side. She reached for a bright yellow rain slicker and realized they needed to purchase one for Kendal in a child's size. "We need to add this to our list," Sully said as she slipped her arms inside the slicker. She picked Kendal up and covered her with the slicker. "Hold on, this will be a bumpy run," Sully said and made a dash for the barn, she and Kendal both giggling all the way until they reached the protection of the barn.

Sully lowered Kendal just in time to be nuzzled by Sunspot, who had met them at the barn door. Their giggling had alerted the filly to their arrival, and she welcomed both with a soft nuzzle.

"Good morning, Sunspot," Sully said, as Kendal wrapped her arms around the filly's neck. "Would you like to brush her while I feed the others?"

"Yes, please," Kendal answered.

"Follow me then."

Kendal and Sunspot followed Sully to a tack room and watched as she took a soft brush down from a shelf. "You are the first to brush her, so be gentle," she said as she handed her the brush. "Let her smell it first before you start to brush, and talk to her while you brush, okay?"

"Yes, ma'am," Kendal answered, wearing a broad smile.

"Come over here, Sunspot," Sully heard her say as she walked down the aisle of the barn to check on the other animals. The young colt was nursing, and Sully swore he had grown several inches over night as she stepped inside the stall to pour grain into the feed trough. She walked over to him and ran her hand down his back.

"You are going to be an amazing animal," she softly whispered to him. Sully allowed her hand to shift to the mare's withers. "You have brought us a beautiful colt, Mama," she said as she stroked the mare.

"This is a brush," Kendal was saying as she held the brush in front of Sunspot's nose for her to sniff. "I am going to use this to brush your coat to keep it shiny and clean," Sully heard her explain to the filly. She leaned against the wall of the stall to observe the interaction between the child and filly, her smile growing as she watched how gently Kendal stroked Sunspot's body with the brush. Kendal talked with her the entire time, even though Sully could not make out what she was saying. When she reached the damaged area of her chest, Sully watched as Kendal dropped down on one knee and gently reached out to touch the fine, soft hairs that were starting to grow back around the now healing scars. "That must have hurt really badly," she heard Kendal say. Sully watched amazed as Sunspot's muscles quivered under Kendal's light touch and strained unsuccessfully to listen to what Kendal was whispering to the filly. A slight nudge to her hip broke her concentration, and she turned to see the young colt standing beside her, impatiently waiting for more attention as his mother began to eat the grain.

"I did not forget you," Sully said, as she scratched the young colt between his ears. "You are so handsome," she said as her hands moved down each leg, lifting each foot to inspect his hooves. It was important for young animals to become familiar with human touch at a young age, and Sully believed it was never too soon to start.

Sully finished tending to the other animals and returned to where she had left Sunspot and Kendal. "How did she do?"

"I think she really likes to be brushed," Kendal answered, almost squealing with excitement.

"I am sure she does, it probably felt very good to her, and you did a very good job."

"Will her scars go away, or will she always have them?"

"In time, as she grows and heals, you will barely know she had an injury," Sully promised. "You can already see how her coat is starting to grow again," she said pointing out the fine, light hairs growing on the filly's chest.

"She must have been hurt really bad."

"She was. We were very lucky that she survived at all, and she has healed remarkably well."

"I think she knows how much we love her," Kendal said.

"I am sure she does, and that helps her out a lot," Sully answered.

Sunspot lifted her head at the sound of a vehicle coming across the cattle guard at the mouth of the driveway, and she trotted to the door to see who was approaching. Kendal and Sully followed her to the barn door to witness Bryn driving up and parking. "You are better than a guard dog," Sully told Sunspot as they watched Bryn dash from her truck to the barn.

"Welcome back," Sully said as Bryn shed the yellow slicker. "I will hang this up and let it dry for a minute."

"How have you both been since I left?"

"We have been busy making lists and doing chores," Kendal offered.

Bryn smiled at Kendal and then Sully. "Let me check everyone, and we will be ready to go shopping then," she stated.

"Do you need our help?"

"No, I won't be long."

"We will wait for you at the house then," Sully said.

She took her rain slicker off the wall and placed it around her shoulders. Looking at Kendal, she asked, "Ready to make a run for it?"

"Yes, ma'am," Kendal said as she reached up for her aunt.

Sully picked Kendal up and made a mad dash for the house. The rain was slowing, or at least she thought it was as she dodged puddles in the yard. When she made it to the porch, she dropped Kendal to her feet. "I need to get our lists and my wallet," she said before disappearing into the house.

Sully walked to the kitchen to retrieve the lists they had made earlier in the day and then into her office to pick up her checkbook and wallet. She picked up the keys to her truck and walked back to the porch to find Kendal waiting patiently.

"Wait here, and I will bring the truck closer."

Sully made a run for her truck, pulled it up close to the porch, and swung the door open. Kendal ran to her, and Sully lifted her up into the truck. "Now let's go get Bryn." She pulled the truck as close to the barn door as she could. Their wait was short-lived, and Sully smiled as she watched Bryn pull the rain slicker around her body and run the short distance to the truck.

Bryn climbed into the truck and pulled the door behind her. "I can't get over how cool the rain is," she said.

"A welcome relief from the heat and drought, though," Sully said.

"Most definitely, but it still sends a chill through me when a drop runs down my spine," Bryn said with a shiver, causing Kendal to laugh.

"Okay, where do we start?"

"Why don't we head into town to the mall? We should be able to get most of what we need there," Bryn suggested.

"Including lunch," Sully said.

"Are you hungry again already?" Bryn teased.

"Breakfast was hours ago," Sully said, feigning a pout.

"I am getting hungry, too, Aunt Micah," Kendal said.

"I swear you two are just alike," Bryn said. "Okay, lunch first, then shopping. What do you want for lunch?"

Sully looked at Kendal. "Pizza sound good to you?"

"That sounds great to me."

"How about a few slices from that place in the mall, then?" Sully asked.

"I can always do pizza," Bryn answered.

"Off we go then," Sully said as she pulled the truck out on the highway.

When they got to the mall, they decided to order a whole pizza instead of single slices which turned out to be a good idea as all but one slice was devoured by the three of them.

†

"I need a nap now," Sully announced as Bryn placed the last slice in a carryout container.

"Oh no, you don't; we shop until we drop," Bryn warned.

"Okay, okay, clothes first?" she asked.

Bryn looked at Kendal, who nodded her head. "Clothes first, so let's go this way."

They found a children's clothing store, and it didn't take long to fill a basket with shorts, jeans, and shirts to Kendal's liking.

"Now for the fun part of trying everything on," Bryn said, as they moved toward the fitting rooms. "Why don't you sit there, Micah, while Kendal and I put on a show for you?" she suggested pointing to a comfortable looking chair.

"That sounds like a wonderful idea."

"Let's get this party started then," Bryn said as she took an armful of clothes and walked with Kendal to a fitting room. She placed the stack of clothes on a small table and said, "Off with the old, on with the new."

Kendal removed her boots, jeans, and shirt while Bryn picked up a pair of jeans. "Let's try these."

"Okay," Kendal said and stepped into the jeans Bryn was holding.

"They are a little long, but I bet you will grow into them fast," Bryn said. "Turn around," she instructed.

Kendal turned slowly so Bryn could check the fit. "They fit good, do you like them?"

"Yes, I do."

"Let's try this top, and you can go model for Micah," Bryn suggested.

Kendal slipped a top over her head and tucked the hem into her jeans. She was so much like Micah,

†

Bryn thought as she watched Kendal. Most kids her age would have left the hem out, but like Micah, Kendal liked everything tucked away neatly.

"All set to show Micah?"

"Yes ma'am," Kendal said.

Bryn opened the door and watched Kendal walk toward Micah and turn slowly so she could see how well the clothes fit.

"That looks really good," Sully said, sitting up in her seat. "Do you like those?"

"Yes, ma'am."

"That is keeper number one," Sully said with a grin. "Let's see what else you have."

Bryn stepped back inside the fitting room and waited until Kendal returned. "What did she think?"

"Aunt Micah said these were keepers," Kendal said with a smile.

"So, what do you want next?"

Kendal picked out a pair of cargo shorts and a T-shirt to try on next. Bryn could imagine just how cute she would look with a pair of Doc Martens and smiled as Kendal turned and looked in the mirror. "I like these," she said.

"I do, too. Go show Micah."

"Oh wow, I really like those," Sully said as Kendal struck a pose almost causing Bryn to laugh out loud.

Kendal grinned at Sully and rushed back to the fitting room. Bryn sat on a small seat and started folding the outfits they would be purchasing.

"Just a few more to try on," she said.

Kendal slipped off the shorts and very casually said, "You love Aunt Micah, don't you Bryn?"

Bryn was glad she was seated as Kendal's question came flying in out of the blue, taking her breath away. She took a breath and answered her honestly.

"Yes, Kendal, I do. Why do you ask?"

"I asked Aunt Micah this morning if you loved her like Mommy loved Daddy, and she said yes, so I was wondering why you don't live with us," Kendal said as she cocked her head to the side.

"Well, Micah and I have discussed living together, but we wanted you to get settled in first," Bryn answered.

"That is exactly what Aunt Micah said. I'm settled," she added.

"Wouldn't you like to spend some time with your aunt?" Bryn asked.

"I can still do that while you are working," Kendal answered quickly.

"You have this all figured out, don't you?"

"Pretty much," Kendal said with a grin.

Bryn felt her cheeks blush. How could this young child be so smart, she wondered? "I will talk with Micah about my moving in later tonight if you are sure."

"I am positive," Kendal said excitedly.

For the next half hour, Kendal paraded past Micah, showing her outfit after outfit for approval. When the final outfit had been approved, Kendal got dressed while Bryn carried the pile of clothes out to Micah. They waited for Kendal, who smiled sweetly at them both.

"You are never going to believe what she asked me in there," Bryn said.

"Was it about you moving in?" Sully asked.

"Yes, as a matter of fact, it was."

"The kid doesn't waste any time," Sully said with a chuckle. "So, what did you say?"

"I told her that you and I would talk about it later tonight."

"I hope I don't have to call Kendal in for back-up," Sully teased.

"Are you sure you are ready to have a house full of women?"

"I have never been more certain of anything," Sully said as she hugged Bryn close.

"I will discuss a move with Doc and probably start moving some stuff over this weekend if that's okay with you."

"Perfect," Sully said as Kendal joined them.

"Okay, now we find shoes and some belts," Micah said.

Kendal smiled even brighter and turned to Bryn. "Lead the way."

Shoe shopping proved to be more to Sully's skills. In a matter of thirty minutes, she had Kendal decked out in a pair of Doc Marten boots, two different pairs of Nike's, and a pair of Roper's, the latter more for working around the barn.

The three of them were loaded down with bags as they left the store. "I think we had better drop these off at the truck before we go computer hunting," Bryn said.

"Oh yes," Sully said from behind a stack of bags.

Kendal rushed ahead of them and pushed a door open for them. The rain had let up for a moment, but the clouds still hung low, full of rain yet to come. They quickly found the truck and placed the bags in the back seat.

"We better hurry before the skies open up again," Bryn said.

Kendal placed one hand in Sully's and the other in Bryn's as they hurried across the parking lot back to the mall. *What a perfect family picture this makes*, Sully thought as they lifted and swung Kendal across a puddle of water, her giggles ringing in Sully's ears.

## CHAPTER TWENTY-SEVEN

---

Two hours later, they once more emerged from the mall complete with three laptops and all the necessary peripherals to make them proficient computer junkies. The sky had opened up again, and Sully made a dash for the truck and pulled in beneath a covered pick-up zone to retrieve Bryn, Kendal, and their growing bags.

"Why don't we take this load to the house? If this rain lets up, we will come back out for school supplies," Sully suggested.

"That sounds like a great idea," Bryn said, as she wiped the rain from Sully's brow. "I think we could all use a break. We have shopped pretty hard today."

"Yes, but we have done very well, I think."

"Me, too, Aunt Micah," Kendal added.

"I think we could pretty easily become shopaholics," Bryn teased.

"Now, hold on one second; let's not go that far."

"Okay, so Kendal and I could," Bryn corrected.

"After today, you two can do all the shopping then," Sully said.

Bryn looked at Kendal, who nodded her head. "That's a deal."

"You know I really do need to start getting ready for Doc's party, too," Sully said. "With everything going on lately, I have lost track of what I need to get done."

"We can help you with that," Bryn said.

"I was counting on that," Sully said with a smile. "I have the invitations printed already, so I just need to get them sent out."

"I think Kendal and I can handle that if you have a guest list with addresses," Bryn offered.

"That I do, and his gift has already arrived, so it's a matter of getting the food organized. Now that we have rain, I think we can do some fireworks."

"You know, I bet Glen would gladly take on that project if you gave him a budget to work with. He seems just the type that would really enjoy setting off a bunch of fireworks."

"You are right, he would probably really enjoy it," Sully agreed.

"By the way, what did you get, Doc?" Bryn asked curiously.

"Well, you will just have to wait and see."

"You won't even tell us?" Bryn said with a pout.

"Nope, you will just have to wait."

"That is so not fair."

"I know, but that is how it is," Sully said with a grin. "Camille usually helps me plan the food, so I guess I had better try to catch up with her soon," she said to change the subject.

"I am not much on the grill, but I can handle vegetables and salads and the like," Bryn offered.

"Thanks, I am sure we can use all the help we can get. Kendal will be my assistant grill master, so if you and Camille can run the inside that would be great."

Kendal perked up at the mention of her name.

Bryn was quick to notice. "Assistant grill master is a great title. Do I get one too?"

"Why of course you do."

"Care to share with us?"

"It's called Camille's flunky," Sully said with a deep laugh so contagious Kendal started laughing too.

"Hey, just because you are an assistant grill master doesn't mean you can laugh at a flunky," Bryn scolded Kendal.

Sully stopped laughing long enough to softly elbow Kendal, who immediately broke out in laughter again after failing to keep a straight face.

"I am sorry, Bryn," Kendal said between fits of the giggles. "It's all Aunt Micah's fault."

"Yes, it is," Bryn said. "She is a very bad role model for you," she added with a wink.

"I am going to pull up as close to the front porch as I can get to keep us from getting soaked. When we stop, Kendal, would you climb in the back and hand us the bags so we can get them inside as quickly as possible?"

"Yes, ma'am," she answered.

With the three of them working together, it only took a few minutes to unload the truck and carry the bags into the house. Bryn took the computer supplies into the office while

Sully and Kendal carried the clothing items into her bedroom.

When they had placed the last of the bags on the bed, Kendal turned around and hugged Sully. "Thanks for all the new stuff, Aunt Micah."

"You are most welcome," Sully said.

"Do you two need help putting the new clothes away?"

Kendal smiled up to Bryn. "Sure, kitchen flunky," she teased.

"I got your kitchen flunky," Bryn said, then rushed forward to pick Kendal up and placed her on the bed for a good tickling.

Sully leaned against the door frame and smiled as she watched the two wrestling on the bed. She felt very proud of her new family. She knew there would be days that weren't filled with joy and laughter, but prayed those days would be few and far between.

When they both fell to the bed exhausted and out of breath, Sully asked, "Do you two need a nap now?"

Bryn looked at Kendal and grinned. "No, I think we are good."

"Fine then, while you two put the clothes away, I will go check on the weather forecast."

"Okay, Aunt Micah," Kendal said and bounced off the bed to start her project.

Sully winked at Bryn and left the room. The weatherman painted a dismal picture for the rest of the afternoon, forecasting rain and thunderstorms throughout the night. He did report good news that the rain would end early the next morning, and the sun would return. That is if his luck was to hold out.

The national weatherman gave a similar forecast. Sully decided it would probably be best if they stayed home the rest of the day and then finished up the rest of the shopping tomorrow. She was pondering what to do with the rest of the afternoon and evening when Bryn and Kendal entered the room.

"That doesn't look promising," Bryn said as she sat next to Sully.

"Rain, rain and more rain," she said. "How about we stay in tonight, cook some dinner, and see if we can find a movie to watch?"

"Fine with me," Kendal said.

"We can finish shopping tomorrow. Do you two like tacos?"

"I love tacos."

"Me, too, but I don't have the ingredients to make them," Sully said.

"Why don't the two of you tend to the animals while I make a store run for taco supplies and some popcorn?"

"I have popcorn in the pantry."

"Okay, so maybe I will look at some other snacks. Anything you like?"

"Some junior mints to go with the popcorn," Kendal said.

Sully looked at Kendal in surprise and shook her head. "I can't believe you just took the words out of my mouth. I was just going to ask for the same thing."

"Two peas in a pod," Bryn said. "I will be back soon."

"Be careful, it is mighty wet and slippery out there."

"I will be back before you know it."

"Be safe," Sully said and kissed Bryn on the lips, shocking both of them, but Kendal did not bat an eye.

"Can I brush Sunspot again?"

"I think she would really enjoy that."

"Go get your slicker, and we will head out to the barn."

"Yes, ma'am," Kendal said and rushed from the room.

Sully walked Bryn to the door. "Do you realize you just kissed me in front of Kendal?"

"Yes, I do believe I am very well aware of the fact," Sully said with a grin. "She seems comfortable with our relationship and can handle a display of affection."

"Not that I minded at all. I was just a little shocked."

"I'm sorry, but it felt the natural thing to do," she said with a smirk.

"Uh-hm, well, I will be back soon," Bryn said and stepped back out into the rain.

†

Sully watched Bryn drive away and then pulled on her rain slicker. She was surprised that Kendal had not returned and went in search of her. She walked down the hall and stepped into the room. Kendal had gotten the slicker on but needed help with a price tag that was left in place when they put up the clothing.

"You need some help?" Sully asked.

"Yes, ma'am. I thought I could get it by myself, but I can't."

"It's okay to ask for help. I do it all the time."

"Thanks, Aunt Micah," Kendal said when her aunt easily snapped the fastener on the price tag.

"My pleasure, missy," Sully said with a grin. "Let's go check on the animals."

They entered the barn together, and Sunspot rushed up to greet them. "I am going to call Glen and check in with him if you want to get started brushing. Can you reach the brush?"

"Yes, ma'am. We will be just fine."

"Okay then, I will join you in a few minutes."

†

Sully walked into the barn office and picked up the phone to call Glen. Cathy answered and, after a brief greeting, yelled for her dad.

"Hello, this is Glen."

"Hello, Glen, this is Sully."

"Is everything okay?" he asked in a panicked voice.

"Yes, things are wet, but everyone is fine, thank you. I was calling to check in on you and to ask you to stop by in the morning for your paycheck."

"Oh, no problem at all. I was hoping this rain would let up soon so I could get back to work."

"Things are just fine here, I promise. Why don't you bring Cathy with you tomorrow so the girls can get acquainted?"

"That sounds like a great idea. I also have a question to ask you."

"What is it, Glen?"

"My blue heeler had her pups, and I was wondering if Kendal might want one?"

"I don't think she has ever had a pet. I will ask her and let you know tomorrow. I like the idea, though."

"She has some really cute pups, and they should be ready to go in a couple of weeks."

"I think it would be safe to say we want one," Sully said with a chuckle.

"I will bring some pictures with me tomorrow, and when you are ready, you and Kendal can come make a pick of the litter."

"That sounds wonderful. Thank you for thinking about us."

"My pleasure, ma'am," he said. "Is there anything I need to do while I am there tomorrow?"

"No, things really are in good shape. We are going to finish up some school shopping tomorrow and get back to work on Monday."

"Okay, see you about eight then?"

"Eight will be fine, Glen. See you then."

"Thanks, Sully," he said and hung up.

†

Sully could hear Kendal talking to Sunspot before she had them in eyesight. It was so sweet how she talked to the filly, and it was apparent they were bonding together.

"You two doing okay?" Sully asked as she passed by where they were standing.

"Yes, ma'am, doing fine," Kendal answered, softly stroking Sunspot's back.

"I am going to check on the rest of the animals but will be right back."

Sully fed the mare and made sure she and the colt had fresh water. She stood at the stall door, looking at him for several minutes. He truly was a beautiful animal and would make a fine addition to her stock. He approached her and nuzzled her hand.

"Hello, handsome fellow," she said as she scratched behind his ears. "You are growing fast, too, I see."

Sully opened the stall door and walked back to where Kendal and Sunspot were. She wanted to see if the colt would follow her and smiled when she heard hoof tracks following behind her.

Kendal looked up and grinned at her. "You have a shadow," she said.

"I thought you two might enjoy some company, but he needs to learn to be brushed, too."

"I will be done with Sunspot in just a bit."

Sully pulled up a stool and watched Kendal in action. The colt watched with growing interest as he inched his way closer to them. Sunspot was older, but the colt was nearly as tall. They made a nice-looking pair, standing close together.

"Okay, Sunspot, you are done for now," Kendal said and then hugged her neck. "Now it's his turn."

"Remember to talk to him and let him smell the brush," Sully reminded her.

"Yes, ma'am." Kendal held the brush out to him to allow him to smell it.

"Stroke his face with your hand. He really likes that."

Sunspot walked over to where she was sitting and nudged her gently. "Hello, my little friend." Sully took the filly's face in her hands and planted a firm kiss on her nose. "You are so bright and shiny after all that brushing."

Kendal beamed up at her aunt's praise. "I may have to put you on the payroll as Chief Horse Groomer," she said.

Kendal grinned even brighter as she slowly lifted the brush to the colt's shoulder. "See how good this feels?" she asked, gently stroking his shoulder. The colt turned his head to watch her but did not move away from Kendal.

"I think he likes the way you brush him."

"I think so, too," Kendal said, moving slowly to keep from startling the colt.

"I know Sunspot loves it," Sully said as she ran her hand down the filly's back.

The colt stomped his foot as Kendal brushed down his leg.

"I think it tickles him," she said.

"Brush a little harder then," Sully instructed. "Glen and Cathy are going to come by in the morning so you two can meet."

"I can't wait to meet her," Kendal said.

"He also wanted to know if you would like to have a puppy."

Kendal stopped mid-stroke and turned to look at Sully. "Can I have one, Aunt Micah?"

"I don't see why not. You take good care of Sunspot. A puppy will be more work, though."

"I can do it with your help," Kendal answered smoothly.

Sully chuckled. "You know I will help, but you will have to housebreak it and teach it not to chew the house to bits."

"I know I can do that."

"Feed him or her every day, and teach it to walk on a leash," she continued.

"What kind of puppy?"

"They are called blue heelers," Sully answered. "They are working dogs, used for herding cattle."

"Are they really blue?"

"Yes, they really are. They come out white with black or brown spots, but turn blue, white, brown, and black as they grow."

"When can I get one?"

"Glen is going to bring pictures tomorrow for us to see, and maybe after we finish shopping, we can stop by to take a look."

"Awesome," Kendal said as she resumed brushing.

Ten minutes later, Kendal had finished brushing the colt.

"Would you like to give them a treat?"

"Yes, ma'am."

"Walk into the office, and on the table is a box of sugar cubes. Get one for each of them."

Kendal placed the brush back on the shelf and rushed to the office. She returned with two sugar cubes. "Open your palm flat and put a cube on it."

Kendal placed a cube on her palm as instructed and offered it to Sunspot. The filly's soft lips gently scooped up the sugar cube, and they heard a crunch as she bit down on it.

"Perfect, now do the same for the colt."

Kendal repeated the process for the colt. He had a little more difficulty scooping up the cube. Kendal giggled as the soft muzzle tickled her palm.

"Tickles, doesn't it?"

"Yes, it does."

†

Sunspot's keen hearing alerted them to Bryn's return.

"I do believe Bryn has made it home. Let's put the colt back in with his mom and head to the house."

The colt followed them down the aisle and trotted back into the stall to nurse from the mare. Sully closed the door, and they walked to the barn entrance.

"Good night, Sunspot," Kendal said.

Sunspot nuzzled Kendal's neck and then watched as they crossed the yard to help Bryn, who had parked and was pulling out bags.

"Welcome home. Can we help with those?"

"Thanks," she said, handing Kendal a bag and two to Sully.

"Guess what, Bryn?"

"What, Kendal?"

"I am getting a puppy."

"Wow, that's great. What kind?"

"A blue heeler," Kendal answered.

"Glen's dog had her pups, and he has offered one to Kendal."

"They are really smart and good dogs," Bryn offered.

"Cool," Kendal said as she rushed ahead of them.

"Whose idea was that?"

"All Glen's, but I like it. She needs a pet she can grow up with."

"I agree completely. I just never thought of you as a dog person."

"I have never had one, but I reckon it's time for a change."

"Very true." Bryn walked toward the house with Sully hot in her tracks.

They found Kendal in the kitchen, already unloading her bag.

"Alright," she exclaimed and pulled out a movie.

Sully looked at Bryn. "I saw the Chipmunk movie in the store and picked it up."

"I can't wait to watch this," Kendal said.

"Well, dinner first, then a movie," Sully said.

Bryn pulled out the hamburger and placed it in a frying pan. She turned on the oven to heat the taco shells. "Micah, will you chop the veggies? Kendal, will you place the taco shells on this cookie sheet?"

"Yes, ma'am," they both said, and Sully saluted Bryn in jest.

Bryn placed the cookie sheet on the table for Kendal and opened the box of shells. "Just lay them flat so they can get warm."

She returned to the stove and seasoned the beef as Sully started chopping the lettuce.

"Do we want tomatoes?" she asked.

Bryn looked at Kendal, who was nodding her head. "That's affirmative," she answered.

Bryn emptied the rest of the grocery bags and placed shredded cheese and sour cream in the refrigerator.

With the three of them working together, it didn't take long to prepare dinner. They made short work of the tacos, and Sully and Kendal squealed in delight when Bryn pulled out a cheesecake for dessert.

"Oh, yummy," Kendal said when she took the first bite.

"This was a great idea. I usually forget all about desserts," Sully said.

"We can't miss out on one of the major food groups," Bryn teased.

"No, I guess we can't."

Bryn and Kendal cleaned up the kitchen and turned the dishwasher on as Sully got the movie ready and popped the popcorn. Finally, with all the chores completed, the three of them settled onto the couch to watch the movie. It was difficult to tell who enjoyed it more, Kendal or the two adults, as they all sat engrossed in the movie and munched on popcorn.

Kendal barely made it through to the end of the movie. Sully noticed her eyelids had grown heavy, and her head was beginning to nod. It had been a long and busy day, and she was sure Kendal was ready for bed. When she turned off the movie, she looked at Kendal.

"Are you ready for bed?"

"Yes, ma'am, I am tired."

"We had a long, busy day."

"Yes, we did," Kendal said with a smile.

"Brush your teeth and get dressed for bed. Bryn and I will take care of the popcorn bowls and will be in to tuck you in shortly."

Kendal left the room slowly, dragging her feet.

"I think we wore her out today," Bryn said with a chuckle as she gathered up the bowls and glasses.

"Shopping is hard work when you are not used to it," Sully said.

"I guess so. So, are you worn out, too?"

"I think I can muster a second wind," Sully grinned.

"Good, I need some you time."

"I was hoping you would."

"Let's go see if Kendal is ready yet."

Sully followed Bryn from the kitchen down the hallway to Kendal's room. Surprisingly, Kendal was already in bed, snoring softly as they quietly approached. Sully turned off the lamp and closed the door behind them as they left the room.

"She is so precious," Bryn said.

"Just like a little angel." Sully closed the bedroom door behind them and reached for Bryn. She took her lover in her arms for a slow, sensual kiss.

"I have been waiting for that all day," Bryn said rather breathlessly when they broke the kiss.

"There is more to come," Sully said as she undressed Bryn, kissing the bare skin as clothing was removed. She took her hand and led Bryn to the bed, pressing her gently onto it. "I will be right back," she said as she lit a candle on the bedside table and turned off the light. She quickly stripped off her clothes and joined Bryn beneath the covers.

†

The sensation of Sully's skin on hers as she moved on top of her made her shiver with excitement. Their bodies moved in a slow rhythm, their desire for one another building rapidly as their mouths melted together in a deep, passionate kiss.

It was late into the night before their desire was finally sated. Bryn curled up next to Sully's body, so happy to be in the arms of the woman she loved.

"I love you," she whispered against Sully's skin.

"I love you, too," Sully answered, her body seconds away from sleep.

Bryn sighed and closed her eyes.

## CHAPTER TWENTY-EIGHT

---

Sully woke to the smell of bacon frying. She slipped into a robe before walking to the kitchen. "Smells good," she said as she walked up behind Bryn and wrapped her arms around her waist. "Good morning, my love."

"Good morning. Did you sleep well?"

"Like a rock."

"Good, me too. I thought we would have a good breakfast to get us going today."

"Do you want me to wake Kendal?"

"No, not yet. Let her sleep a bit longer. Do you like scrambled eggs?"

"I love scrambled eggs."

"Good. Will you crack eight of them and put them in a bowl for me?"

"Sure thing, sweets," Sully said as she walked to the refrigerator.

Bryn chopped green onions on a chopping board and then went to the pantry for parmesan cheese. "I hope you like them a little different."

"I bet I will love them."

"Thanks for getting the eggs for me. Will you get some toast ready to drop, and then you can go wake Kendal."

Sully placed slices of bread in the toaster. "I will be right back," she said and kissed Bryn.

Bryn finished the bacon, whipped the eggs, mixed the cheese and onions, and then poured them into a frying pan. She dropped the lever on the toast and slowly stirred the eggs.

†

Sully walked into Kendal's room. She sat on the bed beside her sleeping niece. "Wake up, sleepyhead."

Kendal stretched, and her eyes slowly opened.

"Breakfast will be ready in a minute, so start waking up," Sully told her.

"Yes, ma'am," Kendal said, sitting up and rubbing the sleep from her eyes.

Sully leaned down and kissed her forehead. "Bryn is cooking a special breakfast for us."

Kendal stepped away from the bed. "I bet I beat you there," she said, taking off running down the hall.

"Oh, you cheat," Sully yelled and ran after her.

With the head start, Kendal beat Sully to the kitchen and rounded the corner laughing.

Bryn was in front of the toaster, removing the last slices of toast when Kendal came barreling into the room. "Whoa, slow down, Nelly," she cried out.

Kendal came skidding to a halt just as Sully rounded the corner. "I win."

"You cheated."

"It's not my fault you couldn't catch me," Kendal teased.

"Regardless, since you lost, you can pour the juice," Bryn said to Sully.

"Don't tell me you're taking her side," Sully said.

"Nope, I just don't want my breakfast to get cold," she said as she placed a plate of toast on the table.

Bryn served the scrambled eggs and brought the bacon to the table. Sully poured three glasses of apple juice and carried them to the table. "Do you want coffee?"

"No, I think I'm good."

"This looks really good," Kendal said.

"Thanks. I hope you like it."

"It smells wonderful, too. Does anyone besides me want jelly?"

"You have grape jelly?"

"Yes, Kendal, I have grape," Sully said as she took the jar of jelly to the table.

They devoured the breakfast like they hadn't eaten in days.

"I guess I need to cook more next time," Bryn said.

"No, I think you did just fine. If I ate any more, I wouldn't be good for anything today," Sully remarked.

"You say that now, but I bet the two of you holler I'm hungry within three hours," she teased.

"Well, that is always a possibility," Sully grinned. "Kendal, would you like to go shower and get dressed while Bryn and I clean up the kitchen?"

"Yes, ma'am." Kendal climbed down from her chair and stopped in front of Bryn. She stood on her tiptoes to kiss Bryn's cheek. "Thank you for breakfast."

"You are quite welcome," Bryn said, her eyes shining with excitement.

"I will see you in a bit," she said to Sully and left the room.

"She is such a sweet kid," Bryn said as she started clearing the table.

"Yes, she is. You rinse, and I'll load," she told Bryn.

"Better yet, why don't you let me take care of this, and you go get ready? Then, while you and Kendal are out with the animals, I can shower and run the dishwasher?"

"You sure you don't need my help?"

"I have loaded a dishwasher or two," Bryn said as she pulled Sully close.

"That was a great breakfast, by the way," Sully said as she brushed hair from Bryn's face. She leaned in to kiss Bryn. "I was starved when I woke up."

"You did work up an appetite last night," Bryn said and lightly smacked Sully on the butt.

"I don't remember any complaints last night."

"No, no complaints at all, ma'am. I hope we can do it again tonight."

"I will see if I can work it into my schedule."

"I would appreciate that," Bryn said, kissing her more passionately this time.

"Mmm, I can definitely work that into my schedule."

"That's more like it. Now off to the shower with you."

†

Bryn finished cleaning the kitchen and sat sipping a cup of coffee. Kendal walked in and sat down beside her. “You look very nice,” Bryn said.

“Thanks. You are going shopping with us today, right?”

“Of course I am.”

“Good. I like it when you shop with us.”

Bryn smiled brightly. “I enjoy shopping with you two. Micah is getting ready, and I will shower and dress while the two of you check on the animals.”

“Cool. What time is it?”

“It’s seven-thirty. Why do you ask?”

“Mr. Glen and Cathy are coming by at eight. I am excited about meeting her.”

“Do you think she would like to go shopping with us?”

“I guess we could ask her when she gets here,” Kendal said.

“Would you like that?” Bryn asked.

“I think I would. Aunt Micah says we will be starting school together, so maybe we can help each other pick out supplies.”

“That’s an excellent idea,” Sully said as she entered the kitchen. “I bet she would love to go shopping, too.”

“I am off to the shower. I will come out to the barn when I am done,” Bryn said.

“Enjoy the shower,” Sully said. “Are we ready to head to the barn?”

Kendal was already halfway to the door. “Yes, ma’am.”

“Would you like to learn how to feed the animals today?”

“Yes, please. I would like that.”

“Okay, and later today, I think we need to ride out and check on the foxes, too.”

“Sweet,” Kendal said and rushed ahead of Sully.

†

Sunspot heard their approach and trotted out to meet them. She was met by a big hug from Kendal.

"Good morning, Sunspot," Sully heard her say. "I get to feed you today."

The three of them walked into the barn, and Sully showed Kendal where different foods were stored. Kendal was still a little shy of being able to reach into the bins, so Sully located a small step stool for her to use. She placed it in front of the bins, and Kendal scrambled up.

"Okay, Sunspot gets two scoops of sweet feed," she instructed as she held a pail.

Kendal carefully scooped out two portions of the sweet-smelling food and poured it into the pail. "Grab your stool. I think you are going to need it in her stall."

Kendal carried the small stool and followed Sully into Sunspot's stall. She placed the stool in front of the feed trough and climbed to the top step. "Okay, you can pour this in for her," Sully said, handing her the pail. "Next, we need to flush her water and fill it with fresh. Push that red lever to the right, and her old water will drain."

Kendal followed her instruction perfectly, and when the old water was gone, Sully said, "Now fill it up about halfway by turning the blue lever."

Sunspot stood patiently at the door of her stall, watching as Sully and Kendal refreshed her water. When that was done, Kendal stepped down from the stool.

"One more job, and we will be done. See that little basket-looking device over in the corner?"

"Yes, ma'am."

"Move your stool over to that, and then follow me."

Kendal placed her stool and then followed Sully down the aisle past the other stalls to a small room filled with bales of hay. There was an open bale on the bottom row, and Sully showed Kendal how the layers peeled off.

"I usually give Sunspot two portions. She will need more as she continues to grow and as the winter comes and there is less grass for grazing."

Kendal carried the hay back to the stall.

"Do I need to hold those for you?"

"No, I think I can get it," she answered.

Sully stood by in case Kendal needed assistance. She watched with pride as she carefully climbed the stool and dropped the hay in the holder.

"All done with Sunspot. Would you like to help me with the mare?"

"Yes, ma'am," Kendal said, grabbing her stool as Sunspot began to eat.

"The mare needs much more food than Sunspot, not only because she is bigger, but also because she is nursing her colt. She needs five scoops." Sully held out a larger bucket as Kendal began dishing out the food, pouring each scoop carefully into the bucket.

"Very good," she praised as Kendal poured the last scoop and carried her stool to the mare's stall. "This one is heavier, so I will have to pour it, but you can refresh the water."

Kendal took care of the water and then moved carefully around the mare as she moved to the feed trough. She placed her stool in front of the hay bin and followed Sully back to the storage room. "How many for the mare?" she asked.

"Four in the morning and four at night," Sully answered. "You carry two, and I will take the other two."

They placed the hay in the bin, and Kendal returned her stool to the feed bin area. "That was good timing," Sully said as she heard Glen's truck pull up. "Let's go greet them."

Kendal smiled as Glen stepped out of his truck, a blonde-haired girl about her height in tow behind him. "Hey, Mr. Glen," she said.

"Good morning, Kendal. I would like you to meet my daughter, Cathy," he said.

"Hi, Cathy," Kendal said with a bashful smile.

"Hi, Kendal," a shy Cathy answered.

"Would you like to see Sunspot?"

"Who is Sunspot?" Cathy asked.

"Come with me," Kendal said and held out her hand, leading Cathy down the aisle to the stalls.

†

Glen and Sully could hear Kendal making the introductions and explaining Sunspot's injuries to Cathy. Glen smiled at Sully.

"I think they will be just fine."

"I do, too. Come with me, and we will get you paid."

"Thanks," Glen said and followed Sully into the office.

"We are going to do some school shopping. Would you mind if Cathy went along, and we could drop her off later today when we stop to look at the pups?"

"I bet she would love that. That reminds me," he said as he dug some pictures from his shirt pocket. "These are the pups."

Sully accepted the photos he offered. "Oh, my goodness, they are adorable."

"Full of themselves already," Glen added.

"How old are they?"

"They are a little over seven weeks old. Mama has started weaning them, and they are beginning to eat some dog food. They should be ready to go by next weekend."

"This one sure looks like a character," Sully said, pointing out a smaller pup.

"The runt in size, but she's got a bigger heart than the bunch of them," Glen said.

"Kendal will have to see these. She is so excited to be able to get a puppy," Sully said as she unlocked a cabinet and pulled out a checkbook. She wrote out a check for Glen and handed it to him. "How much are you getting for the pups?"

"Three hundred," he said. "Don't even think you are going to buy one," he warned.

"It is only fair, Glen."

"Not with everything you do for me and my family," he said. "I just won't have it."

Sully shook her head with a plan already in mind. "Thank you then."

"It's the least I can do for you and Kendal," Glen said with a smile.

The girls were walking down the aisle as Glen and Sully stepped out of the office. They were chattering away to one another.

"Kendal, did you ask Cathy about going shopping with us?"

"No, ma'am, I forgot. Would you like to go school supply shopping with us?"

Cathy looked up to her dad. "Can I?"

"I don't see why not. Have you registered Kendal yet?"

"No, not yet," Sully answered.

"I have a list of supplies the school recommends out in the truck that will help you in shopping. Cathy, will you get the list, and we can make a copy?"

"Yes, sir," Cathy said and ran to the truck to get the list.

"Would you mind picking up some items for Cathy as well and save me a trip?"

"We would love to," Sully answered. Glen started to pull out his wallet. "Stop right there."

"What do you mean?"

"I just won't have it," Sully said with a grin. "Don't even think about arguing with the boss either."

"Yes, ma'am," he said with a blush. "Thank you."

"I am still getting the best of this deal, so no thanks needed."

"Speaking of which, I think Glen has some pictures to show you, Kendal."

"Of the puppies?" she asked.

Glen handed her the photographs. She looked them over with a sparkle in her eyes. "They are so cute."

Cathy came back and handed the list to Glen. "I guess we don't need a copy then," he said with a grin.

"Dad says you want a puppy," Cathy said to Kendal.

"I sure do. I have never had a pet," Kendal said.

"Sugar had a good litter this time. I think you will have a hard time picking one out."

Kendal surprised them all by saying, "No, I think I already know which one."

"Oh really?" Sully asked.

"Yes, ma'am, but I will wait until I meet them all."

"That is very smart of you," Bryn said as she walked into the conversation. "Hey, Glen."

"Good morning, Doc. This is my daughter, Cathy," he said.

"Hello, Cathy. Are you going shopping with us today?"

"Yes, ma'am," Cathy said with a wide grin.

"We are going to have such fun on a girls' day out," Bryn said, rubbing her hands together.

"Well, I will leave you girls to it. Is there anything you need me to do today?"

"Nope, Kendal and I fed everyone, so we are good to go," Sully answered.

"I will see you later today then," he said and left the barn.

Sully slipped the list into her back pocket. "Are we all set?"

The girls nodded their heads and started toward the truck.

"I bet we will be in the same class," Cathy said.

"I hope so," Kendal said.

Bryn opened the back door of her truck, and the girls climbed up. "Buckle up."

Sully slid into the passenger seat and turned around to make sure both girls were secure as Bryn walked to the driver's seat. "This is going to be fun," she giggled as she fastened her seatbelt.

## CHAPTER TWENTY-NINE

---

"We better grab two buggies," Sully teased as they entered the store. "I have a feeling we are going to need them."

"No way, we can make everything fit in one," Bryn answered.

"Okay, where're we going to start?"

"I think we should start with backpacks," Bryn suggested.

"Lead the way."

Bryn, Kendal, and Cathy started down an aisle, followed closely by Sully and a buggy. She would have never believed there would be such a selection in an item as simple as backpacks, but there must have been twenty or so to choose from.

Kendal kept coming back to a blue bag with a big flowery print. “You must like that one,” Sully said. “You keep coming back to look at it.”

“Yes, I do, I think I will get this one,” Kendal said.

“I like it too,” Cathy said. “I think I will get the yellow one.”

That seemed to be the most difficult decision, and the rest of the school shopping went off without a hitch.

“You know, while we’re here, we should look at collars and a leash for your puppy,” Sully said.

“Hey, that’s a great idea.”

“I know where the pet section is,” Cathy said, taking Kendal’s hand and leading her quickly across the store.

“Is that why you wanted a second buggy?” Bryn asked.

“No, but we may need one after all.”

“If we do, I will go get one.”

“Bowls, a bed, food, all those good things a puppy will need.”

“Don’t forget the chew toys and treats,” Bryn said.

“Right, chew toys especially. I can see my favorite boots chewed to bits already,” Sully said.

“If you are referring to that stinking pair of barn boots, I wouldn’t mind seeing them leave the house,” Bryn joked. “I’m not sure even a puppy wants to mess with those.”

“Very funny,” Sully said.

“I’m just being honest,” she said with a grin.

“I love those boots.”

“Uh hmm,” Bryn said as they joined the girls in the pet section.

Kendal honed right in on a purple collar and leash. “Will this be the right size?”

Sully inspected the chosen collar. "At least for a few months, I would think," she said as she extended the collar to its full size.

"Nice color," Bryn said.

"Purple is one of my favorites, too," Cathy said.

Kendal smiled at her new friend. "What about toys?"

Cathy busied herself with a variety of squeaky toys and teething toys. "This would be good, and this one," she said, lifting a small brown teddy bear. "I don't know of a puppy that would pass on a bear."

"That is so true," Bryn added.

Together the small group selected a half dozen toys and placed them in the buggy. The girls moved onto the beds while Bryn and Sully focused on food and treats.

"Okay, Doc, what's your take on food and treats?"

"I would start a puppy out with this," Bryn pointed to a large bag of food. "I would get some of these rawhide chews as well. The teething stage can be horrific."

"Gee, thanks for making me feel at ease," Sully teased.

Bryn chuckled and turned her attention back to the girls. They were looking at small beds. "Do you really think the puppy will be in a dog bed?" she asked Sully.

"Probably not, but we need to have one available just in case."

With some adult guidance, they decided on a blue medium-sized bed and started for the checkout.

"See, I knew we could fit everything in one buggy," Sully joked. "Can anyone think of anything else we need?"

"Lunch," Bryn suggested.

"Lunch sounds good. What are we eating today?"

"Why don't we stop off at the diner so we will have a variety to choose from?" Bryn suggested.

"Sound alright for you two?" Sully asked the girls.

"Yes, ma'am," Kendal said, and Cathy nodded her agreement.

At the checkout they tried to bag the supplies separately for each of the girls to make the unloading process easier and then loaded up the truck.

"Man, that was a workout," Bryn said as they placed the last bag in the back of the truck.

"If we weren't hungry before we are now," Sully replied. "To the diner, James," she ordered.

†

Sully and Bryn settled for chef salads while the girls chose chicken fingers and fries. Sully could see the excitement growing as the girls talked about the puppies while they ate. It felt good to see Kendal comfortable with Cathy and eager to have a puppy.

When the waitress brought the bill, Bryn picked it up. "I have lunch," she said, accepting no argument from Sully.

"Thank you for lunch then," Sully said.

"That was yummy," Kendal added.

"Yes, it was. Are we ready to go look at puppies?" Sully asked.

"Yes, ma'am," Kendal said with a huge grin.

†

They drove past the Trace to Cathy's home. It was a small, modest home that Sully had only been to once since Glen started working for her. There was a small barn with a few beef cattle grazing in the field behind it, and once they stepped out of the truck, they could hear the excited yips and barks coming from the barn.

"Lead the way, Cathy," Sully said. "We can unload the bags later."

Cathy and Kendal took off at a full run toward the barn. "You think she's excited?"

"Maybe just a bit," Sully said with a warm smile.

The girls were met just inside the barn by bouncing fat puppies eager for attention.

"They are so cute," Sully heard Kendal say as she kneeled to pet them.

†

"There you are," she said as she picked up the runt. "Hiya, Munchkin." She lifted the puppy up to her face. The puppy instantly began covering her cheek with loving puppy kisses, and Kendal knew she had found the one.

"Munchkin?" Sully asked.

"Yes, Munchkin like in the Wizard of Oz," Kendal explained. "She may be little in size, but she's full of energy."

Sully roared with laughter.

"I take it Kendal has made her pick?" Glen asked as he walked into the barn.

"I am not sure who picked who, but yes, we have a decision and apparently a name."

†

Glen looked at the puppy Kendal was holding and then shot a knowing glance at Sully. It was the same puppy they had talked about from the photographs.

"I'm glad you had to pick and not me," Sully said.

"Why, Aunt Micah?" Kendal asked with a perplexed look on her face.

"Because they are all so cute, I could never choose," she said with a chuckle as a pup aggressively tugged at her bootstrings. She reached down and picked him up and immediately received a tongue bath.

"Well, there is no limit if you want more than one," Glen said.

"No, no, I think one will do just fine for now," Sully quickly answered.

"You could have a Munchkin and a Wizard," Bryn teased.

Sully whipped her head around to look at Bryn, still playing with the pup in her hands. "You want a puppy to ride with you?"

†

When Sully handed her the surly puppy, Bryn instantly knew she had been trapped. She looked over at Kendal. "What do you think?"

Bryn didn't think it was possible, but Kendal's eyes grew even wider with excitement. "Well, they are cute, and I bet he would make good company as you made your rounds."

Bryn hadn't had a pet since she was a young girl. The idea of a companion to ride with her really wasn't a bad idea either. "Hmm, what do you think, Wizard?" she asked, lifting the puppy up to her face.

The puppy wriggled ferociously with excitement in her hands, and they all broke out in laughter.

"Okay, but under two conditions."

"Which would be what?" Sully asked.

"First, that I pay for this puppy, and second, that he sleeps with Kendal and Munchkin," she replied.

Glen started to protest but was quickly cut off by Sully. "Don't even think about arguing with her," she warned.

"We might need a bigger bed then," Kendal said.

"If so, we will go get one," Sully promised.

"Can they have matching collars?" Kendal asked.

"I don't see why not," Bryn answered.

"Cool," Kendal said.

"I think it's time for the adults to step out," Sully suggested.

"Okay, Cathy. Will you take care of Wiz for me until we can pick them up?" Bryn asked.

"Yes, ma'am, I will," Cathy said with pride as she took the pup from Bryn.

"Thanks."

The three adults walked outside to Bryn's truck. She reached for her checkbook as Sully started separating the bags of supplies. "How much?" she asked Glen.

†

"A hundred," he answered, shooting a glance to Sully, who remained silent, knowing he charged three times that amount normally.

"That sounds like too good a bargain to pass up," Bryn said as she handed him a check. "Thanks."

"Thank you, Doc."

"Let me help you carry these in the house," Sully said as she handed Glen an armful of bags.

"Good Lord, did y'all try to buy out the store?" he teased.

"Just about," Sully said with a grin. "We had so much fun doing it though."

"Thanks for everything, Boss," Glen said.

"You're welcome, but I still came out on top of this deal," she said with a wink.

They carried the bags inside and when they returned, Cathy and Kendal had joined Bryn at the truck.

"I don't know, you will have to ask your dad and Micah," she was saying to the girls.

"Ask us what?" Glen said.

"No more puppies. Two is enough," Sully said.

"No, not that. Cathy has asked me if I want to sleep over tonight," Kendal said.

"Is that okay with you, Glen?"

"Sounds great to me," he answered.

"Let's head home then, and I will bring you back after we pack you some clothes," Sully said.

"I have to go to town in a bit. I could pick her up on my way back," he offered.

"That would be fine," Sully said. "Okay with you, Kendal?"

"Yes, ma'am."

"Let's go get you packed up then."

She opened the door and helped Kendal get settled. She climbed into the front seat and asked, "What all do we need to pack?"

"Pajamas, clothes for tomorrow, a toothbrush and paste," Kendal answered.

"I have a small bag that should hold all of that."

"Can we still check on the foxes when we get home?"

"Yes, I think there will be plenty of time for that."

"I tell you what. You two help me get the bags in the house, and I will pack them for you," Bryn offered.

"Deal," Sully said.

"Shorts, okay for you tomorrow?" Bryn asked.

"That's good," Kendal answered.

†

They carried the bags inside when they arrived home, and then Sully and Kendal struck out for the barn. Sunspot was waiting for them and followed along as Sully carried a bag of food to the golf cart.

"Are you driving?"

"I think it would be better if you did today since we are in a hurry," Kendal said. "Can Sunspot come along?"

"Unless we shut her up in her stall, I don't think we have any choice," Sully said. "You have to be quiet, though," she said to Sunspot. "Let's go."

Kendal climbed in beside Sully, and Sunspot trotted along beside the cart as they made their way to the spot in the woods where the foxes lived. As expected, the food they had dropped off earlier was completely gone, and Sully poured a fresh bag into the container. Sunspot walked over and sniffed the food.

"That is not for you, silly," Kendal said, and Sunspot trotted back to the cart.

"Let's go watch for a few minutes and see if anyone shows up," Sully said. She pulled the cart into her usual waiting spot and cut the power. Sunspot moved close so Kendal could scratch behind her ears as they waited.

Sully caught a flash of red moving through the underbrush and raised a finger to her lips, and then pointed for Kendal to watch. They watched as the mother fox cautiously approached the food they had left. When she bent her head to start eating, two kits bounded out from the bushes to join her.

"They have really grown," Sully whispered.

"They are beautiful," Kendal said.

"Yes, they are. I bet in just a few more weeks the kits will start going off on their own," Sully said.

"Will they be okay on their own?"

"I think there is at least another fox or two in these woods that they can pair up with," Sully answered.

"That's good," Kendal said.

They sat and watched the foxes eat for several minutes until the food was nearly gone.

"I reckon we had better head back to the house."

"Come on, Sunspot," Kendal whispered as Sully started the cart.

They drove off as quietly as possible to prevent disturbing the feeding animals.

Once they drove out of the clearing, Sully picked up speed, and Sunspot cantered beside them, keeping pace.

†

They parked the cart at the barn and went into the house to check on Bryn.

"I have everything ready for you," she said as they walked into her bedroom. "If you want to check, I will pack it up."

"Looks good to me," Kendal said. "May we feed Sunspot before I go?"

"I think we have time," Sully said. Kendal rushed out ahead of them as Bryn zipped up the bag and carried it to the porch.

"May I take you to dinner tonight?" Sully asked.

"Only if we can go for another of those steaks," Bryn teased.

"I was hoping you would suggest that."

"That sounds great. I'm going to get some clothes and talk to Doc and Camille, but I'll be back soon."

Sully kissed Bryn. "Hurry back."

"I will. Tell Kendal I will see her tomorrow."

"Done," Sully said as Bryn walked to her truck.

†

Sully walked to the barn where Kendal was already busy at work, dropping feed into Sunspot's trough and clearing the water. "Should I get the hay?" she asked.

"Yes, please," Kendal answered.

Sully walked into the storage area, took two portions of hay, and carried them back to the stall. As she passed the other stall, she called out to the mare and the colt. "I will take care of you two in just a minute."

She dropped the hay in the bin and stood with Kendal as Sunspot began to eat.

"Thanks for a great day," Kendal said.

"It was fun, wasn't it?"

"Yes, it was. I am glad Bryn is getting a puppy, too."

"I think she is almost as excited as you are," Sully teased.

"You think so, Aunt Micah?"

"Possibly," she said and ruffled up Kendal's hair. "Don't stay up all night playing with the puppies."

"I won't," Kendal said as they walked back to the porch. They could see Glen's truck coming down the driveway.

"Have fun, and call me when you are ready to come home tomorrow."

"Yes, ma'am, I will," Kendal said as she picked up her bag.

"Hey, Glen," she said as he put the truck in park. "Hop in back with Cathy, and I will hand you your bag."

"I will see you tomorrow, Aunt Micah," Kendal said. She hugged her aunt closely. "Love you."

"Love you, too. Have fun."

"We will," she said, scrambling up to the back seat and reaching for her bag.

"Thanks, Glen."

"We'll see you tomorrow," he said, putting the truck in gear.

†

Sully watched them drive away and made her way back to the barn. She fed the mare and colt and then sat on a small bench, suddenly realizing she was all alone. She had grown accustomed to the sound of Kendal and Bryn, so the silence left her feeling a bit odd.

Sunspot finished her meal and joined Sully. "Hey there, little one," she said as she hugged the filly. "Our family is growing quickly. I hope we are ready for all this change."

Sunspot sensed the anxiety Sully felt and nuzzled her gently to comfort her master. "I know everything will be okay," Sully said more to assure herself than anything.

She stood, picked up Kendal's brush, began stroking it across Sunspot, and was just about finished when she heard Bryn's truck returning. "I will see you in the morning," she said as she kissed the filly's forehead and left the barn to join her lover.

"Welcome back, love," she said as she joined Bryn on the porch.

## CHAPTER THIRTY

---

Sully took a small bag from Bryn and followed her into the house. "I can't believe how quickly this day has gone," she said as she placed the bag on the bed.

"It's really been a lot of fun shopping and spending so much time with you and Kendal," Bryn said.

"Yeah, it has," she agreed. "It's also nice knowing we will have some alone time tonight."

"That it will. I don't know about you, but I am getting hungry."

"Me, too. Let's take a shower and head out to dinner, and then we can come back and relax tonight," Sully suggested.

"I am right behind you," Bryn said.

†

After a quick shower, they dressed and drove to town. They ordered their meals and were eating salads when Sully looked up at Bryn. "The last time we were here, all hell broke loose," she said with a sad note in her voice.

Bryn reached across the table and covered Sully's hand. "I know, but we are past the worst of times."

"Do you promise?"

"I will do everything in my power to make life better for you and Kendal," Bryn answered.

When Sully looked up at Bryn again, Bryn saw tears in her eyes. "I promise," she said.

"Thank you for being more than I could ever dream of," Sully said.

"Careful now, or you will give me the big head," Bryn said with a chuckle.

"Here we go, ladies, the two biggest T-bones in the house," the waitress said as she placed two platters on the table. "Enjoy, and let me know if there is anything I can get you."

"Thanks," Sully said, and the waitress left them to enjoy their meal. "These smell fantastic."

"Tastes good, too," Bryn said as she chewed her first bite.

Neither of them could finish the steak, and when Sully gave up and pushed her platter away, she leaned back in her seat. "I know I shouldn't, but I am craving a piece of pie. Will you split one with me?"

"Apple pie with cheese?"

"Yes, that sounds great."

"Count me in then," Bryn said, pushing her plate away.

The waitress took their dessert order and brought the check with the pie. "I will take care of this when you are ready," she said.

"You can go ahead," Sully said, handing her a credit card.

"This is so yummy," Bryn said and then groaned her pleasure.

"If I had known sound effects came with it, I would have ordered two slices," Sully teased.

"You might need to if you want any," Bryn shot back at her.

"Let me dig in quick then," Sully said, taking a bite. "Damn, this is good."

They finished the pie and picked up their doggy bags full of steak before walking to Sully's truck.

"I am so glad you are driving," Bryn said. "I'm stuffed."

"I can't wait to get home and take these clothes off. I feel like they have shrunk a few sizes."

"Can we just snuggle up in bed when we get home?" Bryn asked.

"Woman, you must have been reading my mind again."

"Get us home quick then."

†

The drive home was relatively fast, and Sully placed the leftovers in the fridge before following Bryn down the hall. Bryn had started undressing as she walked, and by the time she made it to the bed, she was nearly naked.

"You weren't kidding about crashing in the bed, were you?"

"No, but would you rather do something else?" Bryn asked.

"Not at all," Sully said as she took her clothes off and laid them across the bench at the foot of the bed. Bryn was already burrowed down in the covers when she walked to the side of the bed and turned off the light. "Would you like a candle?"

"That would be perfect," Bryn answered.

Sully lit a candle, then crawled in beside Bryn, and pulled her into her arms. Bryn settled her head on Sully's shoulder, her hand softly stroking down her stomach. "Thanks for a great meal."

"It was really good, wasn't it?"

"Just what we needed," Bryn said as she snuggled into Sully's body.

Sully's hand caressed Bryn's back as they lay in silence, enjoying the peacefulness of the night.

†

Bryn listened to the beating of Sully's heart deep in her chest. "You have seemed a little off tonight. Are you okay?"

"What do you mean by off?"

"Distracted or lost in your thoughts," Bryn explained.

"I think I may be a bit overwhelmed by how quickly life has changed for me. A little more than a month ago, I was single and had no concerns other than the animals on this farm. Now I have a loving partner and a child to share, and soon we will have two pups to rear as well."

"I can see where that could be overwhelming. Are we taking our relationship too far too fast?" Bryn asked and then held her breath.

"I couldn't do this without you," Sully said, her hand cupping Bryn's chin and lifting her face. "Nor would I want to. Your presence here makes us a family."

It was Bryn's turn to have tears in her eyes, and a tear escaped to run down Sully's chest.

"Why are you crying?" Sully asked.

"I could not have asked for a more perfect family," Bryn said.

"Just remember that when a puppy needs to go out at two in the morning," Sully teased, "or when a little girl crawls in between us, frightened by a bad dream."

"I will care for the little girl if you go out with the puppy," Bryn said with a smile.

"I think it is time we consider a doggy door for when they get house-trained," Sully said. "I don't relish the thought of a cold nose on bare skin in the middle of the night unless it's yours."

Bryn broke out in laughter. "Micah Sullivan, I love you so," she said.

"I love you too, darling," Sully said, holding her tight.

They fell into comfortable silence, content with holding one another close as the minutes ticked by, and Bryn was the first to sleep.

†

Sully continued to hold her close until she stretched and turned onto her side. Then she curled her body around Bryn's and listened to the sound of her breathing. Life had changed very quickly for her, but she was thankful that the woman of her dreams would be waking up next to her every morning.

After that, life should be gravy Sully thought as her consciousness slipped away.

†

Sully woke early the next morning and was almost finished preparing steak and eggs for breakfast when Bryn walked into the kitchen. "Get some coffee, and I will be done in just a minute," she said.

"Okay, baby, that smells good," Bryn said as she poured a cup of coffee.

Sully buttered the toast, slid it onto a small plate, and then placed two fried eggs next to a large chunk of steak left over from last night's meal and carried it to Bryn. "Here you go, my love," she said, placing the plate on the table and kissing Bryn.

"Thanks, baby," Bryn said.

"Go ahead and start while my eggs finish," Sully instructed, pouring them a glass of juice.

"Mmm, this is wonderful," Bryn said from the table. "You could easily spoil me like this, you know."

"We both need to get better about eating breakfast," Sully said. "We are role models now."

"Yes, I know," Bryn agreed. "I wonder how her night went."

"I bet they played with those puppies until Glen made them come inside."

"Probably so," Bryn said. "What are your plans for this morning?"

"I think it is time to take the mare and colt back to the herd," Sully said. "He needs room to run and grow."

"Would you mind if I tag along and check out the herd?"

"Not at all. We have a few mares that are getting close to time to foal. It's going to be a bumper crop this year," Sully said with a grin.

"Plan on keeping me busy then?"

"Oh yes, Doc, I do," Sully said as she sat beside her.

"Good. I have some rounds to make afterward, but I should be back midafternoon," she said.

"I will just fiddle around here until Kendal calls and then go pick her up. How does some grilled chicken sound for supper?"

"Sounds great. I will make a salad and some veggies to accompany it when I get back," she said.

"This is a pretty hearty breakfast, isn't it?"

"Yes, it is. It will take me hours to work this off."

"I could think of some ways to work it off you," Sully grinned.

"I am sure you could, Romeo," Bryn teased.

†

Sully did manage to work a few calories off Bryn in the shower and then suggested they walk out to the herd instead of taking the golf cart.

"Let me take one more look at the mare before we lead her out," Bryn said as they reached the barn, followed closely by Sunspot.

"Okay, you get started, and I will get a lead."

Sully and Sunspot walked to the tack room. She picked out a short lead and tossed it over her shoulder. She noticed a new black halter hanging on the wall and took it down, placing it gently on Sunspot. "There you go, girl. We will have to start some training with Kendal soon."

They walked back to the stall where Bryn was finishing her exam. "She is good to go."

"Excellent," Sully said as she clipped the lead onto the mare's halter. "Ready, Mama?"

The mare followed her out of the stall, and the colt was behind them. Sunspot waited for them to leave the barn and trotted out to follow. The colt was ready to play and took off at a canter, closely followed by Sunspot.

"Someone else is feeling their oats this morning," Bryn said.

"It is such a beautiful day," Sully said, reaching for Bryn's hand.

†

They walked to the back pasture together, and when they stepped inside the gate, Sully unfastened the lead and let the mare run free back to the herd, followed closely by the colt and Sunspot.

"Do you think she will stay this time?" Bryn asked.

"I don't know. It is entirely up to her," Sully answered as they walked into a golden sea of horses. Sunspot quickly located her mother and gently nuzzled into her as Bryn and Sully inspected several pregnant mares.

"In a few weeks, these three will need to come up to at least the front pasture so we can keep an eye on them," Bryn said.

"That shouldn't be any problem," Sully said as she gave attention to several young horses that had crowded around her, hoping for treats. "Sorry guys, no treats on this trip," she said.

†

Bryn noticed how happy Sully was to be surrounded by the animals she so dearly loved. She lovingly stroked each one that came near and spoke softly to those who were shy until they approached her willingly.

"I need to get a move on. Are you going to stay out a while yet?"

"Nope, I will walk back with you and bring some treats back out."

Bryn reached for Sully, and they walked back to the gate together. Sunspot wasn't walking with them, but as she saw them approach the gate, she took off at a full run to catch up with them.

†

Sully heard the approaching hooves and did not have to turn to know it was Sunspot.

"I guess that answers your question," she said, placing her arm around Bryn's shoulder.

"That it does," Bryn said with a smile.

"What took you so long?" she asked as Sunspot rushed beside her. "Let's go home."

They walked hand in hand back to the barn. "I miss you already," Bryn said.

"I will be right here waiting for you." Sully pulled Bryn close for a tender kiss. "I love you."

"I love you, too."

"Hurry back to us," Sully said as she walked Bryn to her truck.

"I will. Have fun today," she said as she climbed into her truck.

"Always," Sully answered.

†

Sully watched Bryn pull away and then walked into the kitchen for a large bag of apples. She placed them in the golf cart and checked to ensure she had her pocketknife. "Are you ready to go spoil some young'uns?"

Sunspot trotted alongside the cart until they reached the gate and then rushed back to the herd. Sully pulled the cart close and opened the bag of apples. She unbuttoned the front of her shirt, stuffed six apples inside, and took another in her hands. Eager foals quickly surrounded her as she started to slice the apple. Sully was always amazed at how fast the apples disappeared, but she ensured everyone had a slice. She left the last apple as she always did for Sam, at eighteen, the oldest of the mares. She sliced the apple into quarters as she approached.

"Hey, old girl, did you think I had forgotten you?" She held her palm out with a quarter of the apple, and the mare gently took the sweet treat from her owner's hand, brushing her palm with silky soft lips. Sully closed the knife and slipped it back into her pocket. She fed Sam the last apple and then scratched behind her ears. "You are still the Queen of this herd," Sully whispered to her. "Keep these young'uns in line for me."

Sully felt her cell phone vibrate in her pocket. She pulled it out to see that Bryn had sent her a text. *Love you.*

She quickly answered with a *love you* in return and started back to the cart. The phone vibrated in her hand, this time with an incoming call. She recognized Glen's number and answered. "Hello."

"It's me, Aunt Micah," Kendal said.

"Are you ready to come home?"

"Yes, ma'am."

"Okay, I'll be there in just a few minutes. Did you have a good time?"

"Yes, it was great. Cathy wants me to come over again soon."

"You can also invite her over whenever you would like."

"Maybe later this week," Kendal said.

"That's fine with me. I will be there soon."

"Goodbye, Aunt Micah," Kendal said and hung up.

"Your buddy is ready to come home," Sully told Sunspot. "Wanna race?" Sully floored the cart, and it took off with a lurch, but it only took a few seconds for the filly to catch and pass her as they left the back pasture headed for the barn. Sully laughed as Sunspot left her in the dust, her hoofs kicked up along the path.

"Show off," she yelled.

## CHAPTER THIRTY-ONE

---

Kendal was very excited to see her aunt when Sully picked her up. She rushed out to the truck carrying Munchkin and said, "Glen says we can bring them home Friday."

"That's great news," Sully said as they walked to the barn.

"Hey, Boss," Glen said as he and Cathy were ushering puppies back into a freshly cleaned pen.

"How's it going?"

"Going well, thanks, and you?"

"Excellent, thanks. You know we need to sit down and discuss you going to some shows this week."

"Yes, the dates are getting close. Should we do it tomorrow?"

"Tomorrow is good. I want to take Kendal to register for school, but after that, I should be free."

"Yep, sounds good to me, Boss. Would you mind if I bring Cathy with me a few days this week so the girls can play before school starts?"

"No, not at all. Bring her anytime you like."

"She will enjoy that."

"I think it is time we girls start going for some rides. Sam looks a little bored, but I know she will be gentle with the girls."

"She's a great horse for kids," he agreed.

"I will have to see about getting some child-sized tack."

"I think you could get away with a bareback blanket at least for a few days," Glen said. "I think a gentle walk would be good for all of them."

"That's true, and they could take her for a swim with that on. Does Cathy know how to swim?"

"Like a fish," Glen said with a grin.

"Well, the rain has brought the lake back up and we may have to take a dip, so bring some extra clothes or a swimsuit when you bring Cathy."

"Will do."

"Kendal, are you ready?" she asked.

"Yes, ma'am," Kendal said. She kissed the puppy on the head. "I will be back for you on Friday." She placed the pup back in the pen.

Munchkin ran to the gate and whined for Kendal. "I will be back, I promise," she said, sticking her fingers through the chain link. Munchkin furiously licked her fingers, causing her to giggle.

"I am not sure we will make it until Friday," Glen teased.

"We may be back earlier," Sully said with a grin.

"That won't be a problem. I think they are close enough to being ready."

"We'll see how this week goes then."

Sully looked at Kendal. "Go get your bag, and we'll hit the road."

Kendal and Cathy ran out of the barn to retrieve her bag.

†

"They seem to get along very well. Did last night go okay?"

"After I ran them out of the barn, they were fine," Glen said with a chuckle.

The girls returned and met them at the truck.

"We'll see you two tomorrow," Sully said as she lifted Kendal into the truck.

"Bye, Cathy."

"Bye, Kendal, see you tomorrow."

"What do you want to do this afternoon?" Sully asked.

"I bet Sunspot needs a brushing."

"I am sure she would love one. How about we pop some corn after and watch a movie?"

"Okay, but where is Bryn?"

"She had to make a few rounds but will return later today. I will grill some chicken while you two make a salad and some veggies. Does that sound okay?"

"Sounds yummy. I love BBQ chicken."

"Great, me too," Sully said as she pulled out of the drive. "I took the mare and colt back to the herd this morning so they can be free to roam and play. I have an old mare, Sam, which I think you and I need to bring into the barn so you and Cathy can ride with me this week."

"That would be fun, Aunt Micah. Can we go get her when we get home?"

"Sure, we can."

†

They arrived home and went to the barn to grab a lead. "How about a walk?"

"Okay with me."

For the third time that day, Sully started for the back pasture, this time with Kendal and Sunspot in tow. She certainly had gotten her exercise today, she thought as they walked and talked.

"Have you ever ridden before?"

"Not that I can remember. I think Dad held me on a pony once when I was little," Kendal said.

"Sam is a very gentle horse, and she loves to swim. She is also very good with new riders, and I think you will love riding her."

"I'm sure I will."

"There will probably be times when you might fall off, and this is to be expected, but you have to get right back up and ride again," Sully said.

"I will, Aunt Micah."

"All around the property, you will see tree stumps that you can use to reach a stirrup. Like that one," Sully said as she pointed to a stump low enough that Kendal could crawl up on. "Go see if you can get on it."

Kendal ran to the stump and easily reached the top. "That wasn't too hard."

"It should be a perfect height for you, especially with Sam."

Kendal hopped down and ran back to Micah. "I'm so excited."

"Riding is so much fun. I know you will like it."

"Will you be riding with us?"

"At first, yes, but I think you can go out on your own soon."

"Does Bryn ride, too?"

"She hasn't in a long time, but I'm sure we can talk her into it."

"That would be sweet," Kendal said, nearly bursting with excitement.

Sam seemed to know what was on Sully's mind. When she saw them walking to the gate, she trotted over to them.

"Kendal, this is Sam," Sully said as she clipped the lead to the mare's halter.

"Hiya, Sam," Kendal said with a gentle stroke down the mare's face. "Who will you ride?"

"There are several young horses in the front pasture that will be sold after some shows this fall. I will ride one of them to give them some exercise." Sully immediately noticed an odd look on Kendal's face.

"I guess I never thought about you selling the horses," Kendal said, a bit concerned.

"I can't possibly keep them all, and they were born to work," Sully explained. "There is no need to worry, though; I make sure each one of them goes to a great home." That seemed to provide some assurance to Kendal.

"You won't sell Sunspot, will you?" she asked.

"Sunspot is your horse now," Sully answered. "She is very special, and I would never dream of letting her go to even the best of farms."

Sully closed the gate behind them, and they started to walk back to the barn. "Would you like to ride?"

Kendal looked up with eyes bright with excitement. "Yes, please."

"Okay, here you go," Sully said as she lifted Kendal onto Sam's back. She placed the lead across Sam's shoulder and handed it to Kendal. Sunspot looked at her curiously and trotted ahead of them.

"Will I be able to ride Sunspot one day?" Kendal asked.

"Yes, after she is fully grown and trained. I think she will make a very good partner for you."

"I heard you tell Mr. Glen that Sam likes to swim. Do you think Sunspot will, too?"

"Once she sees how much fun you're having, I don't think she could resist getting in the lake, too."

"That would be so fun," Kendal said.

"Horses are naturally good swimmers, and it's a welcome relief from the heat for them."

"Just like us?"

"Yes, just like us."

The smile on Kendal's face as she rode Sam warmed Sully's heart. She seemed right at home on a horse, which was perfect in Sully's world. When they reached the barn, she asked, "Can you slide down on your own?"

"I think so," Kendal answered, easily sliding down from Sam's back.

"That was perfect for a bareback dismount. I will try to pick up a small saddle for you this week, but until then, you and Cathy can use a bareback blanket."

Sully led the mare into a clean stall and removed the lead. "Will you feed Sam while I muck out the other stall?"

"Muck it out?" Kendal asked.

"Clean it and put down fresh wood shavings," Sully explained.

"Oh, I see," Kendal said as she went to the feed bin. "Two scoops for Sam?"

"Yes, and some fresh water for now. She has been grazing, so she won't need hay tonight."

Sully used a small wheelbarrow and a rake to clean the stall and then scattered a large bucket of shavings inside.

"Follow me," she said to Kendal, pushing the wheelbarrow around the barn to a large pile where she dumped its contents. "This is a compost pile," Sully explained. "Waste from the stalls is dumped here and turns into great fertilizer for gardens and flowers."

"Smells a bit," Kendal said, wrinkling up her nose.

Sully chuckled. "Yes, it does, but you will get used to it."

"Should I start mucking Sam's stall every day?"

"Yes, that would be a good chore for you. If you do it every day, then it doesn't pile up, so to speak."

Kendal laughed at Sully's joke. "That was corny, Aunt Micah," she teased.

"Yeah, but you laughed," Sully quickly reminded her. "You ready to brush Sunspot?"

"Yes, ma'am."

"You get started, and I'm going to see if there's a decent movie coming on. I'll be back shortly."

Sully went inside the house and took a package of popcorn from the pantry. She turned on the television in the den, scrolled through the channel guide, and found an animated movie that would begin in twenty minutes. "There should be plenty of time to finish up," she said to herself. She tuned in to the channel and went to check on Kendal.

Kendal was almost finished brushing down Sunspot.

"Your brushing makes her coat shine," Sully commented as she ran a hand down the filly's back.

"She is pretty, isn't she?" Kendal said.

"Yes, she is pretty rotten and pretty apt to stay that way," Sully teased. "I think there are a few baby carrots left in the office refrigerator. Would you like to give her a couple?"

Kendal put away her brush and went to get the carrots. "She really likes these," she said as Sunspot took them gently from her hand and crunched loudly.

"Yes, I think those and apples are her favorites," Sully said.

"I like apples, too," Kendal told Sunspot.

"We will have to get more when we go back to the store."

"Didn't we just buy a bag?" Kendal asked, confused.

"Yes, we did, but they disappeared this morning when I went to treat the young horses," Sully answered.

†

They walked into the house together and headed for the kitchen. "Do you want to make the popcorn?"

"Sure, if you will tell me how."

Sully moved the step stool in front of the microwave. "Open the door and place the bag this side down." She demonstrated. "Close the door and push this button. It's already programmed for popcorn."

She handed Kendal the bag and went to the refrigerator to check the chicken she had thawing for dinner. Satisfied that it was coming along well, she reached up and pulled down a bowl for the popcorn. "What do you want to drink?"

"May I have a soda?"

"I think we will both have a soda," Sully answered and placed them on the counter.

When the popcorn was finished, she opened the bag and poured it into the bowl. "If you carry this, I will bring the drinks and napkins."

"Deal," Kendal said.

They placed the goodies on the coffee table in the den. "I guess we had better take our boots off before Bryn gets home and catches us," Sully teased. They walked to the porch and removed their barn boots, scurrying back through the house in sock feet. Sully turned up the volume of the movie that was beginning, and they settled in on the couch to enjoy their popcorn and movie.

Once the popcorn was finished, they decided they would stretch out on the couch to finish the movie. Kendal placed her head on Sully's arm and snuggled in as they watched the movie. It was no surprise to Sully that Kendal began to nod off as they watched the movie and was soon napping on her arm. Unable to resist the allure of a nap, Sully closed her eyes and fell asleep.

†

Two hours later, Bryn returned home to find the house quiet except for the television in the den. She crept through the house and found Sully and Kendal sleeping on the couch. They looked so precious and snuggled up together; she decided to let them sleep and went to the bedroom to shower and change clothes.

†

Sully heard the water in the bathroom turn on and was startled awake. Her movement woke Kendal, who rubbed her sleepy eyes.

"We fell asleep, didn't we?"

"Yes, we did, and I think Bryn came home and caught us napping." Sully looked at the clock. "It's getting late. We better get started. Will you help me outside for a few minutes?"

"Sure will," Kendal said. She stood and stretched.

"We will have to watch that movie again," Sully said. "I like what I saw of it," she giggled.

"Me, too," Kendal agreed as they walked to the porch and slipped back into their boots.

"I need to start up the grill. Will you bring the lighter fluid and lighter and follow me?"

Kendal picked up the two items Sully requested and followed her off the porch and to the side of the house where a grill sat beneath a small covering. Sully opened the lid and poured charcoal into the base, dowsing it with starter fluid. Sunspot joined them to see what they were doing and watched curiously.

"You might want to move her back while I light the grill," she told Kendal.

Kendal took Sunspot by the halter and walked her back from the covering while Sully ignited the lighter and started a flame burning in the base. "Let's see if Bryn is out of the shower and ready to start in the kitchen."

†

Bryn was coming down the hall when they walked in. "Hey, sleepyheads," she said with a grin.

"We thought we would check on you to see if you needed some help while the coals burn down a bit."

"We can start working on the salad."

"Let me rinse off the chicken first and get it soaking, and you two can have the whole kitchen," Sully said.

"What kind of veggies do we want?" Bryn asked.

"Can we have corn on the cob?" Kendal asked.

"Most definitely. What else would you like?"

"How about some baked beans?"

"That would go well with the chicken," Sully agreed.

"I better get started on those, and then we can work on the salad," Bryn said as she searched the pantry.

Sully busied herself at the sink rinsing the chicken and placing it in a large bowl to soak in her special ingredients, as she called them, while Kendal and Bryn pulled out cans of baked beans and a container of brown sugar and placed them on the table.

"There, all yours," Sully said as she threw away her garbage and placed the soaking chicken on the counter. "I am going to grab a drink and go check on the fire," she said, taking a bottle of beer from the fridge. "See you in a bit."

"We will be right here," Bryn said as she opened cans of beans and poured them into a glass dish for baking. "Kendal, will you get that pack of bacon out of the fridge for me, please?" Sully heard Bryn ask as she walked towards the door.

†

The sun started setting as Sully walked outside to check the coals. A subtle breeze had come up from the east, promising a nice night. Sully sat in a well-worn chair and took a long drink from the beer. The cold liquid flowing down her throat felt good as she tried remembering the last beer she had tasted. She remembered she and Josh had drunk a few as he grilled one night in Atlanta. It had only been a few days, but it seemed ages ago. She sat back in the chair and listened to the sound of the night as the sun slowly set and the crickets began to chirp in the distance. Down by the lake, she could hear bullfrogs as they began their nightly chorus. *There is no sound like this in the city*, she reminded herself as she finished her beer. She heard the screen door close and the sound of footsteps approaching. She saw Kendal walking toward her, carrying a fresh beer.

"Bryn said you would probably be ready for another drink," she said as she handed Sully the beer.

"Thank you. That was perfect timing."

Kendal crawled up in her lap. "The beans are in the oven, and the salad is in the fridge. Bryn said I could come out with you if I wanted to."

"I am so glad you did. I was enjoying the music of the night. Can you hear the crickets and bullfrogs?"

"Yes, I can," Kendal said.

"You know, later tonight when you go to bed, if you listen carefully, you might even hear Henry," Sully said.

"Who's Henry?"

"Henry is an old barn owl who has lived in the barn for many years. He keeps the mice from getting into the horse feed and making nests in the hay."

"Everything seems to have a job around here," Kendal said, surprising Sully.

"You are so right, and it is clever of you to have figured it out," she said.

"What is my job?"

"Well, aside from caring for Sunspot and now Sam, you are my gopher," Sully said.

"Your gopher?" Kendal asked.

"Yep, whenever I need something from the barn or the kitchen, I can tell you to go for this or go for that," Sully teased.

It took a second for Kendal to comprehend the joke, but when she did, she broke out in laughter with Sully.

"You are crazy, Aunt Micah," Kendal said.

"Are you just now figuring that out?" Sully said as she tickled Kendal's side.

"Hey, what's all this laughter? I thought you two were working?" Bryn said as she stepped off the porch.

"I am just about ready to break in my gopher," Sully said with a straight face.

"Your gopher?"

"Yep," she looked at Kendal and said, "Will you go for another beer?"

Kendal started laughing again, walked into the house for another beer, and returned it to Sully.

"You haven't finished that one yet," she said to Sully.

"This one isn't for me. It's for the chicken."

"Chickens don't drink beer, Aunt Micah."

"Nope, but they bathe in it, and it makes them so juicy," she explained.

"Are the coals ready for the chicken?" Bryn asked.

"Yes, ma'am, I believe they are. Kendal, will you go with Bryn and bring back a pair of tongs for me?"

"Yes, ma'am."

They returned a few minutes later with the bowl of chicken and a pair of tongs, which Sully took and placed on a shelf attached to the grill. "Thanks, ladies."

They watched as Sully opened the top of a spray bottle, poured in the bottle of beer, and then placed the chicken out across the grill before soaking it with sprayed beer. “That should get us started,” she said as she closed the lid. “Do you have time to have a beer with me?” she asked Bryn.

“Sure do.”

“Gopher, can you go for two beers this time?” she asked Kendal.

“Yes, ma’am,” Kendal said and returned to the house.

Bryn kissed Sully and sat down next to her. “What a nice night out.”

“It’s beautiful, isn’t it?”

“Very much so, even better now that I am here with you.”

“Such a smoothie you have turned out to be,” Sully teased.

Kendal returned with the beers. “Here you go.”

“Thanks,” Sully said as she opened them and handed one to Bryn.

“You make an excellent gopher,” Sully said as Kendal climbed back into her lap.

“Smells good,” Kendal said.

“I am so glad you love chicken,” Sully said.

“I like anything you cook.”

Bryn chuckled. “Now, who’s the smooth talker?”

“Hey, I’m thankful she can eat my cooking.”

“You cook good, Aunt Micah,” Kendal said.

“Thanks, Kendal,” Sully said, ruffling her hair. “I haven’t killed anyone yet with my cooking.”

“That’s comforting,” Bryn said, taking a long drink of her beer.

Sunspot heard their laughter and came trotting from the barn.

"Hey there, little one," Sully said.

Kendal climbed down from her lap and walked over to Sunspot. She softly stroked her face as she whispered to her.

Bryn smiled at Sully. "How's the chicken coming?"

"Let me check." Sully stood and walked over to the grill. She inspected the meat and turned it, revealing a golden-brown side. "It's coming along quite well," she said as she coated the meat in another dowsing of beer. "I should be ready for sauce in about twenty minutes."

"I will put the corn on unless I need to do it now."

"On the cob or off?"

"On, those little mini ears you had in the freezer."

"I think you would be safe to wait, but you might want to go ahead and get the water on."

"I will be right back then. Do you need anything?"

"I'm good, thanks. When you go back in, I will send my gopher with you to bring out the sauce and a brush," she said with a grin.

†

Bryn shook her head and walked back into the house. She placed a pot of water on the stove to boil and searched the kitchen until she found a basting brush and put it on the counter. She then searched for barbeque sauce in the fridge and, finding none, walked to the pantry. She found a new bottle and placed it beside the brush.

†

When Bryn returned, Sully was lost in thought, staring across the lake.

"A penny for your thoughts," she said, sitting beside her.

"I was watching for the fireflies to come out. It's good and dark now, so they should be out dancing by now."

"Do you think the recent rains have affected them?"

"No, I wouldn't think so, but I guess anything is possible."

Bryn leaned over to look past the grill. "There," she said, pointing at the small cluster of woods surrounding the lake. "They just haven't made it out into the open yet."

"Ah, I see them now, thanks."

"What's a summer without them?" Bryn asked.

"Very dull," Sully answered. "I can't remember ever having one without them."

"This is the perfect spot, not too hot, not too wet. I could sit and watch them all night."

"There have been many nights I have nodded off down at the lake, mesmerized by them," Sully admitted. "I would wake up late, when the dew started to fall, to find them lighting up the night with their glow and shuffle up to the house to collapse in my bed."

"Sounds like you were lonesome."

"I was lonesome, lost, in despair until you came home."

"You didn't seem that way at all," Bryn said.

"I have gotten very good at hiding my feelings," Sully said. "But now there is no reason."

†

Bryn looked deep into her eyes and saw the sincerity in her words. "I love you, Micah Sullivan."

"As I love you," she said, stroking Bryn's face.

They shared eye contact for a moment until the hoot of an owl broke the silence.

"Is that Henry?" Kendal asked as she walked over to them.

"I do believe it is," Sully answered. "He's letting us know he's awake and on the job," she said with a smile.

"Speaking of which, I better get back to mine. Kendal, will you come with me and bring the sauce back to Micah while I start the corn?"

"Yes, ma'am," she said, walking into the house with Bryn, leaving Sunspot with Sully, who walked over to the young horse.

†

"Hey there, little one," Sully said as she stroked down her back.

Sunspot looked back at her with dark eyes. Sully's hand ran down her shoulder to her chest. She was amazed by how well she had healed from the trauma inflicted by the wild dogs. "Holy shit," she whispered to herself when she realized that they were about to bring two dogs into the family. She worried how Sunspot would respond to them after her attack. She would have to be very careful to introduce the pups to her slowly so as not to bring the terror of the attack back to her. Sully was still caressing Sunspot when Kendal returned with the brush and a bowl of sauce, which she handed to Sully.

"You know, I just thought of something," she said as she laid them on the shelf.

"What's that, Aunt Micah?" Kendal said as she climbed onto a chair.

"We will need to be very careful around Sunspot when we bring the puppies home, so we don't scare her, and she doesn't try to hurt them."

"Why would she do that?" Kendal asked, confused.

"Because when she was little, she was attacked by wild dogs that caused her injuries."

"I didn't think of that."

"I know, me neither, so we will have to be careful."

"What will happen if she is scared of them?"

"I don't know. I guess we will have to keep them out of the barn to keep them safe."

"I think she will be okay with them. She is such a gentle animal," Kendal said.

"I hope you're right," Micah said as she started to baste the chicken. Once finished, she turned the meat and basted the other side.

"Smells yummy."

"Are you hungry?"

"Starving would be more like it."

"Will you ask Bryn for a platter and see how she is coming in the kitchen?"

†

Kendal nodded and walked back into the house.

"Aunt Micah wants a platter for the chicken and wants to know if you are ready?"

Bryn handed her a platter. "Almost done. Will you come back and help me set the table?"

"Sure," Kendal said and returned to the grill. "Bryn said she is almost done and wants me to help her set the table."

"Thanks. I will come in as soon as the chicken is finished."

†

Sully gave the chicken a final turn, and when she was pleased with the product, she took the chicken and placed it on the platter. She picked it up with the brush and bowl and carried it into the kitchen. Kendal sat at the table watching as Bryn carried the baked beans and placed them on a hot pad.

"Where would you like the chicken?"

"You can set it right in the middle. I will get the corn and salad."

Sully washed her hands at the sink and then joined them at the table. She reached out for Kendal and Bryn and bowed her head. "Dear Lord, bless this food and our family and friends. Amen."

"Amen. This all looks so good," Bryn said.

"Let's eat."

Bryn, Kendal, and Sully ate until they were completely stuffed. Kendal was sent to shower while Sully and Bryn cleaned the kitchen. She walked back, dressed in pajamas, as they sat at the table sipping coffee.

"You look all bright and shiny," Sully said. "Are you ready for bed?"

"I think I am," Kendal said.

†

"I will be right back," Sully said, then took Kendal's hand and walked to her bedroom. "We will have a busy day tomorrow, so get some sleep," she said as she pulled the covers over Kendal's body.

"I will, Aunt Micah. Good night. Love you."

Sully leaned down and kissed her forehead. "Love you, too. See you in the morning." Sully turned off the lamp and partially closed the door behind her before returning to the kitchen.

†

"That was a great meal," Bryn said when she returned.

"We make a good team."

"Yes, we do. Are you ready for a shower and some sleep, too?"

"Just waiting on you, my love," Bryn said, her eyes burning with desire, making Sully's heart jump with excitement.

Sully showered quickly and took Bryn in her arms for a long, deep kiss. Bryn's hands were urgent as they moved between Sully's thighs, stroking deeply inside her lover until Sully's body shuddered, and she dropped to her knees. She lifted Bryn's leg and draped it over her shoulder as her lips sought Bryn's center. Bryn's hands found the back of Sully's head and guided her to her throbbing center of need. Sully's fingers filled Bryn's body as her mouth gently suckled her lover into a soul-shaking orgasm.

Bryn joined Sully on the shower floor, and they embraced in a deep, loving kiss as the water washed over their bodies.

When the warmth of the water began to fade, Sully reached behind Bryn and turned the water off. "Let's go lay down," she whispered.

They dried their bodies, slipped between the soft sheets of their bed, and fell asleep, bodies entwined and heartbeats echoing in the silent night.

## CHAPTER THIRTY-TWO

---

The next morning blossomed into a bright midsummer day. After breakfast, Sully and Kendall tended to the horses as Bryn began her daily rounds. As they were finishing, Glen and Cathy arrived at the barn.

"Good morning, Boss."

"Morning, Glen, how are you today?"

"Doing fine, thanks, and you?"

"No complaints on my side either. Would you mind if Cathy went with us to the school?"

"No, not at all. I can get some chores done around here while you are gone."

"Good. I want you to work the three horses we have entered in the show, and then when we get back, I will take the young filly for a ride with the girls."

"I will work her first and keep her saddled for you."

"Sounds great. Is there anything we need from town?"

"Not that I can think of at this moment."

"Alright, we will be back shortly. Kendal and Cathy, are you ready to head to town?"

"Yes, ma'am," the girls said as they finished brushing down Sunspot.

"Let's go, then, so we can come back to ride."

The girls rushed out of the barn and were crawling into Sully's truck when she caught up with them. "Y'all aren't excited, are you?"

"We can't wait to ride," Cathy said.

"Did you remember a swimsuit?"

"Yes, ma'am, I have it under my shorts," Cathy said.

"Good deal," Sully said as she started the engine and pulled onto the drive.

†

Two hours later, Kendal was enrolled in school and as hoped, would be in the same class as Cathy. The principal was pleased they had already completed shopping and looked forward to seeing the girls in a few weeks when school started.

They chatted excitedly in the back seat as they rode back to the Trace.

Sully pulled the truck to the barn when they reached home and shut off the engine. "Kendal, did we get you a swimsuit?"

"I already had one, Aunt Micah."

"Why don't you put it on under your shorts like Cathy while I get Sam ready?"

"Ok, I will be right back," she said as she climbed down from the truck.

"Can I help you?" Cathy asked.

"Yes, ma'am, you can," Sully said.

Cathy followed her into the barn to the tack room. Sully looked through a window and saw Glen working one of the colts in the corral with a small group of cattle. He was much more relaxed on the horse as it made sharp cuts and turns. She was very proud of how much he had learned in such a short time. She smiled to herself as she reached for a bridle and a bareback blanket.

"Can you carry this for me?" she asked as she handed the bridle to Cathy.

"Yes, ma'am," Cathy said, beaming a smile up to Sully.

She followed Sully into Sam's stall and watched as she smoothed her hand down the horse's back. "Are you ready to go for a walk?" Sully asked the animal.

Sully placed the blanket across Sam's withers and pulled it slowly down her back. She then reached beneath the mare and smoothed the cinch against her skin, running it through the D ring and fastening it to keep the blanket in place. The blanket had no stirrups, but it did have some hand loops for riders to hold onto if needed.

Kendal came rushing into the barn, followed by Sunspot. She watched as Sully removed Sam's halter and reached for the bridle Cathy was holding. The girls observed as Sully placed the bit in Sam's mouth above her tongue and slipped the earpiece over her head.

"Does that hurt her, Aunt Micah?"

"The bit itself doesn't hurt her, but if the rider is too forceful with the reins, it can be painful, so be gentle when using them."

"What do the reins do?" Cathy asked.

"They are basically like a steering wheel on a car. They tell her when you want to turn left or right and when you want her to move forward, backward, or stop."

"That sounds confusing," Kendal said.

"It's not hard, but I will show you how to steer. Let's take Sam outside, and we will get started."

Sully draped the reins over Sam's shoulders and placed her hand on the bottom of the bridle. She led her to a small stump and stopped next to it. "Okay, who is going to steer first?"

"I think Kendal should," Cathy volunteered.

"Okay, Kendal up on the stump."

Kendal quickly scrambled onto the stump.

"Grab hold of that handle on the saddle, swing your right leg over Sam's back, and pull yourself on," she instructed.

Kendal slid onto Sam's back like a natural.

"Very good," Sully praised. "Okay, now to get your rider safely on behind you. There is another handle toward the back of the blanket, but I will show you an easier way. Kendal, put your right hand through the handle in front of you and hold your left arm out like this," she instructed.

Kendal followed her direction and bent her arm at ninety degrees. "Okay, now hold your arm still. Cathy will use it to steady herself as she climbs on behind you." She looked at Cathy and then Kendal. "Ready, girls?"

Both girls nodded, and Cathy climbed onto the stump. "Okay, take Kendal's arm and slide your right leg across Sam."

Kendal slipped slightly when Cathy placed weight on her arm, but she quickly righted herself, and Cathy made it on behind her easily.

"Very good job, girls."

Both girls grinned back at her as she moved to the front of Sam.

"Now, Kendal, I want you to pick up both reins and place them in your left hand. You always want them to lay flat against the horse's neck, so you must always check to ensure they aren't twisted."

Kendal looked closely and saw the reins were flat.

"Okay, now the steering. Bring your left hand forward, releasing the tension on the reins, and softly squeeze your legs into Sam's sides. That tells her you want to go forward."

Sam stepped forward slowly, following Sully, who was walking backward to watch the girls. "If you want Sam to turn to the right, you move your hand toward the right, which presses the rein into the left side of her neck. When she has turned like you want, you move your hand back to the middle."

Kendal guided Sam through a right-hand turn and turned her left when they were walking straight again. "That's it, you got it, just remember to be gentle."

"Now, to stop, you pull the reins back toward your belly button. That's it, nice and easy," Sully said. "No need to jerk or do it too fast. Release the tension when she comes to a stop."

Sam came to a stop just as Kendal had asked. "Okay, now the tricky part," Sully teased. "Backing up is a little more difficult, but you need to know how. Tighten your grip on the reins just a bit, Kendal, and squeeze Sam's sides with your knees while pulling the reins backward toward your belly button and keep gentle pressure until she has backed up to where you want her to be."

Sam backed up quickly to Kendal's command, and Cathy slipped off balance just a bit at the movement and grabbed for Kendal. Sully caught her just as she began to slide. "If you find yourself sliding as a passenger, you need to remember to reach for your rider's waist. If you grab Kendal up high, like on her arm, all you will succeed in doing is having both of you go toppling off, but if you grab around her waist, you can pull yourself back up safely."

Sully held Cathy in the position she had slid into. "Try pulling yourself back up using Kendal's waist."

Cathy was very successful in righting her body. "Good job, Cathy."

†

"Both of you feel pretty secure?"

"Yes, ma'am," they said in unison.

"Good, I want you to walk Sam to the back pasture gate and back while I get my horse saddled and ready to go."

Sully watched as Kendal gently guided Sam, just as instructed, to turn to the right, and they started toward the back pasture. Sully turned to walk back to the barn and saw Glen watching, too.

Glen leaned against a stall and watched the lesson progress, looking proud of both the girls.

"They are going to be fine," she promised.

"That they are," Glen said. "I already have the filly saddled for you."

"I figured you probably did, but I wanted them to feel secure and not need me to follow their every move."

"I reckon that's smart, and there's not much trouble they can get into going there and back."

"The worst, I reckon, is they might fall off and not be able to find a stump and have to walk back home leading Sam," Sully said.

"As stubborn as those two are, they would find a way to get back on."

Sully chuckled at Glen's remark. "You are so right, my friend."

She followed him into the barn to the filly he had just finished working. They adjusted the stirrups to Sully's length. "How did she do this morning?"

"She's a natural. Once we cut out a cow, I just sat back and let her work. I have a feeling she could dance for hours," Glen said, referring to the way a cutting horse rested most of its weight on the back legs while the front legs moved from side to side to keep the cow separated from the herd.

"Excellent," Sully said as she led her through the barn. "Will you work the other two today as well?"

"That's where I am heading next."

"Thanks, Glen. When we finish our ride, why don't you join us down at the lake, and we can discuss those show schedules while the girls swim."

"Okay, will do, Boss," he said, walking back through the barn.

†

Sully mounted the young horse and cantered down the driveway and back while she waited for the girls to return. She was a strong young horse and very smooth in her movements. It seemed like forever since Sully had been on a horse, and she welcomed the slight breeze blowing through her hair. When she returned to the barn, she saw the girls returning and Sunspot dancing alongside them.

"How was it?"

"It was great, Aunt Micah," Kendal said.

"Are you two ready to swap places?"

"Sure," Cathy said.

"Okay, Cathy, swing your right leg over Sam's rump and slide down to the ground. Hold onto the blanket loop if you need to."

Cathy easily slid off Sam to the ground, followed closely by Kendal.

"Take Sam over to the stump, and Cathy, you get on first this time."

With only a second of shaky balance, the girls were able to remount Sam, and they were off on a walk again. Instead of going to the back pasture, Sully took them off to the left and to the spot where the fox lived. "If we are lucky, maybe we can sneak up on them today," she told Kendal.

"On who?" Cathy asked.

"The foxes I told you about," Kendal answered.

"Oh, that would be so neat," Cathy said.

Sunspot trotted beside them, happy to be included in their trip. The girls chatted excitedly until Sully pulled the filly to a stop, and Sam stopped instinctively. "We will need to be very quiet if we are going to sneak up on a fox," she warned, and both girls went silent. "Let's see if we can see them before they see us."

When they made the final turn into the small clearing where she had first seen the mother fox, Sully heard sharp yips and yelps. She was delighted to see two fox pups chasing one another through the clearing, one nipping at the other's hind legs. They were oblivious to anyone watching them as they romped and rolled together. Sully pulled them to a halt and scanned the forest's edge until she spotted the mother keeping a watchful eye out for her young. Sully and the fox made eye contact almost simultaneously, and the fox seemed to smile at her and then return her gaze to the playing pups. Both girls were completely enthralled with the pups and had to work hard to stifle the laughter that threatened to erupt between them.

They watched the pups romp in the open field until a sharp yip from their mother brought them running back to her, and they disappeared into the dense woods. Sully silently turned the filly around as they headed back to the barn. When they emerged from the cover of the woods, the sun shone brightly.

"I do believe it's time for a swim."

"Yay," Kendal squealed.

†

They stopped off at the barn long enough for Sully to remove the saddle from the filly, and then she placed Cathy on her back. She took the reins and walked the filly down the drive as they made for the lake. They stopped off at a small picnic table, and the girls dismounted to remove their clothing before swimming with the horses. Sully helped them mount up and then walked to the lake's edge.

"Go ahead, squeeze your knees, and let them know you want to go in."

Kendal was eager and nudged Sam with her knees until she stepped into the water. The filly soon followed, and the girls giggled with delight as the horses walked deeper and began to swim.

Sully sat down on the top of the picnic table and watched the girls swim with the horses. Glen walked up from the barn with Sunspot following and handed her a soda bottle before sitting beside her.

"It's hard to tell who is having more fun, the girls or the horses," he said as he watched.

"Yeah, I think it's a toss-up."

They sat in silence until Sully saw a flash off to the left and looked to see the sun glaring down on Bryn's windshield as she drove toward the driveway. "It looks like we are going to have more company," she told Glen who looked up to see Bryn turning into the drive.

"The more the merrier," Glen said. "I am going to the barn to grab a few more sodas. Is there anything else you need?"

"No, I think I'm good. Thanks, Glen."

Glen waved at Bryn as she drove up, and he started off to the barn.

Bryn parked the truck and stepped out carrying two large bags and wearing a big smile. "Hey, baby," she said as Sully walked toward her. "I thought it would be a great day for a picnic."

"What a perfect idea, my love," Sully said as she took a bag from Bryn. "It sure smells good."

"I stopped off for some chicken and fixings," Bryn said, placing a bag on the picnic table.

"Glen went back to the barn for sodas."

"Great, I didn't think to get drinks."

"Hey, you two, start making it back to the shore," Sully called out to the girls. "Bryn has brought us a picnic."

Glen returned with the drinks, and they set out plates for their picnic. When the girls brought the horses from the water, he and Sully went to help them.

"Just tie the reins and let them graze while we eat," she instructed as she helped Cathy down.

"They won't go away?" Cathy asked.

"No, they will stay close," Sully answered.

"Yummy, chicken," Kendal said as they reached the picnic table.

They ate a beautiful picnic lunch, and, after cleaning up, the girls took the horses back in for another swim. Sunspot followed the girls into the water and went for her first swim. Glen took the bags and returned to the barn to finish some chores. Bryn sat beside Sully and watched the girls having fun, her hand resting on Sully's knee.

†

An hour later, as the sun began to sink, Glen returned. "I have a few things I need to pick up in town, and I promised Cathy a movie at the theater. Would you mind if Kendal went with us?"

"No, not at all," Sully said.

"I will tend to the horses, then, if you will get the girls dressed and ready."

"You have a deal, Glen. Girls, it's time to head to the barn," she yelled.

They returned to the barn together and met Bryn, who had driven her truck. "You girls are going to the movies," Sully said.

"Awesome," Kendal said.

"Let's head into the house to get you cleaned up and ready to go," Sully said as Glen took the horses back to the barn.

†

A half-hour later, the girls ran out to meet Glen. Bryn and Sully watched them enter the truck and head down the drive.

With a heavy sigh, Sully turned to Bryn and held out her hand. "Come with me."

Bryn took her hand and walked with her to the barn. Sully climbed the steps to the hayloft and led Bryn to the loft door, where a bale of hay sat before the open door. Sully sat down and waited for Bryn to sit beside her. She placed an arm around her shoulders and pointed off to the west.

"Look," was all she said.

Bryn laid her head on Sully's shoulder, and they sat in silence as the bright orange sun melted into the horizon, ending another beautiful day at the Trace.

## About the Author

---

Ali Spooner lives in beautiful northwest Florida with several fur babies. Ali's writing began as a hobby, and with the assistance of the Affinity Rainbow Publishing team, her love of storytelling has advanced to a new level.

Ali's characters are primarily everyday people, from cowgirls to psychics. Ali also has created a few supernatural characters in her paranormal series. Several of her thirty-plus books have been Amazon-rated number-one choices, and always include a happily ever after. Ali's hobbies include photography, reading, travel, college sports, and spending time with family and friends.

Let the author know what you think please write a review.

## OTHER AFFINITY BOOKS

---

Love Sins by Annette Mori

Jessica Green's life is predictable and boring. As the chief engineer for Solar Flair, her career is right on track. Her love life, not so much. The last thing she expects is a call from her estranged father's attorney. Too curious to ignore the message, she can't resist meeting with him and discovering more about specific instructions related to his estate, as well as the letter her father left for her. Rattled by what she finds at her father's home, she promptly dials 911.

Special Agent Amanda Forrester is perplexed by a call to join a homicide investigation until she arrives at the scene and learns the victim is not only a serial killer but an elite assassin the authorities have been after for years. To Amanda's increasing irritation, the daughter recognizes a picture of the last target and insinuates herself into the investigation. As the case takes a surprising turn, Amanda finds she has landed smack dab in the middle of a complicated and dangerous situation. The facts lead her to a puzzle weaving together the recent suicide of a wealthy businessman with the activities of several prominent politicians. Amanda must join forces with a mysterious organization and the persistent woman she finds increasingly hard to resist. Her instinct to protect the alluring and vulnerable Jessica Green kicks into high gear, taking the reader on a roller-coaster journey for the last book in *The Next Generation* series.

<u>A Wild Moon Rises by Jen Silver</u>

Successful author, Malory G Holmes, has had a rough year. Wounded by an emotional breakup and writer's block she returns home after eight months travelling to discover the startling results of a DNA test. Apparently, through her mother's side, she is related to a baronet with an estate in Briarbay, Northumberland. She decides to visit the place to find out more about this unknown side of her family.

Selene Wylde is content with life, running a bookshop in the small hamlet of Briarbay. She also looks after her father, Reginald, who is grieving over the recent death of his husband, Sir Alan Guyatt. Reginald is worrying about his claim to stay at Briarbay Hall as the Will of Sir Alan has not yet been found.

With the arrival in her shop of a very attractive, well-known writer, Selene's world begins to tilt alarmingly. Malory and Selene become entangled in a web of secrets and deceptions with the added complication of a rapidly growing attraction.

<u>The Wolf and The Unicorn by Ali Spooner (Erotica)</u>

Ready to explore a steamy, passionate, and tantalizing erotica romance….

Keagan and Celeste have built a solid relationship on trust and independence. A successful surgeon, Keagan understands Celeste's supercharged libido and her desire to experience a variety of sexual encounters. Everything changes when Sky, a new doctor, arrives at the hospital, and Celeste is immediately drawn to the younger woman. Keagan is surprised when she is also attracted to Sky, who shares common interests with Celeste and her. When more than a physical attraction develops, the three women discover a loving relationship beyond the bedroom.

<u>The Blank White Page by Ali Spooner</u>

Tatum Chastain, Corporate Officer of Chastain International, her family's real estate empire, accepts the challenge her father, Charles, has set forth. Charles has tasked Tatum and her brother, Charlie, to survive in the wilderness for six months to prove their skills in taking over the family business once he retires. Charles fails to realize that Tatum would fall in love with the southeastern Alaska cabin he has chosen for her to test her resilience and creativity. Tatum prepares for life in the bush, and shortly after she arrives, Poe, a beautiful raven, becomes her companion and guardian. When River Foster, a designated hunter for her village, crosses Tatum's path, she finds a different kind of love awaits her.

<u>Love Hacks by Annette Mori</u>

Joy Stiles is adrift. Having finally finished her graduate degree at the National Defense University, the only thing keeping her interest is an ongoing feud with a fellow hacker to gain access to sensitive information. Against all odds, the person snuck their way into her tech and kept leaving taunting messages. It's driving Joy crazy. She doesn't have time for this. Operation Elephant Bites isn't working as The Organization thought it would when they started down that path two years ago. Now they have a new worry. Someone is desperately trying to find out more about The Organization, believing they are behind the attacks on the mines. Whoever that person is has not only ties to the Chinese and Russian governments but also members of the US Government. Top secret files at the NSA call their unknown group The Crusaders. Joy's efforts to uncover the identity of the enemy lead The Organization to a lot more than evil plans, and it's up to The Next Generation, with support from senior members of The Organization, to thwart the inevitable trajectory, perhaps with the assistance of Joy's irritating foe.

Strength Within by Mia Barnes

Samantha Wilson is an award-winning freelance writer with a passion for being the voice of others. Despite vowing never to go back, she returns to Milwaukee, Wisconsin, for an assignment. Her return awakens memories that force her to confront her sad and lonely childhood, including the violent attack she'd rather forget. Moving away and making a quiet, successful solo life for herself, leaving the life she knew behind cannot keep Sammie from facing her past.

Fortunately, her best friend, Zoë, flies in from New Mexico to be by her side while she confronts the demons of her past. Sammie has a knack for helping others find their happy endings. Will she finally let Zoe help her become whole again and maybe discover her happy ending in the process?

Mom's Last Wish by Charlene Neil

After fifteen years away from home, Lucy Donald receives an email from her mother's personal assistant, Cameron Bishop, compelling her to return. Soon after Lucy's arrival, threatening letters start to appear, and Lucy realizes her life is in actual danger. She seeks comfort in the arms of the alluring Cameron Bishop, but can Cameron really be trusted?

Lucy's return home and the events that unfold lead to an intense and suspenseful atmosphere.

Left to uncover the mysteries by herself, she finds herself grappling with the dilemma of not knowing whom to trust.

The Next Generation by Annette Mori

Despite Toni's legendary brilliance, even she could not stop the march of time. After learning her daughter, Joy, and Joy's two best friends, Pepper and Alina, attempted to deceive the senior agents in The Organization with a bogus Spring Break cover story, she convinces her wife it's time to let the Next Generation take over.

The last thing Pepper Maggio expects after agreeing to lead a mission is literally running into the woman she's followed for years. Not only is Grace Turner beautiful, but she's a passionate crusader for the same innocents that The Organization vows to protect. Along with her two best friends, the three young women embark on an adventure to save the day. But the mission quickly gets out of hand as the human traffickers target not only Grace and her film crew, but also the young Mexican woman who managed to catch Alina's eye. Maria might be the bravest of the bunch as a survivor of one of the Mexican mines, but she's a sitting duck if they don't intervene. They might be the Next Generation, but they'll need the full support of The Organization, including Pepper's lethal mother, Val, to get out of Mexico alive.

Turn the Page by Ali Spooner

Continue the journey with Whit and Eli in this final installment of the Cast Iron Farm series. The brilliance of their twins, Mack and Zack, rapidly develops, challenging Whit and Eli to keep up with their education. Their sensitivity to others and kindness are far beyond their youth and a testament to the family's efforts to help them grow into young adults. In addition to more adventures, a budding romance, and wedding bells ring for the Fortner family once more as a new generation begins life on Cast Iron Farm.

A Breath of Scandal by S Anne Gardner

Adele Visconti, Contessa de Caravagio, is passionate and wild and doesn't know the meaning of the word no. One day by chance she turns her head and in a very old cliché fashion she sees a face across the expanse of a Polo field and goes to meet it. Unknowingly this would change her life forever.

When Gillian meets Adele, she is in a committed relationship. The last thing she wanted was to be sucked into the maelstrom that is Adele. However, Adele was something that she could not fight against and her world was turned upside down from the moment they met.

Will their relationship survive against a tide of intrigue, manipulations, passion, family, and most importantly reconnecting the magic of their love for each other.

Affinity
Rainbow Publications

eBooks, Print, Free eBooks

Visit our website for more publications available online.

https://affinityebooks.com/

Published by Affinity Rainbow Publications
A Division of Affinity eBook Press NZ LTD
Canterbury, New Zealand

Registered Company 2517228

www.ingramcontent.com/pod-product-compliance
Lightning Source LLC
Chambersburg PA
CBHW050029030726
47506CB00001B/184

* 9 7 8 1 9 9 1 0 4 0 8 5 5 *